BOOMER ANGERS

LIKE A BOOMERANG, WE ALWAYS END UP RIGHT BACK WHERE WE STARTED.

USA TODAY BESTSELLING AUTHOR
HEATHER M. ORGERON

Boomerangers
Copyright © 2017 Heather M. Orgeron
ALL RIGHTS RESERVED

ISBN: 978-1546458739

No part of this publication may be reproduced, transmitted, downloaded, distributed, stored in or introduced into any information storage or retrieval system, in any form or by any means, whether electronic, photocopying, mechanical or otherwise, without express permission of the publisher, except by a reviewer who may quote brief passages for review purposes.

This book is a work of fiction. Names, characters, places, story lines and incidents are the product of the author's imagination or are used fictitiously. Any resemblances to actual persons, living or dead, events, locales or any events or occurrences are purely coincidental.

Edited by Edee M. Fallon, *Mad Spark Editing, www.madsparkediting.com*

Cover Design, Interior Design & Formatting by Juliana Cabrera, *Jersey Girl Design, www.jerseygirl-design.com*

Other Titles

Vivienne's Guilt
Boomerangers
Breakaway
Doppelbanger
Heartbreak Warefare
Pour Judgment

*For Maw-Maw Agnes and promises kept from the grave.
We had no idea what we were missing, but you did.
Thank you.*

Chapter One
SPENCER

I love sex. I love the power, the intimacy, the euphoria it brings.

Don't misunderstand, I'm not a slut. God, the mere thought of the word makes me cringe. I'm simply a woman unashamed of her desires. A woman who knows her own body and wants you to know yours just as well.

For instance, did you know that the clitoris has roughly *twice* the nerve endings as a penis? In fact, it is the *only* body part, male or female, that exists solely for pleasure. That's right, ladies. Sex is supposed to feel *good*. If it doesn't, call my office and make an appointment. I'll see what I can do to help.

No, I'm not running some scandalous operation. I am a family psychologist specializing in sex therapy, or more commonly known simply as a sex therapist, and I *love* my job. There are few things I find more rewarding than knowing I've helped an individual or couple learn to find pleasure in what I consider to be one of the most vital of ways.

There are many reasons, beyond the usual emotional connection, that make a healthy sexual relationship important.

Sex contributes to your overall well-being. It has *magical* powers. I'm serious. It's scientifically proven that sex releases hormones that both calm and relieve stress. It is a natural antidepressant as well as pain killer. Therefore, next time you feel like pushing your man away because you have a headache, consider taking one for the team. By the time you reach orgasm, that headache will have been long forgotten. I swear by it.

So, if I'm such an expert, you may ask yourselves how I ended up here. A thirty-three-year-old woman with three children by two different men—not presently married to either. Stop judging me. Some problems can't be solved in the bedroom, and apparently, I attract those kinds of problems.

You see, I've only had sex with three men, and consequently, two of those relationships resulted in tiny humans whose sperm donors wanted no part in raising.

When I was nineteen, and in my sophomore year of college, two years into a broken heart, I met Tate Tenning. He was a senior and the star of the football team. His blond curls, blue eyes, and perfect ass were just too much for my drunken mind to refuse. We hooked up in the backseat of his Explorer during a frat party, and a whirlwind romance ensued. We hit it off in a big way. That man could make my body scream, and he was a good boyfriend, too. Tate was kind, attentive, and he worshipped the ground I walked on. We traveled a lot and partied even more. About a month after he graduated, we took a trip to Vegas to celebrate, and when we returned, I had a ring on my finger. He was a good husband, for the most part, and we were happy, young, and in love. Fast forward a few months, a positive pregnancy test, sonogram, and two heartbeats later... Well, I'm sure you can piece together the rest of that story.

Lake and Landon were born six months after our

divorce. Tate didn't even bother coming to the hospital, but I'd wanted my children to have a father. I had hopes that he would eventually come around. So, I put his name on their birth certificates, and at my father's insistence, filed for child support. For a few years, he was no more than a check in the mail. His measly seven hundred dollars a month barely put diapers on their asses and clothes on their backs. My parents paid for their daycare so that I could finish school and made sure we always had food on the table. They'd already been paying for my apartment since I'd started college, so they simply upgraded me from a one bedroom to a two, and we made it. It was hard as hell, but we did it.

The plan had always been to return to my hometown of Cedar Grove after school, but my best friend, Gina, who was sticking around to work for her cousin, Dillon, at his new practice begged me to join her. I'd already completed my masters in psychology, so Dillon paid for our additional training, and once we'd completed our obligatory hours of observation, Gina and I went to work at NOLA Sexual Health.

Around the time the boys turned five, Tate suddenly decided he wanted to be a part of their lives. You know, after the hard stuff: the crying, constant diaper changing, and up-all-night feedings. Legally, he had visitation rights, so I couldn't stop him from taking them on his weekends. Sometimes, he did; other times, he didn't. He gets them just often enough to ruin all of my hard work, returning two disrespectful little shits. And just when I've finally whipped their little asses back into shape, he miraculously shows up and the cycle starts all over. But the worst part of him blowing in and out of their lives by far is the way he hurts my boys. There is nothing worse than seeing the disappointment on my babies' faces when that man promises them he'll show and then doesn't.

For a very long time, it was impossible for me to date. Between being a single mother to twin boys and living almost three hours away from any family, it was difficult to find time for myself. I barely had time to shower. *Trust me*, a man was the least of my worries. But, on the weekends the twins left to go to Tate's house, I found myself with nothing but time. Gina grew tired of watching me mope and declared his weekends girls' weekends. I had forgotten how fun it was to drink, dance, and to not have to be the responsible one all of the time. And, I may have allowed myself to get a little carried away.

While we were out one night almost three years ago, I met a Latin god by the name of Alex and apparently got drunk enough to forget that sperm makes babies. Alex and I had only been seeing each other for a few months. Wait, that sounds so formal. I'll just call it like it was. We'd been fucking, but only while the boys were away. I was obsessed with Alex's body and addicted to the things he did to mine. After having been responsible for my own orgasms for so long, it was nice to pass that task over to his more than capable hands and, um...appendage.

When I found myself unable to get out of bed and puking my guts up for a solid week, Gina showed up at my house with a drugstore bag, which she shoved into my chest before she ushered me into the bathroom. She wished me luck and shut the door. I don't know why it hadn't dawned on me before. Maybe I was in denial. But when I saw that little rectangular box, my reality hit me like a ton of bricks. *Not again.*

If you do the math, you already know that little booger came out with a big fat positive. I was thirty years old, unmarried, and pregnant with my third child.

When I told Alex, he offered to pay for an abortion. I may have been irresponsible in failing to use protection, but I was not going to end my pregnancy. I'd already come to terms with the fact there *was* going to be a baby. The only question in my mind at that point was whether or not he would be involved. I wasn't fooling myself. We were not a couple, and I had no intention of trying to force a relationship between us just because I'd wound up pregnant. But, I wasn't going to make the same mistake that I had with Lake and Landon. If he wasn't going to be an active part of this baby's life, then I wouldn't force it. I left him with the knowledge that I was having this baby, with or without him, and that if he chose to be a real father to our child, I would not stand in his way. But if he wasn't going to be there, and I mean really be there, then I didn't want his money, and he could pretend the whole thing never happened. Alex didn't even take a full day to think it over before texting me back. His message simply read, "I'm out."

You would think that all of this would make me a cynic. Believe it or not, I'm not. I know there are good men out there, but I have neither the time nor the energy to search for my prince charming anymore. My three boys, my job, and my vibrator will just have to sustain me for the foreseeable future.

But, my clients give me hope. They prove to me every day that there are still princes living among the pigs. Men who are willing to humble themselves in order to do whatever it takes to save their marriages. I may not know how to pick 'em, but I've got a list of clients a mile long that will tell you I know how to fix 'em.

And that, dear friends, is how I became a walking contradiction—a thirty-three year-old sex therapist with absolutely no sex life.

Chapter Two
SPENCER

"Spencer?" my secretary, Annie, blares through the intercom, interrupting my daydream.

I reach out to press the intercom button on my phone. "Yes?"

"Boss is here to see you."

Just great.

I sure hope he isn't here to give me shit about the episode with Mr. Monroe yesterday. I've been seeing the Monroes for a few months, trying—successfully, I thought—to help them work through their intimacy issues. Then out of nowhere, they show up, turning my office into a freaking Jerry Springer episode. My bookshelf was tossed on its side, papers and glass from broken picture frames strewn around the room. It was a complete disaster. Apparently, Tom had walked in on Sue and her best friend, Rosalie, going at it on the couch. He'd rushed right on over here without even making an appointment to rat her out. Only, I'd had other clients in my office. He'd barged in with Sue hot on his heels. A shouting match ensued, my office was destroyed, and we'd had to call security to escort them out of the building. I'd apologized profusely to the Boudreauxs for the interruption. It was all I could do. In the seven years I'd practiced here, nothing like that had ever happened.

I slide my mouse across the desk to wake my computer then click the little X on Facebook before buzzing her back. "Send him on in."

A lump forms in my throat as the French doors to my office swing open and Dillon Bourque saunters in. *Damn, that man is sex in a suit.* The whole room fills with the scent of his spicy cologne. It usually gets me all flustered, but today it's just making my stomach churn with nausea.

"Spencer, we need to talk." He looks so serious. There's not the slightest hint of a smile on his lips, and his eyes aren't the lust-filled orbs that normally make me uncomfortable in an entirely different manner.

Oh God, Is he going to fire me?

I try not to freak out, but I can't help it. When I'm nervous, I tend to develop diarrhea mouth. "Dillon, what happened yesterday was completely out of my control. I wasn't aware that there was another woman involved. I only know what they tell me and—"

He holds up his hand, cutting me off. Dillon, who is usually amused by my rambling, is stone cold—almost lifeless. "I know…that's not why I'm here."

My hands begin to sweat as he starts pacing around my small office. I'm going to vomit if he doesn't put me out of my misery soon. I try swallowing down the sick feeling lodged in my throat then nod, signaling for him to go ahead.

"There's no easy way to tell you this, Spencer…"

Spit it out already!

"Try using words." It comes out flat, lacking my usual

sarcasm, but patience is not my greatest virtue.

"We're shutting down the clinic."

My fingers dig into the leather arms of my chair as the room begins to spin. There's no way that I just heard him correctly. "No." The lone word comes out as a plea as my head begins to shake from side to side. I feel faint. I can't breathe. Dillon's voice morphs into something resembling the teacher from Charlie Brown, but I completely tune him out in my panic. All of my focus is on the ability to draw air into my lungs, which seem to be failing me at the moment.

Before he has even finished speaking, my office door flies open and Gina bursts into the room. Her short, blonde hair that's usually styled to perfection is sticking up on all ends, her pasty white skin a nice shade of crimson. She's a wreck. *Guess he got ahold of her first.*

"Goddamnit, Gina!" Dillon growls, fisting his hands in his hair.

She glares at him before turning in my direction. "I'm so sorry, Spence." My best friend rushes over, wrapping me up in her arms as her tears soak my shirt. "He just left my office. I wanted to come right over, but he insisted on being the one to tell you."

My lip begins to quiver. "Why?"

Dillon's throat clears, his exasperation with the two of us evident on his face. "All right, I'll leave you girls to it. For what it's worth, I'm really sorry, and you'll both have nice severance packages."

Gina breaks from our hug, spinning around lightning fast and leveling him with devil eyes. "Oh, you buzz right the fuck off, Dillon Bourque." She's like a possessed little pixie. I have never seen her get mad at Dillon, ever.

Dillon's jaw ticks for a moment before he finally shakes his head in defeat and turns to walk out. On his way, I hear him stop to tell Annie to cancel all of my upcoming appointments and to let my clients know that NOLA Sexual Health is no longer seeing patients.

As soon as the door clicks into place, I leap to my feet, pacing a hole into the floor. "What's going on, Gina? We have plenty of business. There's no way we're going under. This can't be because of that shit yesterday, can it?"

I've never seen my best friend this angry. Well, except maybe when I showed her that text from Alex a few years ago. She is beet red, and that little blue vein throbbing in the center of her forehead looks ready to pop. "That fucker fucked one of his fucking clients and we're being sued!"

My eyes bulge. *Well, that is not what I was expecting.* "He-he did what?"

"Apparently, it's been happening for a while. She got pissed at her husband and threw it in his face a couple of days ago. The husband is suing."

It's going to be okay. We're going to be okay. I just need a plan.

What's the plan, Spencer?

I drop the final box of my personal belongings into the back of my Tahoe and slam it shut. This all feels like a sick dream. It's hard enough to earn respect in our profession without people assuming we're running a fucking brothel, but with Dillon bringing the damned stereotype to life, Gina and I will never be able to practice in this town again.

I can't believe that asshole. How could he be stupid enough to sleep with a client? In his damned office, at that. How could he do this to us? To Gina and to me? It's not like he couldn't get any piece of ass he wanted. He's freaking gorgeous, smart, successful...I just can't wrap my mind around it. But then again, I know better than anyone men always think with their fucking dicks.

I can't stop the steady stream of tears that are lining my face as I pull the door open and curl into my seat. My hand is shaking so violently that it's hard to get the key into the ignition. After several attempts, I finally insert the key and the engine roars to life. The air comes on, blasting cold wind in my face. *God, it feels good.* I rest my head on the steering wheel, allowing the air to cool my flaming skin. When I finally get control of my tears, I pluck my phone out of my purse and scroll down to the letter M, pressing my finger on Momma.

"Hey, Spence! What's up?" The comfort in her voice wraps around my heart like a warm blanket as my eyes fill with new tears.

You know that feeling when you're barely holding it together and someone asks you what's wrong and you just kind of lose it? *It's gone.*

"M-Momma," I stammer, sobbing into my hands.

So much for that control.

"Are you okay, baby? Are the boys all right?"

"They're, umm...They're fine. It's just...well, Dillon fucking slept with a client and now they're shutting the whole place down. I have no freaking job because of his dumb ass. How the hell am I going to support three children with no job, Mom? He ruined everything just to get his fucking dick wet and—"

"Slow down and stop using that filthy language. You know

I hate it when you talk like that. I raised you better, Spencer Rose!"

I snort out a laugh, choking on my tears. Leave it to my mother to chastise me for my unladylike mouth in the middle of a breakdown. "Sorry," I mutter.

"Now, as for the rest of it...you're gonna get your ducks in a row, hire some movers, and *come home*. You can stay with me 'til you sell your place there and find a decent job. Hell, you can stay here even after that."

"Mom, I don't wanna inconvenience you. It's not just me, you know."

"Nonsense. I've been all alone in this big house since your father died last year, and I would love the company. You always said if you could move the clinic to Cedar Grove you would. Well, now there's no need. Come home."

She makes it sound so simple. Like it's not a big deal for me to just pack up three kids and move hours away. Like my maniacs won't completely disrupt her life. I don't think she has any clue what she's in for, but what other choice do I have right now? As much as I don't want to leave the city, I won't be able to start over here. Not with the scandal Dillon created.

It's Monday. If I tell the kids tonight, that'll give them the rest of the week to say their goodbyes. My job was really the only thing keeping us here, and it would be nice not to constantly worry that I might run into Kyle's sperm donor around town.

Guess we're going back home. Small town Louisiana, here we come.

"We'll be there Saturday. Thanks, Mom."

"Love you, baby. It's gonna be all right. You'll see. Change is hard, but sometimes it's a blessing in disguise."

There's a lilt in her tone that leads me to believe that there's something she's not telling me. I just hope she knows what she's in for. Living with three boys is a hell of a lot different from a week-long visit every couple of months.

After ending the call, I switch over to my messages, which had been blowing up while I was on the phone. With a quick glance at the clock, I note the time: 3:30. The boys are just getting home from school. I was a nervous wreck about letting them stay home alone for the few hours after school until I get home in the afternoons, but since they turned twelve last summer and aged out of the sitter, I didn't have much choice. I'm normally staring at the phone, waiting for their texts letting me know they've made it home. I've gotten so caught up in the drama today that I wasn't even aware of the time.

> Landon: Hey, Mom. We're home. Can you get burgers for dinner from that deli near your office? Pleeeeeeease? No onions, extra pickles.

> Me: Sure thing, baby. Do your homework.

> Landon: Thanks! Don't have any.

> Lake: Mom, don't be mad at me. I have a project. Can you pick up a poster board and colored Sharpies on your way home?

> Me: Why would I be mad at you for having a project?

I already know why. I'd bet my ass this project is due tomorrow.

> Lake: Uh, it's due tomorrow.

> Me: Figured. I got it. Do the rest of your homework.

> Lake: Yes, ma'am. Sorry, Mom.

Oh, these boys.

They are going to be so upset. They've been attending Saint Augustine with the same kids since pre-k. They're going to hate me for making them leave.

I stop by the burger joint to grab dinner, hit up Walmart for supplies, and finally make it to Kyle's daycare just minutes before they close.

"Mommy," he squeals, running toward me on his wobbly little legs before wrapping himself around my calf.

"Hey, baby, did you have a good day?" I ask, bending to lift him into my arms.

He nods, his eyes widen, and he sniffs. "You 'mell *good*, Mom."

"I do? Well, you smell stinky! Did you poop in your pull-up?"

Kyle shakes his head. "I not did dat. Mya do dat."

Mrs. Stevens and I both suck in our lips and cheeks, trying not to laugh. "Mya pooped in *your* diaper?"

"Her did," he insists with the most innocent puppy dog eyes ever.

"I did not," Mya, Mrs. Steven's four-year-old granddaughter, shouts, stomping her foot on the floor and crossing her chubby little arms across her chest.

"Liar, liar," Kyle chants, tilting his head from side to side.

Mya's bottom lip starts to tremble and fat tears drip from her eyes.

"It's okay, Mya. I know you didn't do it." I pat her little, blonde head and that seems to appease her. "That wasn't nice, Savage. We don't lie, and we aren't mean to our friends." My eyes narrow at my son, who every day is more and more deserving of the nickname his brothers gave him. Thank God he's impossibly cute. The bad is strong with this one.

I make Kyle apologize to Mya and give her a hug before walking over to the changing table to clean his mess, putting him in a fresh pull-up for the ride home. I'm just about to walk out of the door when it hits me that he won't be coming back.

With my heart in my throat, I take a few extra minutes to explain what happened at work and that we'll be moving this weekend. By the time I finish, Mrs. Stevens and I are both in tears. She's been his sitter since Kyle was two months old. I'm going to miss her, and I know that she will miss Kyle very much. Goodbyes suck.

As I pull up to my house, the wind is knocked out of me. It's small and it's old, but it's ours. We live in a great neighborhood, and this has been our home for going on five years. I'm going to miss it, even if I do complain about the lack of space.

Am I doing the right thing? I can't help but wonder. That's probably the hardest part of being alone—having to make all of the major life changing decisions for this family myself.

Before I've even turned off the truck, Lake and Landon come barreling out of the house. Lake goes right for Kyle and begins unbuckling him, and Landon straight for the food. He's eating out of the bag before he even gets inside of the house.

"Did you had a good day, Yake?" I hear Kyle ask his brother.

"It was all right, Savage. Did you make anyone cry today?"

"I in shrouble, brudder. I make Mya cry."

I watch their interaction in the rearview mirror, and it takes everything in me not to laugh at Kyle's pitiful face.

"That's okay. Tomorrow's a new day, my man. Do better."

"Lake!" I shake my head, pursing my lips. "Don't tell him it's okay to be mean."

"But, Mom, look how sorry he is. He won't do it again."

Lake is Kyle's biggest champion. He adores that little boy. It warms my heart to see how good he is with him because I know one day my boy is going to make an amazing father.

"Just get in the house." I wave them off as I grab the Walmart bags and Kyle's diaper bag from the back seat then kick the door shut. "You have a project to do."

I decide on waiting until homework is done and we've all eaten supper before breaking the news to the twins. But, as I take my seat at the kitchen table, my pulse begins to race as it dawns on me. This is Tate's weekend with the boys.

Fuck my life.

Just when I thought this day couldn't get any worse.

Fighting back the urge to hurl, I pull out my phone, scroll to his name, and press send. It rings three times, and I breathe out a sigh of relief thinking I've gotten off the hook, but then I hear his voice…like nails on a fucking chalkboard.

"Listen, Spence," he answers in that fake, apologetic tone he uses when he's getting ready to blow off his kids. No greeting, not that I'm surprised. "This weekend is bad for me."

Bad for him? Hah! "You don't say?" I ask condescendingly. "Well, we would hate to inconvenience you. What is it this time? Taking Whorey Spice on another vacation?"

"Jesus, Spencer, grow the fuck up."

I'm sure I sound certifiable when I begin cackling into the phone, because I damn sure feel crazy enough to chop his fucking pecker off and shove it down his throat. "Oh my God," I finally say, dabbing tears from the corners of my eyes. "Wow, Tate, that's rich coming from you."

He groans. "You can be so immature sometimes, I swear to God."

"Well, you know what, Tate? You've got me beat in the immaturity department on my worst day. Maybe you should have grown the fuck up when you planted two kids in my uterus then hauled ass and disappeared for five fucking years. Huh? Maybe you should have grown up then? Or maybe now? Now would be nice. Maybe you should grow the fuck up and put your children first for the first time ever. I was left with no choice but to grow up when I was left alone to raise our children."

"Oh, man. Not this spiel again." I can practically see his eyes rolling up into the back of his head.

I'm so angry, it feels like my veins will explode. He's such a piece of shit and not even worth the stress he adds to my life. "Nah, it never helps, anyway."

"Good, so we're done?"

I wish. "No, I actually called for something other than to see if you were picking up the boys, although they will be absolutely devastated, as usual."

"Why do you always try to make me feel bad?"

What did I ever see in this man? "I'm so sorry, Tate. I forgot for a second that the entire world revolves around you. I'm actually calling to let you know that we're moving."

"And I care where you live because...why, exactly?"

Jesus, Mary, and Joseph, this man better thank his lucky stars he's not standing in front of me right now. "Oh, I don't know...maybe because your children live with me and I thought you might want to know where they are?"

He sighs. "I'll get the new address from you next time I come get them. It's not that serious that you had to make this big of an ordeal out of it."

"We're moving back to Cedar Grove."

That gets his attention. "That's over three hours from here!" he shouts. "Look, I don't give a shit where you live, but I'm not driving that far to pick them up. You'll have to bring them here or something."

"That's not how this works. It's your responsibility to facilitate your visitations, and that includes getting the children to your home on your weekends—whenever you decide to actually take advantage of those. I have no problem meeting you halfway. Unlike you, my life revolves around their happiness, and for some unknown reason, they still enjoy being with you."

"Whatever. I've got to go. Tell the boys I'm sorry I can't take them this weekend, okay? We'll discuss the rest of this when the time comes."

"Why don't you tell them you're sorry? Why don't you tell them you have better things to do? Why the hell am I always the one who has to do your dirty work, Tate?"

He huffs into the line. "Look, I gotta go. Tell the boys I love them."

"Always such a—" *pleasure talking to you*, I finish in my head when I realize that the line is dead.

I hate that Tate doesn't take more interest in our children. They deserve so much more from him. And, once again, I will bear the brunt of their disappointment. Then, I'll add the icing to the cake with news of our move.

Here goes nothing.

"Boys!" I shout, cupping my clammy hands around my mouth. "Can y'all come in here for a bit? I need to talk to you about something." I rub my palms nervously on my pants as I wait, pulling in a few deep breaths to calm myself.

Landon arrives first, and with one look at my face makes

his own assumptions as to the reason I've called them over. "He's not coming to get us, is he?"

Lake appears in the doorway with the little savage clinging to his leg just as his brother finishes asking the question. The anxious looks on both of their faces makes me sick to my stomach.

Well, if I'm gonna break their hearts tonight, I might as well give 'em a double whammy, right?

Fuck you, Tate.

Fuck you, Dillon.

Swallowing hard, I give them my most sympathetic face. "Sorry, guys. He's not coming."

Landon shrugs. "I didn't really wanna go, anyway." His eyes glisten with unshed tears. My poor love. He's trying so hard to pretend it doesn't bother him. Landon's at that age where he thinks he's too big to cry. Instead, he bottles up his emotions until they are forced to come out in angry outbursts.

"I don't even care anymore," Lake adds without an ounce of emotion. "I'd be more stunned if he actually did show up." He shrugs. "I'd rather be home, anyway."

"Can we go now?" Landon asks, trying to mask his pain.

Time to twist the knife. "Actually, there's more. Can you two sit, please?" I pat the chairs on either side of me and they each take a seat. My kids stare at me expectantly while I take a few more deep breaths before delivering the blow. I clear my throat, feeling my pulse speed up. "The clinic is shutting down. I, uh...I lost my job today."

Both boys stare at me with stunned expressions. It's Lake who finally speaks up. "What's that mean? Are we going to lose our house?"

"It means that we're going to sell our house and move in

with Gramma Elaine for a while. We're moving to Cedar Grove...this weekend." I force myself to smile, hoping that if I seem excited about it, they will be, too.

"What the fuck!?" Landon shouts, shocking me speechless.

It takes me a moment to register that my child just said that word...to me.

"Excuse me, young man?" My eyes narrow.

Landon doesn't apologize or seem remorseful. Instead, he places his hands on the table and stands, sending his chair crashing to the floor behind him. "You can't do this to us. It isn't fair!"

Lake stares at his brother like he's lost his damned mind, and I'm fairly certain he's right. We've both kind of gotten used to Landon's blow ups, but this...this is taking it to a whole other level. I don't even know how to react.

Kyle starts running in circles around the dining room table, yelling, "Fuck, fuck, fuck." I'm seriously about to have a freaking nervous breakdown.

Shutting my eyes, I pinch the bridge of my nose, and with all the restraint I can muster, grit out between clenched teeth, "Get to your room, Landon Michael."

"I'm not moving." Landon fists his hands at his sides, shaking his head. "I'm staying with Dad."

I bark out a humorless laugh and have to stop myself before I say something really ugly about his piece of shit father. "You will do whatever I say. Get. To. Your. Room. Now!" I slam my fist onto the table, and all three pairs of my children's eyes jerk my way. I can feel my blood boiling beneath my skin, and I know that I can't go near my son feeling this way. For both of our sakes, he better get out of my face.

"Dude, listen to Mom," Lake finally says, shoving his

twin out of the kitchen. Landon must realize how pissed I am because he rushes off to his room without another word. Their bedroom door slams shut, rattling the thin walls of our shotgun house, and I don't even flinch, fully expecting his dramatics. Lake scoops Kyle up as he comes back around. "Don't say that bad word, little man. That's not nice."

"Fuck not nice, Yake?" Kyle's little hands cup his brother's cheeks as his face screws up in confusion.

Lake stifles his laugh, shaking his head. "Want me to get him ready for bed, Mom?"

This kid has such a tender heart. I know he's upset as well, but where Landon is explosive with his feelings and reacts without thinking, Lake always puts others' feelings above his own. Always.

I scoot my chair back and walk over to where Lake is standing with Kyle in the entryway. "I'm sorry, Lake."

"It'll be okay. He'll calm down. You know how he is." He should be upset about his father and the move, but all I see in those big blue eyes is sympathy for me. This boy is mature beyond his years. I don't know what I did to deserve such a great kid, but I'm so very thankful. He's the calm to our storm.

"Thank you for understanding." As I take Kyle from him, I wrap my free arm around Lake's shoulders before placing a kiss on his cheek. "Get to bed, baby. I've got Savage."

"'Night, Mom. Love you."

"Love you, too, baby."

That went well...

Chapter Three
COOPER

"Coop," Momma calls from the sink where she's washing dishes. "Can you go grab the mail? I just saw the truck pass and I'm waiting on some Avon."

That woman and her Avon. I close the case files I've been working on for the past two hours. My eyes could use a break, anyway. "Sure, Ma."

As I'm making my way into the foyer to grab my tennis shoes, I can't help but notice how everything is still exactly the same as it was when I lived here fifteen years ago. The same pictures hang in the same spots. The floral sofa set that no one's ever been allowed to sit on still sits in pristine condition on the white carpet that years later still looks brand new. I open the front door, stepping out onto the wraparound porch. The same two rocking chairs that have been there for as long as I can remember sit to my left, and the old wood swing still hangs on the right. It's like stepping into a time capsule.

When I sprint down the steps, the bottom one gives a little, creaking beneath my weight, just like I expect it to.

I'm jogging down the long drive that runs parallel to

the LeBlanc's, who've been our neighbors since before I was born, when my eyes wander over to their house and spot an unfamiliar vehicle. I've been back here for almost two weeks and I've never seen that black Tahoe before today. I slow my gait, being the nosy neighbor that I am, curious to see who's paying Mrs. Elaine a visit this early on a Saturday.

I hear her before I see her. "Landon, I've had about enough of your attitude for one day already."

Spence is still raising hell. The sound of her screeching brings a nostalgic smile to my face. I used to love to get that girl's panties in a twist. Hell, I used to love to get into that girl's panties.

I switch directions, heading toward the LeBlanc house to say hello.

As I'm approaching the truck, I hear her yell at Landon again. "Go help your brother get our stuff out of the car." I watch as two dirty blond teens walk around to the back and pop the hatch open. Bags begin tumbling out. Damn. How long are they planning to visit?

The driver's side door swings open and Spence climbs out. Immediately, our eyes lock. She looks me up and down as I take in the beautiful chaos that stands before me. Her raven hair is in a huge knot on top of her head. She's in yoga pants and a threadbare tee with flip-flops and not a stitch of makeup on. Although I can tell she's both tired and stressed, her face hasn't aged a bit. Creamy white skin, crystal blue eyes, and dimples for days.

"Coop?" She blinks a few times as if she's surprised to see me. Her mother must not have told her that I moved back, much like my own hadn't bothered mentioning to me that Spencer would be in for a visit this weekend. She must have known. I don't think either of our moms can take a shit without telling the other.

"Heya, Princess." The old nickname rolls easily off my tongue.

Spencer looks down at her ratty clothes and her cheeks flush. "What're you doing in Cedar Grove? I thought that you and Kristy had moved to Texas."

"We did. Our divorce has been finalized for a few months." Spencer's blue eyes widen in shock. Did her mom not tell her that, either? "I moved back about two weeks ago," I add, stuffing my hands into my pockets as I begin rocking back and forth. Spencer makes me feel like a nervous teenager. I never thought I'd ever feel uncomfortable around this girl. There was a time we'd known all there was to know about each other. But, since we broke up, every interaction feels awkward. Like we're ignoring the huge fucking elephant in the room, because we are, and we've been doing it for almost fifteen damn years.

"Oh," she gasps before clearing her throat. "I, ummm. I had no clue." She swallows as her thumbnail moves to her mouth and she begins chewing. "I can't believe my mom didn't mention that. I mean, it's kind of a big deal." She huffs, blowing upward to push the hair out of her eyes.

"I assumed you already knew."

Spencer's head shakes slowly. "Wh-what happened?" she asks, fiddling with the bottom of her shirt.

The last thing I want to discuss with this woman is my ex-wife and our failed marriage. I shrug. "We just...we didn't work out. Kristy wanted things I couldn't give her." Spence nods, but her face is screwed up in confusion. It's as if she doesn't understand a word that's coming out of my mouth. "There was no sense in either of us being miserable. It was for the best," I answer carefully, both wanting to make sure she knows that I'm not still hung up on my ex-wife and not wanting to come off as an uncaring asshole, either.

"Wow." She gulps, staring at my face as if she's waiting for more. I have no more to offer.

The truth is, that while I cared about Kristy, I never loved her. Not the way I should have. I guess she's expecting me to be more upset, but all I felt the day I signed those papers was relief. I can't exactly say that, so I opt for changing the subject.

"What about you? Last I heard you were still teaching women how to orgasm in NOLA." I laugh, throwing that out there to try and lighten the mood. I hate it that she's so nervous. But, my attempt at humor backfires.

Spencer's face pales as a little voice calls from the back seat. "Hi, man. Hiii!"

That must be number three. The last time I saw him was at her father's funeral. He was barely walking, and certainly not talking yet. It's a lot harder to ignore him when he's calling for me.

Her eyes narrow to slits. "Don't be a pig, Cooper. I loved my job."

Well, this just got interesting. "Past tense?"

"The clinic I worked at is closing down, so the kids and I are moving in with Mom 'til I find a job and we sell our house." Her voice is thick with emotion. She's definitely not happy about being back here, and she doesn't seem too thrilled with the fact that I'm here, either.

"Yet me outta here! Yet me out, man!" baby spawn yells from the back seat as his little fist pounds on the tinted glass. Spencer pretends she doesn't notice.

"You gonna take the kid out or what?"

"I'm sorry?" Her hand goes to her chest in an unspoken "Are you talking to me?"

"The little one." I dip my eyes toward the back seat. "You can't tell me you don't hear him yelling to get out."

"I know it's been a while, Coop, but I'm missing a vital piece of equipment to be addressed as man." Her brows do a sexy little bounce as she dips her head toward the car in challenge. A smirk plays on her lips.

Shaking my head, I hold my hands palms out and slowly begin backing away. "Oh no. Sorry. I don't do kids." Especially not kids that the woman who was supposed to bear my own children had with other men.

Apparently, she finds this amusing. With a giggle, she mocks, "You don't do children?" Spence raises her hands, making air quotes.

"I don't."

"Wow." With that single word, all humor is wiped from her face. I'm truly fascinated by how quickly this woman is able to switch her emotions. I try not to stare in awe as she continues. "I'm not asking you to take him home or anything. He just wants you to get him out of the truck. He's a two-year-old, Cooper...not a fucking viper."

Well, this is going downhill real quick.

"I'm just not around kids much. They make me uncomfortable," I say by way of explanation, hoping to calm her tits a little. The last thing I want is to piss her off, but I seem to have a knack for it.

Spencer's mouth falls open in surprise. "Are you really not going to take that baby out of the car?" She is downright pissed, and this time, her anger is directed at me.

Fuck. I don't remember her being so scary. She's got those

momma eyes down to a T, yet, somehow...on her, they are hot as hell. The term M.I.L.F. now makes all the sense in the world.

Spence throws her hands up in resignation as she tries to move around me. "Get out of my way so I can get him."

My hand darts out, grabbing ahold of her upper arm. "Are you angry with me, Princess?" I ask, pulling her close. I find myself fighting the urge to smile. She would fucking murder me.

Spence growls with annoyance. "Fuckin' right I am. You don't come over here acting like my baby has a damn disease or something." Her manicured finger is right in my face. I reach out, pinching it between my thumb and forefinger, and bring it to my lips, dropping a kiss on the tip before lowering her hand to her side. That earns me a glare, but she's not unaffected. In fact, she's stunned speechless. My heart is racing. I can feel it pulsing in my throat.

"Man! Hi, man. Take me out!"

"Fine, I'll do it."

Spencer's sparkling blue eyes roll up in her head as she jerks her arm out of my grip and crosses them on her chest. "Just go home." Her head shakes slightly and she huffs a disgusted breath. And fuck if that doesn't make me want to prove to her that I'm not the loser she thinks I am. Her anger, I can handle. Her disappointment, I cannot.

She starts to walk around me again to open the door, but I stand in front of it, legs and arms spread wide, blocking her. "I said I'd do it."

"You look like a five-year-old," Spence snaps, backing away a few paces.

I open the truck door and the little booger smiles a big, cheesy grin. "Hi, man!"

"Hey, little guy," I say with a smile. I can do this. I can hold her kid.

"You a fuck!"

Whoa! I jerk back in surprise, knocking my head on the doorframe.

"Shit!" Goddamnit. That fucking hurt.

"Shit!" the little potty mouth repeats.

"Don't say that," I whisper, hoping the she-devil behind me didn't hear.

"Are you teaching my baby bad words?"

"I think your baby could teach me a few bad words," I call back as I finish untangling his arms from the straps and pull him out. The way he looks so much like his momma takes me by surprise. Her smile. Her dimples. Her little button nose.

"What're you talking about?"

"This kid just called me a fuck." I make sure to mouth the last word as to not get myself into any more trouble. I hold the kid out to Spencer so she can take him, but he pushes away from her.

"Hole me, man! I yike you."

Spencer's cheeks redden like a ripe, juicy tomato. "He probably just said truck. Two-year-olds don't always pronounce words correctly."

"I not say shruck, Mommy. I say fuck!"

I smirk and cock my brow, daring her to tell me that I didn't just hear what I know I heard. "Your baby just called me the F word."

"Landonnnn!" Uh oh.

"Ma'am?" he says, coming around the truck with a fresh load of bags in his arms.

Spencer's hand flies out, connecting with his shoulder.

Landon flinches at the same time that I hop back in surprise.

"How many times have I told you to watch your mouth around your baby brother? Huh?" Landon shrugs as she leans in closer. "He just called Cooper the F word!"

"Mommy, you mean! Not hit Yannon, Mommy. Dat not nice!"

"Shhhhh," I whisper to the little dude in my arms. "Didn't anyone ever teach you not to poke the bear?"

"Not helping, Cooper," Satan grumbles without turning from her kid.

"Can I go now?" Landon mutters, still rubbing his arm.

"Go!"

I wait until the kid is out of sight before risking my life. Why I'm choosing to put my life on the line for the enemy, I have no fucking clue, but apparently I am going for the gusto. "I know I'm not a parent or anything, and I don't even think I'd be a good one, but you think maybe you shouldn't have hit him?"

Her head spins, and I half expect green vomit to shoot out of her mouth. "Did you just call me a shitty parent?"

I look around as if the person she's talking to will just magically appear, because I know damned well that I did not just do that. "I didn't say that."

"No," she says, ripping her baby from my arms. "You just said that you'd be a shit parent and even you wouldn't hit your kid."

Umm. What the hell is happening here? "I don't think that's what I said."

Her big blue eyes well up. Oh shit. "You think this is easy, Cooper? Huh? You think you could do better?" Her eyes overflow as big, fat tears drip from her chin. "Guess where their perfect fathers are?"

I shrug, wishing I could take back what I said.

"Out...living their lives, because you know what, Coop? They don't do children, either."

Her other son, Lake, silently walks between us, giving me a "Now you've gone and done it" look while shaking his head to himself. He grabs the little one from Spencer's arms. "Come on, Savage. Let's go say hi to Gramma."

"Otay, Yake. Bye, man!"

I lift my hand and wave, watching until they've made it inside before apologizing. "I'm really sorry, Spence. You're right. I don't know shit about raising kids. I shouldn't have said anything."

Her face crumbles. "But, you're right. I-I shouldn't have hit him. He's not handling the move well, and his father stood him up. He's just been so ugly to me this last week, and he taught the baby to say fuck. I was just so embarrassed, and I took it out on him."

She still does it. My heart clenches tightly in my chest as I listen to her ramble on, the way she always used to when she was upset. It's crazy how little things like that stay with you.

Opening my arms, I whisper, "Come here, Princess."

She shuffles forward until her chest is flush with mine then rests her forehead on my shoulder. Slowly, Spence snakes her arms around my waist as I do the same. I hold her while she cries it all out, stroking her back lightly with the tips of my fingers.

I look up to find her mother watching us from the front window, and when her eyes meet mine, she gives me a thumbs up.

It's at this moment I realize that these old ladies are up to something. I'd be willing to bet that when I get to Momma's mailbox...that son of a bitch is empty.

Chapter Four
SPENCER

Remember when I told you I'd had exactly three sexual partners in my lifetime? That broken heart I spent years getting over before Tate? Well, that third spot and broken heart can both be accredited to Cooper Hebert. And yet, being in Cooper's arms like this again feels like heaven. Even if he is a big, dumb, kid-hating jerk.

Stop staring, Spencer. Fuck. I can't. Somehow, he's managed to get even more gorgeous with time with his stupid boy band hair and the way the light sheen of sweat on his hairline causes brown wisps to stick to his forehead. How those amber brown eyes catch the light from the sun so perfectly. The way they're staring into mine right now and I'm suddenly finding it hard to swallow. Those lips. Dear God in heaven, I want to suck on those lips. No. No, I don't. *What's wrong with me?* I will not be lured in by that sexy scruff, chiseled jawline, or that fucking dimple in his chin that still makes my heart race. Goddamnit.

"Still mad, Momma Bear?" He whispers the question in my ear, and the warmth of his breath makes me shiver.

I shrug, burying my nose in the fabric of his shirt. The scent is oddly comforting. It's the smell of childhood sleepovers, first dances, first kisses, and first love. Coop smells exactly the way he did when we were kids. For a moment, I convince myself that nothing has changed. But, although this place may look the same and he may even smell the same, I can't allow myself to forget that we are very different people.

"Let me make it up to you? I'm meeting Roy Nelson at T-Boy's tonight for a beer. Why don't you take my number and call me if you can sneak away? Let me buy you a drink?"

God, I haven't been to T-Boy's bar since we were kids. Hell, I haven't been inside of a bar since discovering that I was pregnant with Kyle. I'm not sure how wise it'd be to go out drinking with my heart's most unhealthy addiction. I am dangerously close to falling back under his spell. Hell, maybe I've been fooling myself into believing I've ever truly gotten out from under it.

I pull back, feeling embarrassed for so many reasons. The way I'm dressed, losing it on my child, breaking down in front of him. It's definitely not a novel worthy reunion, that's for damned sure.

"Say you'll come..." he pleads, giving me a pouty lip as he holds out his business card, offering it to me between his pointer and middle fingers.

"I'll think about it. It's been a hell of a day, Coop. Shit. It's been a hell of a week." I take the card from his hand and flip it around in my fingers.

"All the more reason you should sneak away with an old friend for an adult beverage or two, or even ten. I won't judge."

Old friends. Such a shitty title for all that we were.

"Is that what you consider me? An old friend, Coop?"

He reaches out, tucking a tendril of hair behind my ear

as his eyes meet mine. "Princess, I don't know that there are words to adequately define what I think of you and us. Old friends felt most appropriate considering...But, if you need me to stand here and list all of the roles you've filled in my life...the voids you left when you took yourself out of it...I can."

I can smell the coffee on his breath and have to fight the urge to lean in and taste it. Suddenly, I'm finding it extremely difficult to breathe. Why does the world always disappear when I'm with this man? How can a few words still ignite a fire in my blood?

"Mommmmy," Kyle screams, banging on the screen door. "Mommy, hole me!"

I pull my bottom lip between my teeth and laugh. "I'll think about it, Coop. I should get inside and say hi to Momma... tend to my children."

Cooper hangs his head, studying his shoes. "You're still as beautiful as ever, Spence," he says as he lifts his brown eyes to meet mine. "You still make it hard to breathe."

"And you," I say, swallowing as I try to rein in my overeager heart, "are still the same old charmer you always were."

He chuckles, mostly to himself. "Was good seeing you again, Spence. Call me if you change your mind, okay?"

"Mommmmy!"

"I will. I gotta run."

Cooper takes both of my hands into his, squeezing them gently. He looks into my eyes and stares a little too long. A little too hard. And I feel way too much.

I step back, letting my hands slip slowly out of his, and then I tear my eyes away. I don't trust my voice enough to utter another word as I go. I want to turn back. I miss him the second I move away. Coop's eyes burn holes into my back as I climb the steps and pull the screen door open. Even then, I don't have the courage to glance in his direction. I let the door slam shut behind me, continuing into the kitchen where Momma is spoiling my boys with junk food and sodas.

"Mommy, you baack!" Kyle calls from his booster seat, reaching out with his Cheeto-covered fingers, making grabby hands.

I blow him a kiss from the doorway. "Not a chance, Savage. You finish your snack and I'll hold you after you get all cleaned up."

He doesn't argue, digging right back in to the mountain of chips and candy before him.

"Welcome home, Spencer." Momma dries her hands on the towel that hangs from the oven handle and walks over with glossy eyes and a smile that splits her wrinkly face. She grabs my head in her hands and places kisses on each of my cheeks before wrapping me in her arms. "I'm so happy you've finally come back."

I know why she didn't tell me that Cooper was home. It's never been said, but she knows me better than anyone. Well enough to know that the reason I've stayed away all these years was to distance myself from the boy who broke my heart. The heartbreak from which I've never fully recovered. I thought I'd be safe now that he was married and living in another state. If I had known that Coop was back, there's no way I'd have come. I'd have been too afraid to face him. And yet, I still have to ask..."Why didn't you tell me?" My voice cracks.

"You wouldn't have come," she answers simply, crossing her arms on her chest.

I shake my head. "No."

"Well, there ya have it. Now go wash up. You look like hell.

I got these hooligans for a few hours. Take a nap."

This woman. My eyes well up as my heart swells. I've gone it alone for so long with no one there to worry about me. The simple offer of a bath and a nap in the middle of the day is the greatest gift she could've given me.

"Thanks, Mom."

"No problem, baby girl. It's time you start taking better care of yourself. You aren't gonna win that man back walking around looking like something off that walking zombies show."

I choke. "It's *The Walking Dead*, Momma."

"Whatever, you get the point. Now's your chance, Fancy... Don't let me down."

My Momma is obsessed with Reba and has been since I was a little girl. The reference brings a smile to my face, even if her meaning sort of pisses me off. "Momma, I'm not looking for a man."

"Of course you aren't lookin'. The only one you ever wanted is right under your nose," she says, tapping her pointer finger to the tip of my nose. "Don't fuck it up this time," she whispers so the kids can't hear.

What the ever-living hell? Why does everyone seem to think I'm to blame for Coop and I not ending up together?

"You're going senile, old lady. Coop dumped me. Not the other way around. And did you just say fuck?"

"Sometimes sentence enhancers are necessary to get one's point across."

"Well, your point is out of line. And anyway, Cooper doesn't like kids. So, you can get those thoughts out of your head. You should've seen the way he acted with Kyle. It was insulting. Cooper isn't the same boy he was when we were growing up, Momma. He's sort of an ass."

But, God, does he have a fine ass...and his face. That body. It's better than ever. My skin begins to tingle remembering the way it felt to have my body pressed against his just moments ago.

"He just needs time to fall in love with 'em, baby. I was watching the two of you out there. I saw the longing in his eyes when he looked at you. That boy isn't over you, not by a long shot. And we both know that...well, you never got over him, either."

The truth hurts, and now it will be staring me in the face each and every day. But, what if she's right? What if he still loves me, too? Would it even matter? The answer is a resounding no. My life isn't about me anymore. I gave that up when I had children. They come first, and I could never be with a man who couldn't love my babies.

As tears begin to creep out the corners of my eyes, I excuse myself. "I'm gonna go lay down now, Momma. Thanks for everything."

"Oh, baby. It's gonna be okay," she whispers after me with a little catch in her voice as I rush off.

"I'm fine, Mom," I yell from the top of the stairs before making my way across the hall and into my room.

I shut the door and lean back against it, taking in my old bedroom fit for a princess. The white, four-poster bed dons a pink canopy adorned with bows in each corner. The pink netting drips down to the floor and is pulled back at the middle and tied to the posts on each end. The bedding is white and fluffy, decorated with varying shades of pink throw pillows.

My first ballet shoes still hang above my old desk and on top sit four ornate picture frames, each holding a memory of Coop and me.

There's one from when we were toddlers, both of us in only our diapers, running in the field between our houses. I looked like the Stay Puft Marshmallow Man with all of my rolls, and Coop was a skinny little thing. His hair was a lighter shade of brown, thin and wispy, curling at the ends. Mine jet black and already past my shoulders.

In the next picture, we were in junior high. He was in his football uniform with his helmet held in his right hand, which was also gripping one of my legs to keep me from falling from his back. I matched him in my cheerleading getup. My long hair in pig tails, topped off with bows. My smile was huge, and there was a sparkle in my eyes. But, what I love most about this picture is the way Coop stared up at me instead of the camera. Even then he looked at me like I was the only thing that mattered. I never had to wonder where I stood with him because Coop wore his love for me loud and proud.

That's why I don't understand how things ended the way they did. How we ended up where we are today—living, and then again, not really living separate lives.

The third frame holds a picture of the two of us standing in front of the limo the night of our senior prom. Coop was so handsome in his tux, and I felt like a princess in that white dress. The bodice was fitted and strapless with sequins, and the skirt consisted of layers upon layers of tulle. He stood with his legs about a foot apart with me cradled in his arms. I remember thinking that this was a prelude to our wedding day. The white dress, the tux, the limo...I'd dreamt of our wedding for practically all my life.

By the time my eyes drift to the fourth and final frame, the tears are steadily falling. Graduation day...Judging by the smile on his face, I'd have never guessed he was planning to break my heart later that night. We stood hand in hand under the large oak in my front yard. Piano key smiles on both of our faces. We were happy. We were in love. Or at least I was. God, I was so crazy in love with that boy.

After graduation, we'd gone out to a fancy dinner with our parents at Marceaux's Steak House. From there, we rode together in Cooper's single cab Chevy S10 to join our class for the after party: a bon fire in the cane fields. Old Mr. Dugas pretended not to notice the hoards of teenagers who invaded his property every weekend. There's no way he didn't know. We left behind plenty of evidence. I think he just wanted us to have a safe place to hang out. We lived in the middle of nowhere. There wasn't even a movie theater within fifty miles.

Looking back on it now, I can't believe our parents allowed us to be so stupid. We drank, we smoked, and Coop and I made love for the last time on a pad of blankets in the bed of his truck. Coop drove us home, and when we parked in his spot, he asked me to stay because we needed to talk. A few different scenarios ran through my head. He had changed his mind and was coming to New Orleans with me instead of taking that stupid scholarship to Boulder. He was going to propose. But never did I imagine he'd kept me there to crush my heart.

"I don't know how to say this, Princess." His beautiful brown eyes swam with unshed tears. "I think we need a break."

I was in shock. I didn't have the ability to utter a single word as my heart shriveled up and died. I stared at the boy I'd loved for all of my life like he was a complete stranger, and I guess he was. I didn't know this person at all.

"Don't do that, baby. Don't cry..." His own tears began to fall, but that didn't stop him from digging that knife in and gutting me. "All we've ever known is each other. And I love you. I know you probably don't believe that right now, but I love you, and that's why we need to do this. I need to know. I need to know that you're with me because there's no one else out there, not because I'm the boy you've shared a bed with since we were in diapers. Not because it's convenient or because it's how it's supposed to be. I want us to come back from college in four years and know without a doubt that this—" he waved his finger between the two of us "—that what we have is the real thing."

His hand darted out and he cupped my cheek, wiping my tears with the pad of his thumb.

I shoved him away. "Don't. Don't you dare. You don't get to break my fucking heart and touch me like you care."

He sniffled and began crying harder. "That's not fair. You know me. You know how much I care about you, Spence."

I scoffed. "No, Coop. I thought I knew you. But, the boy I love wouldn't need to fuck other girls to decide if I was good enough."

I gripped the door handle and pulled before the door swung open. I moved to get out, but Coop's hand reached out, wrapping around my wrist.

"I love you, Spence. Don't give up on us."

Was he freaking serious with this shit? "I never would have. This...this was all you. Now let go of my fucking arm before I lose my shit, Cooper."

He closed his eyes and took two deep breaths before releasing me from his grip. As I climbed down from his truck, he started crying louder and harder, his fists pounding on the dash.

I slammed the door shut, and without looking back, ran through the wet, muddy yard that separated our houses. My chest heaved and tears blinded my vision. I slipped, falling over one of the roots of the big oak tree. I didn't even have the strength to lift myself up.

Cradling my hands to my chest, I cried with a broken heart.

Sometime during the night, Daddy came out and found me lying there. I was soaked to the bone, freezing, trembling, wailing. He lifted me into his arms then carried me up the stairs to my room. He called for Momma. Daddy sat on my bedroom floor and rocked me. And as Momma rushed about gathering clean clothes and dry towels, he cried with me.

Momma dried me up and helped me into my pajamas. She got me into bed, and in that bed is where I stayed for weeks on end. Cooper tried to visit. I heard Momma and Daddy send him away almost every day. He called. I deleted every voicemail without listening to them. And the day I left for college, I made a promise to myself that I would fall in love again.

Boy, did I ever fuck that promise straight to hell. My chest feels tight as I swat at the tears that are rolling down my face. God, I feel like such a fool to still be crying over Cooper all these years later. My stupid heart is nothing but a big fucking vagina.

I fall back onto my childhood bed, and just as I'm starting to drift off, my phone buzzes in my back pocket. With sleep-bleary eyes, I strain to read the message.

Gina: Did you guys make it yet?

Me: Yeah. We're here. Sorry, it's been a little overwhelming. About to take a nap.

Gina: Did something happen? Landon still being a little fucker? Want me to come over there and give him some Auntie Gina tough lovin'?

God, I love this girl.

Me: Nah. I mean, yeah, he's still upset, but it's okay. Coop's here.

Gina: Here as in with you right now? Spencer...he's married.

Me: He's not.

Gina: Not there or not married?

Me: Both.

Gina: Well, if he's not married, then why the fuck aren't you fucking his brains out and showing him what he's been missing out on for the last fifteen goddamned years?

Me: The whole reunion was a freaking disaster. I'll call you later and fill you in. He invited me out for a drink tonight, but I don't think I'm gonna go.

Gina: Uh...yeah, you are. You haven't had sex in like three years, Spence. You could have twat rot for all we know. Take a nap. Groom the lady bits. Put on something sexy and a pair of fuck me heels and go get you some!

Me: Maybe...Going to sleep now. Love you, Gigi!

Chapter Five
COOPER

She didn't call.

I don't know why that surprises me, but it does. I haven't been able to stop thinking about Spence since I held her in my arms this morning. I thought for sure she'd felt what I had. The pull. The spark. The electricity buzzing between us.

I unlock my phone, checking one last time for any missed calls or messages, finding none. Ah, well. There's always tomorrow.

I turn off my truck and step out onto the gravel parking lot in front of T-Boy's. There are exactly three other cars in the lot. Much to my disappointment, none of them are a black Tahoe.

The sinking feeling forming in the pit of my stomach is pissing me off. I know better than to get too attached to Spencer. Those kids aren't going anywhere any time soon, and I can't handle being around a constant reminder of what Spence and I should have had—what we'll never have because she's already given away our chance at a family. I can feel the bitterness threatening to consume me.

Taking a deep inhale of the cool, night air, I head for the hot pink neon sign that reads T-Boy's in cursive letters.

T-Boy's bar is a hole in the wall that's been here for forever. The outside is dingy cypress, and the inside is exactly what you'd expect in a small-town bar. There's a stage in the far right corner where local bands sometimes play on the weekends. The stage is empty tonight. In the center of the room are two pool tables with Budweiser lights dangling above and straight ahead is the bar. Working behind that bar is T-Boy's niece, Josie.

Roy is already seated, chatting up the pretty blonde with a drink in hand.

"Howdy, stranger," Josie shouts as I pull out the stool next to Roy. "What brings you back 'round these parts? Thought you done got married and hauled off to Texas?"

Good old Cedar Grove, where everybody knows all your business half the time before you do. I'm surprised word of my divorce hasn't made it around town yet.

"Heya, Josie. You look good." And she does. Always has. Josie has big, blue eyes and long, blonde curls that reach the middle of her back. She has perky tits and a nice, firm ass, which are both on display tonight in a low-cut crop top and booty shorts that do little to cover her *ass*-ets.

"Nuh uhn, don't you try flatterin' me, thinkin' you're gettin' outta answerin' my questions." She shakes her long, bony finger in my face.

"Nothing gets by you, does it, girl?"

"Not a thing." She reaches beneath the counter and pulls out a Bud Light, popping the cap and setting it on a cocktail napkin directly in front of me. "Now, spill."

"All right. All right." I hold up my hand, indicating for her to hold on while taking a long pull from my beer. "By the way, hi, Roy."

"Hey, man." He hits me with a handshake and a firm slap to the back. Then with a smirk, he dips his eyes at Josie. "Go on, now. Don't keep the lady waitin'."

"Get on with it," she encourages.

I chuckle to myself, shaking my head as I answer. *Guess they'll all know by tomorrow.* "I *was* married, and I *did* move to Houston for about three years. Got divorced a few months ago, and since Pops is getting ready to retire, I figured it was time to come back home and take over the firm."

I know better than to think that's enough to satisfy nosy-rosy. "I'm not tryin' to be nosy or nuthin'..." I do my best not to roll my eyes. "But why'd y'all end up gettin' divorced?"

I hate sharing the reason behind our divorce because people always give me that same "What the fuck is wrong with you?" look. But, I am nothing if not honest.

Josie and Roy both stare at me in anticipation.

"She, uh…Well, Kristy wanted children and I didn't—don't. So…yeah. That's kind of a deal breaker."

Just like I'd expected, Josie looks at me like I'm the devil incarnate. *What kind of man doesn't want to give his wife children?* Even Roy has to clear his throat and take a pull of his beer to keep from reacting.

In Cedar Grove, marriage is still forever and divorce is just not done…That I threw a perfectly good marriage away over what is to most a natural progression when you've committed to sharing your life with another person will be the talk of this little town for years to come.

There's an awkward moment of silence before Josie's eyes widen and a shit-eating grin spreads across her face.

"Well, hot damn, if it ain't Spencer LeBlanc." Her hand starts waving wildly over her head.

*She came...*I spin around in my chair to find her, but I don't have to look too hard. Because there she is, standing a foot behind me with an expression on her face that tells me she's been there for a while. Long enough to confirm her suspicion that I'm some child-hating ass.

Fucking hell.

"Hey, Princess," I say with feigned confidence. I'm fucking shaking in my boots beneath the glare in those haunting blue eyes. "You're, umm, giving me that Momma look again, Spence."

She crosses her arms on her chest, pushing her tits up in her low-cut black top. "Yeah, well. I can't help that I look like a mom, Coop. As much as that may disgust you."

My eyes roam over her body. From her waist-long black locks, mouthwatering cleavage, painted on jeans, and fuck me heels...Kids be damned, I need to touch this woman tonight. It's been too fucking long.

Spencer's hands move to her waist as she cocks one hip to the side, continuing to stare as if she's waiting on me to do or say something.

I rise from my stool, taking a few steps forward 'til I'm close enough to feel her body heat without actually touching her. *God, she smells so damned good.* I snake my right arm around her waist, cup her ass, and pull her body against mine. Dipping my head down to her ear, I whisper, "I'm finding you very—" I thrust the evidence in my jeans forward, making damned sure she can feel it "—very not disgusting right now."

Her breath hitches and her eyes go all soft and wanting. Slowly, I begin to lean in, sure that she's about to let me kiss her, when Spence pushes me away with both hands on my chest. "I'll have that drink...or ten you promised me earlier." She slaps her hands together a few times like she's shaking off something dirty then walks over to the bar.

My heart is racing. My dick twitches as I scrub my hand over my face with a groan. Biting my lip in frustration, I return to my seat beside her.

It's gonna be a long night.

"Is it just me, Roy Nelson, or did it just get awfully hot in here?" Josie chimes, fanning herself with exaggeration.

Roy laughs, Spencer blushes, and I take deep breaths trying to cool myself down. For once, I am definitely in agreement with Josie.

"Hey, girl," Spence offers, ignoring her comment. "I'll have a Crown and Coke." Her eyes dart in my direction and she smiles. "Go ahead and make that a double, will ya?"

"Sure thing, girl...and can I just say that you do *not* look like you have three children."

Again, I'm in agreement with Josie. Spencer is hotter than ever. But, I can't look at her without seeing those kids. Three. Fucking. Kids. I half expect one of 'em to pop up at any moment, demanding her attention. *Leeches.*

My skin pricks as I down the rest of my beer, tapping the counter before I've even finished swallowing, indicating for Josie to bring me another.

"Thanks, Josie. It's really sweet of you to say that," Spencer says meekly, as if she doesn't believe it. Her cheeks pinken slightly and her smile is flat. It doesn't reach her eyes. *How can she not know how drop dead gorgeous she is?*

Spencer makes it a point to ignore me for the most part, catching up with Josie and a few other locals who've trickled in.

She's like a fucking celebrity or something. Everyone expresses their shock and excitement over having her back. But that's always been Spencer...the life of the party. Everyone's best friend, unless you cross her. Then she can be a cold-hearted bitch. I'm on the receiving end of that treatment tonight.

The more I drink, the more it really starts to bother me. How can she be so fucking pissed at me for not wanting kids? According to my parents and my college roommate, Derrick, I have no right to be angry at her for having children, even though I kind of am. Yet, she can give me the cold-shoulder for not having them? I'd have been fucking ecstatic to learn that she didn't want kids with another man.

After another beer, I really want to call her out on this shit. I'm tired of the distance. We've been keeping each other at arm's length for years because of boyfriends or girlfriends or spouses, or *kids*. I turn in her direction, ready to do just that, but the smile on her face stops me. I haven't seen her smile like this in years. Spencer is enjoying herself, and I'm not selfish enough to ruin her night. It can wait.

After a few beers of her own, Josie is feeling even more audacious than usual. While only half paying attention to Roy, I hear, "Okay, girl. I've got to know..." Josie's beer bottle lands loudly on the bar in front of Spencer and me. "Is it true you worked at some clinic teaching people how to have sex? I mean, I ain't judgin' or nothin'," she slurs. "Just curious."

Apparently, everyone else is, too, because it's suddenly quiet enough to hear a pin drop.

I swivel in my chair, facing Spence, who is choking on her drink. "Jesus, Josie," I mutter as I pat Spencer on the back.

Josie doesn't apologize, just continues staring at Spence, awaiting her response.

Spencer clears her throat, scanning the room nervously. "I'm a sex therapist, Josie. I don't teach people how to have sex *or orgasms*," she says pointedly at me. "We talk. It's nothing physical. I would never touch my patients." Her head hangs forward just a little, her long hair shielding her from prying eyes.

"Huh." Josie's face falls with disappointment. "Well, that sounds a lot less exciting than I've been picturing all these years."

Spence begins absentmindedly picking at the label on my beer as her face heats from all of the attention. "Sorry to disappoint you, Josie." Without realizing it, her body moves closer to mine, and it feels good to know that even when she's pissed at me, she's still comforted by my presence.

Slowly, the noise level picks up and the beginning chords to our song start to play. *I Don't Want To Miss A Thing* by Aerosmith.

"Dance with me?" I ask, grabbing her tiny hand in my own and tugging.

She's still mad, but Spence allows me to lead her out to the dance floor, grateful for the opportunity to escape the hot seat. We're the only two out here, but I don't care. I just wanna hold her. Smell her. Breathe her air.

I wrap my arms around her waist and Spencer's body stiffens. "Come on, babe. Dance with me." My heart is pounding. So is hers. I can feel her pulse racing against the hand that's gripping her wrist.

Spencer's beautiful blue eyes glisten as she hesitantly lifts her arms and places them on my shoulders. "I don't like you very much right now."

I chuckle to myself. "That's okay," I whisper in her ear,

pulling her closer. "Just give me one dance...for old time's sake, huh? You can go back to hating me after."

I feel her heart beating against my chest as she rests her chin on my shoulder, linking her hands behind my neck. Each time she exhales, her warm breath sends a jolt of electricity through my body.

I slide my right hand slowly up her back, and when my fingers trail over the clasp of her bra, it takes everything in me not to unhook it and undress this woman here and now. I've yearned for this moment for so long.

Every word of the song rings true. There is nothing I want more than to stay in this moment forever. To pretend that it's still just me and Spence. No divorces. No kids. No regrets.

I can't be certain, but I think I feel her lips brush the skin at the base of my neck. With my right hand, I grip her chin, turning her face up to mine. I meet her eyes and allow my own to drift down to her trembling lips and back up to her eyes. It's a question, and when her tongue darts out to lick her bottom lip, I have all the answer I need.

My mouth crashes onto hers, and as our bodies sway in time to the music, our tongues dance to a rhythm that's all their own. Spencer tastes of liquor and spearmint gum. She smells like heaven.

It's as if we were never apart—like we've been kissing for all of our lives. Spencer moans against my lips, and I grip the back of her neck, kissing her harder, determined to leave my mark.

I haven't felt this much with anyone since Spencer. I'd started to believe that maybe I'd imagined that kissing could be this good. But, my memory did not deceive me.

Soft touches turn frantic. Gentle kisses become bruising.

Rapid breaths progress to sensual moans. I allow the moment to completely take me; getting lost in the way her body responds to mine.

There's a slow clap and the bar erupts into cheers.

I feel her body stiffen at the attention, but she doesn't pull her lips away. We stand there making out like two kids 'til long after the music has stopped. When Spence finally breaks for air, she grabs my hand, tugging me off the dance floor and down the hall to the women's restroom.

"What're you doing, Spencer?" I ask as she shuts and bolts the door behind us. When she looks up at me, the hunger in her eyes is unmistakable.

Spencer's body slams against mine, and her hands fist into my hair as she thrusts her tongue into my mouth.

I groan, swirling my tongue around hers before pulling back. "Answer me, Princess, 'cause I am seconds away from ripping your clothes off and fucking you against this wall."

She whimpers. "The kids..." Leave it to Spencer to bring them up at a time like this.

"Aren't here," I grit out, trying not to let my frustration show. *It's always about those damn kids.*

She tilts her head back, offering me her neck to feast on. "Tell me what you want, baby," I urge as I trail my tongue along her throat, feeling her body melt beneath me.

"I-I...Oh God." Spencer's head falls back as her eyes begin to roll up.

Fucking hell, she's close already.

"I'm not looking for a relationship," she rushes out.

I remove my lips from the skin above her breasts. "What *are* you lookin' for, Spence?" I lower my hand, cupping her between the legs through her jeans and squeeze.

Spencer's entire body jerks, shaking with need. "A friend?" she asks. "With, ummm...Oh God, that's so good," she breathes out as I trace the shell of her ear with my tongue.

"With?" I urge, continuing to rub her through her tight ass jeans.

"Benefitsss," she says, bucking against me. "No st-strings."

"You want me to fuck you, baby?"

Her head bobs as her legs begin to buckle. Spence can barely hold herself upright, and I can't take her on the floor of this nasty ass bathroom. We don't have many options, but I'll make it work. There is no way in hell I'm missing this chance.

I unbutton her jeans, tug them down, and she slips out of her heels, holding on to me for balance as she works her way out of her pants. I lift her top over her head, taking a moment to admire the beautiful woman Spencer has grown into. She's thickened up in all the right places, no longer a waif of a girl.

"Put the heels back on," I rasp, admiring her long legs, and she does. "Goddamn, you are the sexiest woman I have ever seen, Spencer LeBlanc."

She smiles, slipping her hands under my shirt, allowing her fingers to trace the muscles of my stomach as she slowly raises it higher.

Reaching over my shoulders, behind my back, I grab my shirt and pull it over my head, tossing it to the counter. She fumbles with the belt and button on my jeans, growing impatient as she jerks them down past my hips.

My cock springs free, and she gasps audibly. I'm rock hard already. Her soft fingers are drawn to me like a magnet. Spencer starts off slowly running a finger from base to tip and then testing the size in her hand. "I need you," she pleads almost desperately.

"You can have all you want, baby girl." I bend down to retrieve my wallet from the jeans that are now pooled around my ankles and grab a condom. "Put your hands on the sink and bend over."

She does as I instruct. Her ass on full display. Her hungry blue eyes staring right into mine through the mirror as I roll the condom onto my throbbing dick. She licks her lips.

I place the head of my shaft at her entrance. But before pushing inside, and because I am a bit of a dick, I have to ask, "You aren't just using me for my sperm, are you, Princess?" I let my hand rest on her flat stomach. "Ready for number four?" I goad.

Her eyes flame. "I'd rather pull my twat hairs out with tweezers than procreate with you."

"Ouch."

"Now get on with it before I remember I'm still mad at you."

Such a fucking lady. And I almost lose it. *Almost.* "Well, all right, then," I say, trying not to laugh, before pushing inside of the woman who always should have been mine.

Chapter Six
SPENCER

Did that just happen?

The softening dick in my hoo-hah tells me that indeed it did. The throbbing between my legs says that I want it to happen again...

Shit. I'm so fucked—literally, figuratively, in all ways.

My head and my heart are raging a shitstorm of a battle and I'm too buzzed to try and make sense of it right now. All I want is for this man to make my body feel this way every day—every minute of the rest of my life. And it's the one thing I know that I can never have.

I will not cry. I will not cry.

"You all right, Spence?" he purrs into my ear, and like a kitten, I nuzzle the side of my face into his.

"I don't know," I answer honestly. Because, what just happened?

He kisses the side of my face. "We should get dressed. Someone's been knocking on the door."

Oh shit.

I just had sex with my high school boyfriend, after spending *maybe* a total of three hours with him, in the bathroom of a bar...and now I'm going to do the walk of shame in front of half the town on my first day back.

Coop notices the panic in my face as he rights my thong and passes me my jeans. "Fuck 'em, Spence. Who are they, anyway?"

I know he's right. I don't know why I even care. Maybe it isn't their judgment I'm worried about but my own. "We shouldn't have—"

Coop spins me around to face him. "Don't." His eyes plead with mine. "Please don't discount what just happened here, Spence. I know we aren't together. But, we are two consenting adults, and we both wanted...no, *needed*. We *needed* this. Don't turn it into something dirty."

I glance around the single-stall restroom, taking in the piss on the floor and the horrendous smell, and I can't help the giggle that escapes. Surely he has to see the hilarity in that statement.

Coop's eyes dart around the room, and he huffs out a laugh. "You know what I mean."

Suddenly, a fist starts pounding on the door. "All right, you two. I need to fucking piss like a goddamned racehorse. Come out with your pants up!" *Fucking Josie.* "No, wait! Cooper, you can keep yours down if you'd like."

Cooper's eyes grow wide as saucers as we both burst into a fit of laughter while scrambling to get back into our clothes.

"Coming," I yell out as I tug on my jeans.

"Yeah, you did," he whispers, and a blush works its way from my cheeks to my neck.

"T.M.I., lover girl. Hurry up!" *Bang. Bang. Bang.*

I stand directly behind Cooper, trying to hide as he twists the deadbolt and the door flies open. Josie rushes in, cursing us to hell and back, but neither of us pays her any mind. We walk right through the bar, ignoring all the knowing smiles and judging eyes, and make a beeline for the parking lot.

"Ride with me?" Coop asks as he pries the keys to his truck from the pocket of his tight jeans.

I take a moment to appraise him being that I had been too upset earlier at the conversation I'd walked in on to really drink him in the way a beautiful man like Cooper deserves. His brown hair is a wreck from the sex we just had...and it's utterly delicious. His deep brown eyes are thick with emotion—with hunger and love? *Maybe?* He can't possibly still love me after all these years. *It doesn't even matter*...Moving along, I take in the way his muscles bulge against the fabric of his charcoal V-neck and how just the very front is tucked right behind the buckle of his belt, almost begging me to look at the bulge in his pants. The bulge that still has my sex clenching. *Did the temperature just go up twenty degrees?*

"Spence?" Coop chuckles.

I snap out of my daze, lifting my face to meet his. "Huh? Yeah?"

He rolls his bottom lip through his teeth with a smirk. "My eyes are up here," he says as he points with his first two fingers at his sockets.

Busted.

"Just checkin' out the, umm." I gulp as his dick literally jumps in his jeans. I rub my eyes with my fingers. *Am I seeing things?* I can't be that fucking drunk. I only had four of my ten drinks. *Note to self: Coop still owes me drinks.*

"Yes?" he taunts, giving me a knowing smile.

"The merchandise."

"What merchandise?" he asks, and I swear to baby Jesus it jumps again.

"Do that again."

"Do what again?" Fuck that fucking smirk right off his damned perfect face.

I tilt my head to the side, lifting my brows. "You know what I'm talking about. Make it jump."

He snorts out a laugh. "Make what jump, Princess?"

I let out an exaggerated sigh. "Your...*thing*..." I wave my hand over the general area of his crotch.

Coop's brows lift. "My...*thing*? Is that what they teach you to call it in sex therapy school? 'Cause I've got to say, baby, you aren't sounding very professional at the moment."

"Ugh," I growl. "Just forget it. I'm going home." I start to fish my keys from my purse as I turn toward my truck and instantly his hands are on my waist, spinning me around 'til his body is flattening my back against the passenger door of his truck. He's breathing heavily against my neck, and suddenly I'm out of breath. It's just gone, along with every ounce of common sense I used to possess.

His tongue traces a path from my shoulder to my ear, and I think if he asked, I'd give him round two right here in the damned parking lot.

"I was just messing with you, Spence. Didn't mean to piss you off again," he says, sounding sincere.

Was I mad? I can't remember. My heart is beating so hard. So fast. It scares me. The depth of what I still feel for this man scares the shit out of me. "I need...I need to go home, Coop." My eyes well up, and I have a sudden urge to cry.

He nods, trailing the side of his hand along my face. "Let

me drive you? We can pick up your car tomorrow."

I think I'm more drunk on him than the alcohol, but in either case, in my current condition, I probably should not be driving. "Okay."

His smile is flat as he grips my chin with his thumb and forefinger, placing a whisper soft kiss on the tip of my nose. With both hands, he pushes off the truck, lifting his body away from mine, and leaving me feeling empty, alone, and so confused.

I hear the sound of the lock clicking as he rounds the truck to his side. I pull the door open and climb into his truck, breathing in the scent of Coop's cologne and leather.

Riding through town beside Coop again is surreal. This truck is different. *We* are different, yet in my heart, nothing's changed. It knows this boy, these back roads, and draws comfort from the familiar cadence that only Cooper James has ever evoked.

The five-minute drive home is made in complete silence, although I feel like we've said so much.

As he shifts his truck into park in the very spot where he broke my heart all those years ago, I feel a sense of dread. I reach for the handle and turn to leave when his hand darts out, gripping my wrist. *Déjà vu.*

"Spence?" His voice is clogged with emotion. His eyes reflecting the same hurt and confusion I feel deep in my chest.

"Yeah?"

"You didn't wait...I-I thought you'd wait." His eyes are rimmed in tears.

"No," I choke out, shaking my head. *The fucking nerve.* "I wasn't your toy to play with and then put on a shelf for another day when you were ready to play with her again. You don't get to blame me, Cooper," I grit out as a tear slips down my cheek. "This..." I gesture between the two of us as tears flood from my eyes. "You alone are responsible."

"Well, you got your revenge, didn't you?" he sneers. His eyes drift over to Momma's house where my babies lie asleep.

I gasp, shocked that he would go there. "Let me make one thing crystal fucking clear to you right now. My children were not revenge, and my having them had not one Goddamned thing to do with you—"

"No?" Cooper shakes his head in disbelief.

I yank my wrist from his grip. "No, and if you so much as look at them the wrong way, this *friendship* is over."

His jaw ticks as he turns his head, staring absently into space, and just as I'm climbing down from the truck, his fist slams down into the dash. *Fuck him.*

As I cross the yard back to our house, I put my momma hat back on. I'm not the fragile little girl I was back then. Being a mother has toughened me up in a way that I don't think anything else could. Where I may not have been able to find the strength to hold myself together for me, I have an endless reserve when it comes to my boys.

With my cheeks still sticky with dried tears, I creep into the room where Landon and Lake are asleep, and for a moment, I stand in the doorway, watching the steady rise and fall of their chests. I listen to the gentle hum of their breaths and I wonder when my little babies started to turn into men. And I pray. I pray that my boys will be good men. That they will know how to treat the women in their lives, and more than anything, I pray to God that they will be good fathers, despite the fact that they've had no one to show them how.

I walk over to Lake, placing a kiss on his forehead, and

then move to Landon's bed and do the same.

His eyes pop open, and he smiles a dreamy smile. "Night, Mom. Love you."

That strength I spoke of earlier? Yeah, it's gone. These boys are the ones with the power to bring me to my knees. Suddenly, I'm sniveling like a fool.

Landon sits up in bed. "Are you okay, Mom?"

I wrap him in my arms. "I'm sorry. I-I shouldn't have hit you earlier." I haven't had a chance to apologize to him yet, and it's been eating me alive.

My baby hugs me back, his chest vibrating with tears. "I'm sorry, too, Mom."

"It'll be okay," I assure him as I rub my hand in circles on his back. Somehow, it soothes the ache in my own chest as well.

I feel him swallow and nod his head. "I know."

I tuck Landon in, just like I used to when he was little, and leave his room feeling ten pounds lighter. I peek in on Kyle sleeping soundly in his crib and make my way to my old room.

Immediately, I strip out of my clothes, bra, panties and all. I can't stand the smoky smell imbedded in them from the bar. Grabbing fresh underclothes, a camisole, and sleep shorts, I make my way into the adjoining bathroom and take the world's fastest shower.

When I return to my room, I pick up my phone from the side table. There are messages waiting from a number I don't recognize.

Unknown: I'm sorry for what I said. I'd really like to meet your kids.

Me: You met them already. And how did you get my number?

Unknown: I mean really meet them. Get to know them. I called myself from your phone when you were busy gossiping with Josie. I'm not sorry for that.

Me: You don't even like kids.

Asshole: I never said I didn't like kids. I said I didn't want any and they made me uncomfortable. That's not the same thing.

Me: Don't try to lawyer me, Coop. Why the sudden interest?

Asshole: They're part of you...and you're important to me.

Oh, my heart.

Me: We'll see.

Asshole: Okay. 'Night, Princess. See you tomorrow.

Me: 'Night, Coop.

Asshole: BTW, thanks for the strip tease. Forgot to close your curtains.;)

I roll over, and sure enough, the curtains are wide open.

Me: Did your "thing" jump?

Asshole: Like a dick in the box.

Me: You are so corny.

Asshole: Get it? Like a jack in the box, but it's a dick in the box? BTW, I think you typed C by accident when you really meant H.

Me: Yeah...I got it. Thanks. Now you've got me corny with an H, too, picturing JT with his dick in a box. MMMM.

Asshole: I've got a package you are more than welcome to unwrap. Let me take care of you, baby. I promise you won't be disappointed.

Me: I'm an independent woman, Coop. I've gotten really good at taking care of myself. ;)

Asshole: Nothing's as good as the real thing.

Me: I don't know. Fabio is ginormous and thick. He has five settings and NO SPERM. #winning.

Asshole: But can he suck those beautiful tits of yours, Princess? Does he fuck your mouth with his tongue? Make your heart feel like it's going to explode in your chest? Does he make you cry out when you cum the way half the town heard you scream for me tonight?

Holy fuck. I'm panting. Shaking. Aching. He's a man, Spencer. Another fucking man who doesn't do kids. Remember that.

Me: No. But, he won't break my heart, either. He's safe. You're a lesson I've already learned, and one I don't care to repeat. Goodnight, Cooper.

Chapter Seven
COOPER

I'm up before the sun, staring at the last text I received from Spence before finally drifting off into a few hours of restless sleep. Talk about a punch in the gut. "He's safe..." I tsk, slamming the phone face down on the bed. It's a sad day when you're playing second fiddle to a fucking vibrator.

There is nothing I regret more in this life than letting that woman go. I should've gone after her when I'd heard that she and that douche she was married to had split. But, I'd allowed misplaced pride and hurt to get in the way. She was supposed to marry me. Her children were supposed to be mine...ours. Blue eyed, raven haired, little babies. They'd have her dimples and my cleft chin. They'd be the perfect blend of two parents who'd loved each other their entire lives.

As hard as it is to admit it to myself, I fucked up all those years ago. I set all of this into motion. I can't go back. I can't change any of it, no matter how badly I want to. I know that I don't stand a chance in hell of getting Spencer back if I can't accept her kids. And how long will she be content with just fucking? I can't risk another asshole coming along and stealing her heart. So that's the challenge I have to overcome, and as hard as it is to look at those children whose features are a mix of the woman I love and the men who's arms I pushed her in to, I'll have to give it an honest shot. Because I don't think I'll survive losing Spencer a second time.

After a quick shower, I head down to the kitchen to grab a cup of coffee before going out to the front porch to watch the sun rise.

The screen door squeaks as I push it open, stepping out into the cool morning air. Immediately, my eyes wander to Spencer's bedroom window. I feel a pang of disappointment when I see that the pink frilly curtains are shut tight. *Message received.*

"You're up early," Momma chirps from behind me. My body jerks with surprise, splashing hot coffee onto my hand.

"Jeez, Mom! You scared the shit out of me." I move the cup of joe to my other hand and shake most of the liquid off, wiping the rest on the fabric of my jeans.

Momma's eyes are narrowed and shooting daggers my way, her arms crossed on her chest. She doesn't even offer an apology to her baby boy, which is really unlike my mother. I must've fucked up bad.

I comb my fingers nervously through my hair, looking around to be sure that there's not someone else behind me, but nope. Those eyes are definitely intended for me. I'm not sure what I did to piss her off, but I try my best to flatter my way out of it. "Mornin', Momma," I say with a megawatt smile. "Is that a new dress? Looks good on you."

Her dark brown eyes, identical to mine, roll back in her head. "Oh, cut the shit, Cooper, and sit down." She points to one of the old, wooden rockers, and I take my thirty-three year-old ass and park it right where she's pointing. Mom nods her head as if to say "Yeah, you better sit." It makes me smile on the inside. Not where she can see it. I don't have a death wish.

I sit quietly while she works out whatever it is she wants to say in her head, and I scramble around in my own thoughts, trying to figure out what I've done that could possibly warrant the ugly looks crossing her face as she glares in my direction. I can't come up with a thing.

Finally, she throws her hands into the air and whisper-shouts, "In the fucking bathroom, Cooper? What the hell were you thinking? Huh?"

"I, uh—" *How the hell does she know about that already?*

"You weren't. You. Weren't. Thinking." She paces around in front of me in an exasperated manner that I haven't witnessed from her in years.

"Momma, I—" Each time I open my mouth, she cuts me off.

"Do you honestly think you're gonna win that girl's heart by screwing her in a public restroom, Cooper James? I mean, I can't even fathom what goes through that dense head of yours son. You're gonna screw this all up."

I feel my hackles rising and try to tamp down my anger, knowing better than to blow up at my momma. But I'm close. "How'd you—"

"How'd I find out? Seriously? Did you forget where we live? I just got off the phone with Earline." *Josie's momma.* "And she filled me in on your disgusting behavior. As if that sham of a marriage and divorce aren't enough of an embarrassment. The whole town knows!" Her hands once again are over her head, waving around like a psychopath.

I grit my teeth. No one else would get away with talking to me this way.

"Well," she says expectantly, "don't you have anything to say for yourself?"

I shrug. "That depends. You gonna stop yelling long enough for me to talk?"

Her mouth falls open in a gasp. "Don't you sass me, young man. I'm still your momma, and you will respect me in my house." She looks around before adding, "And outside of my house."

I bring my fingers to the bridge of my nose, pinching and releasing to try to relieve the tension.

"Well?" She crosses her arms as her foot taps a steady rhythm on the wood beneath her feet.

"It just happened," I mumble.

If smoke could shoot out of her ears, she'd have two chimney stacks on the sides of her head. "Sex doesn't *just happen*, Cooper. I'm gonna need better than that."

I cannot believe I am having this discussion with my mother. "I am not talking about what happened between Spencer and me. We are adults, and what we do is none of yours or anyone else's business." I press my hands to the arms of the rocking chair and start to rise then swiftly fall right back into my seat when I see the tears filling my momma's eyes.

Shit.

"Excuse me for caring, son. Excuse me for wanting my only child to find some happiness in his life." She sniffles as the tears begin to roll down her cheeks. "Excuse me for wanting to be a grandmother someday."

There she goes again with the grandchildren. Her tears make me feel like utter and complete shit.

I clear the lump from my throat. "Sorry, Momma. I wasn't thinking. I shouldn't have treated her that way. But, you need to understand something. I don't know whether Spencer and I will end up together or not, and you need to be prepared for this to go either way."

"You l-l-love her."

I nod. "I do. But it's not that simple. We're not kids anymore, and it's not just me and Spence."

"Those children are beautiful, Cooper. We could love them. You...you could love them." She nods, wiping her leaky nose on the sleeve of her pretty blue dress.

I feel my own eyes start to burn as I shout, "They. Aren't. Mine!"

"And whose fault is that? Huh?"

It feels as if my head is about to implode. "Don't you think I know that, Mother?" I swallow hard. "I don't need you to tell me how badly I've fucked everything up, because I already know. But, just because I know it, doesn't change the facts. And the fact is that I just don't know if I can accept...*truly accept* someone else's children as my own, and Spencer would accept nothing less...and she shouldn't!"

"It ain't those children's fault."

I sigh. "I know."

"And it ain't Spencer's fault, neither."

"I know."

She swipes her fingers beneath her eyes, swatting away tears. "Just so you know," she says on a nod.

I gulp. "I do."

"All right, then." She steps around me, pulling the screen door open. "I'm not gonna lay into you for your filthy mouth or the way you just spoke to me, because I know you're upset with yourself right now and have every right to be."

I suck in my lips, trying not to smile.

She puts one foot in the door before turning back with her finger pointed at my face. "Fix it, son." The door slams shut behind her, rattling the rickety old porch.

Before I can get up from my chair, my father comes through the door, coffee in hand and a smile in his eyes. *This ought to be interesting.* Round two.

"Mornin', Pops." I nod and force the best smile I can manage.

He laughs a little under his breath as he bends to sit in the chair beside me. He glances in my direction and completely loses it.

"Glad to see you find all of this so funny," I say, fighting a smile at how very different my parents are.

He coughs as his laughter fizzles out. "Oh no, son. I don't find *all* of it funny, only the ass chewing your momma just gave you."

I shake my head. "Happy to amuse."

"So the bathroom, huh?" He nods his head as if to answer his own question.

"Oh, for fuck's sake."

The old man lights a cigarette and takes a long pull, holding it in for a few seconds before slowly blowing it back out. "Heard you two put on quite the show." His laughter vibrates the porch.

"Can we not?"

"My boy," he mutters to himself with pride.

We sit in silence for a few minutes, Dad puffing away and me silently praying that he will just let this go.

"So...how you gonna fix this—" he waves his hand back and forth between our two houses "—situation, you've gotten yourself into here, son?"

"I don't know that it can be fixed, Dad. But, I'm gonna try."

His eyes get serious as he says, "Try *real* hard, boy. You're not gonna get another chance to fuck this up again."

"I'm aware."

"Probably shouldn't screw her in anymore bathrooms, either."

Shoot me. "Noted."

"And, uh...try to be a little...you know, charming."

I take a deep breath and release it. "Will do it."

"The kids," he says, pursing his lips and nodding. "You gotta win her heart through those boys, Cooper. That's your ticket."

The kids. It all starts and ends with those kids. "I don't know if I can. Y'all make it sound so easy, but, Dad...I can't just forget that they aren't mine. She should've had my kids. They should be ours, not hers."

"Ya know, Cooper, you need to stop dwelling on the things you can't change. Stop focusing so much on the fact that they're not yours and remember that they're hers. Those boys are a part of the woman you love and that alone should make them worthy." He nods in agreement with himself. "Elaine's confided in your momma a lot over the years, and those boys' fathers aren't worth a damn. That girl's been raising them practically on her own. You could change their lives, son. You could change all of our lives." He slowly pushes himself up from the rocker, and as he walks toward the door, turns back to add, "You let that marinate for a bit."

And I do. For over an hour, I think about how I can go about winning those kids over. But if I get the chance to fuck my girl in another bathroom...I'm sure as shit takin' it.

I check the time on my phone. It's 7:30. Spence has a baby. I deduce from that fact that she's probably an early riser and tap out a text while yelling through the screen door, "Hey, Dad, I might take the boat out today, if that's all right."

Momma's head appears in the window of the door. "You planning on taking Spencer out?"

Her nosiness knows no bounds. "I'm planning to extend the invitation," I say, raising my brows.

She smiles from ear to ear. "Take it. Just be back in time for dinner. I just invited the whole gang over for a crawfish boil!" I watch her pump her fist in the air as she walks toward the kitchen. *That freaking woman.* She means well.

Me: Good morning, beautiful. Hope you slept well. I must say that I'm a bit disappointed to see you shut the curtains. :p

Her reply is almost immediate.

Princess: Yeah, well, you never know what pervert might be lurking around getting his rocks off.

I choke.

Me: There aren't any other perverts around for miles.

Princess: Exactly.

Me: Ouch.

Princess: No freebies, "friend."

Oh yeah, she wants me.

Me: Understood. Hey, I wanted to see if you and the kids wanted to come out in the boat with me today. It's gorgeous out.

Princess: You don't have to try so hard, Coop. I just said be nice to them. You don't need to force yourself into their lives just to fuck me. I've already told you I wanted it, too. No strings. Stop trying to make strings.

Me: No agenda, babe. I just really want to spend time with you, and I think your boys would enjoy it. If you don't wanna come, just say no.

About ten full minutes pass before she finally responds.

Princess: You can't so much as touch me in front of my children, Cooper. No lingering looks or innuendoes. Lake and Landon will catch on, and I don't want them thinking I'm some kind of whore.

Me: Whore? Jeez, Spence. A bit much? I promise to behave.

Princess: Okay.

Me: Okay?

Princess: We'll come. Thank you for inviting us.

Chapter Eight
SPENCER

"Okay, so...make sure you're nice to the boy, Spence. You can't keep holding all Coop's past mistakes against him." Momma offers her unsolicited advice as she packs a backpack with toys for Savage.

"I'm not going so I can make the man miserable, Mom," I retort as I throw in a few extra pull-ups and changes of clothes for Kyle.

She tilts her head to the side, offering me a soft smile. "I know, baby. I'm just nervous, is all."

"Don't be," I say, shoving the sunscreen in with Kyle's things. "We're just going out in the boat, Momma. *With* the kids. I don't know what you think's gonna happen."

"Wanna know what I think's gonna happen?" she asks, smiling so hard the veins in her neck pop out.

"No."

She shuffles her feet excitedly while rubbing her hands together. "All right, I'll tell ya. Those three boys over there—" she tilts her head in the direction of the kitchen where the kids are having breakfast "—are going to steal that man's heart away." She nods to herself. "And we already know, he never got it back from you."

She's spouting off every dream I have like it's just going to all fall into my lap without realizing how much it fucking hurts. I'm trying to keep a level head here, and Momma is somewhere off in Neverland. I will be alone for the rest of my life because I won't put my own desires above my children, and I will not force another man into their lives who doesn't wanna be there. No one's gonna show up to wave their magic wand over this mess and fix it. If life has taught me anything it's that it is far from a fairytale.

"Stop. Please, stop putting so much pressure on me. I'm happy to just have his friendship again. Can we not put expectations and labels on whatever's gonna happen between the two of us?"

She walks around the bed to my side, and I think she's about to hug me, but she puts her lips close to my ear and deadpans, "Friends don't *hmmhmm* each other in bar bathrooms, Spencer Rose."

What the ever-loving fuck did this woman just say to me?

"I…ju—huh…what?" I sputter.

Her brows do a sassy little bounce as she rounds the bed back to the bag she's still stuffing. "Yeah, I got *that* call this morning." She tries to give me a stern look but the smile on her face makes it impossible. "You really should think about your reputation, though, Spencer. You already have kids for two guys…and you aren't married. That kinda stuff stays with you. Luckily for us, I don't think anyone realizes they aren't with the same man."

Did my mother just call me a slut? I'm pretty sure that is exactly what just happened here.

"You need to stop." I point at her with the pack of wipes I'm now stuffing into the bag.

"I'll do no such thing. You two have been screwing this up for the last fifteen years. Nelly and I are gonna help you little love birds fix this right on up."

Great, Coop's mom is in on this master plan too. We don't stand a freaking chance.

"The neighbor guy's here," Landon calls up the stairs.

"I'm coming," I shout back as my phone instantly dings.

Asshole: Liar.

Me: I said no funny business.

Asshole: They can't hear me.

Point made.

"Stop playin' on your phone, girl, and get down there," Momma hisses.

I grab the bags and follow her down the stairs.

"Hey, Coop! Don't you look nice." She nudges me with her elbow. "Right, Spence? Doesn't he look nice?"

A knowing smile spreads across Cooper's face. "Thanks, Mrs. Elaine."

"I'm just gonna go make sure the kids are ready," Momma says, nervously backing out of the room.

The second we are alone, Coop's eyes caress every inch of my body, and my skin heats under his perusal. "Like what you see?" I tease, nibbling on my lip.

His eyes go all soft as he clears his throat. "Very much," he whispers just as Mom and the kids enter the room.

Coop hops up from the arm of the couch, any and all traces of desire have vanished. "Hey, guys, ready to go have some fun?" He looks genuinely excited...like a big kid.

Kyle runs right over to Cooper with his arms outstretched "Hi, man! Hole me. I yike you."

God, my child is so desperate for a man's attention that it breaks my heart.

Without hesitation this time, Coop lifts him into his arms. "What's up, little man? My name's Cooper. Can you say Cooper."

"Pooper." Kyle giggles. *Little shit.*

Lake and Landon both laugh at the little comedian, and Coop answers with an exaggerated shrug and a simple, "Close enough."

We leave the kids with Mom for a few minutes to run over to the bar and get my truck.

I keep feeling his eyes on me, but the moment I turn to look at him, he darts them back to the road. The drive is only minutes long, but being this near to Cooper for any amount of time has my body going haywire.

As we make the last turn, he finally speaks. "You look really beautiful, Spencer."

"So do you," I say. "I mean good. You look good, Coop."

He chuckles. "Don't be nervous with me."

"I'm trying," I say under my breath. "It's just...it's been a long time, Coop."

He rolls into the parking lot, pulling up next to my truck. Coop shifts into park and turns his body to face mine. He ghosts his fingers down the side of my face, fingering them through my hair, and letting his thumb trail down my jaw line, whisper soft, before pulling his hand away. "It's been way too long," he agrees with a heavy swallow.

My breath catches in my throat as a chill makes me shiver,

leaving gooseflesh in its wake. My eyes latch on to his, pleading with him to kiss me.

Coop closes half the distance between us and stops. His tongue darts out to lick the seam of his mouth and all of the blood rushes to my head. "You're gonna have to meet me halfway, Princess."

I don't lean in, but rather slide my body to the center of the bench seat so that I can feel his heat pressing against mine. Reaching up with shaky hands, I cup the sides of his face, tracing my thumbs along the light stubble on his jaw. "Kiss me," I breathe out against his lips.

His mouth moves over mine. His kiss is soft, gentle, and exquisitely slow. Our breaths mingle as we take our time exploring forgotten territory. Last night, at the bar, this man's tongue may have fucked my mouth. But this...this kiss is filled with heart and soul...and so much longing.

I both feel and hear my phone buzzing in my back pocket but nothing short of this truck exploding is going to make me be the one to pull away.

Coop's phone dings and then dings again and again. With a frustrated groan, he tears his lips from mine. The sound of our labored breaths fills the space around us.

Coop barks out a laugh and then holds his phone out for me to read the messages.

Mom: Elaine just called. Did Spencer forget her phone or something?

Mom: It doesn't take this damned long to go pick up a car down the street.

Mom: Don't let me find out y'all are back in that bathroom, Cooper James, or there will be hell to pay when you get home. You better treat her like a lady.

My cheeks warm. "Oh my God. They all know..."

"Welcome back to Cedar Grove, Princess. Did you honestly believe they wouldn't find out?" God, his smile is so beautiful.

"I'm so embarrassed, Coop. I'm never leaving the house again. And your parents. They've always treated me like the good one. Now they'll think less of me. We are so freaking stupid."

Coop narrows his eyes at me. "Hold up, little lady. One... you have three kids. They know damned well you've been getting busy. Two...most of those gossip mongers are probably just jealous. Have you seen the size of what I'm packin'?" The goofy smile on his face makes me laugh.

My eyes fall on his package, which just so happens to be fighting to escape from his jeans. Guess I wasn't the only one getting carried away.

"Watch out!" he shouts at the same time his dick hops again. "Stare too hard and he might come get you."

I decide against telling him that I'd be perfectly okay if that situation were to occur because we really don't have time for all that right now. "That is really some talent you've got there, Mr. Hebert."

He leans in close. "It's even better without the pants."

Phew. Lord, it's getting hot in here. "You'll have to show me some time, *friend*."

Just then his phone pings again.

Mom: Lord help me, if I have to come drag y'alls' asses out of that bathroom...

"We should go," I say, peaking over his shoulder, but not really wanting to leave at all.

Coop nods. "Yeah. I'm starting to think she might well

show up." He laughs. "Let's go. We have the whole day to spend together."

Coop's dad has a really nice bow rider with U-shaped seating in the back, and in the open bow at the front there are two more bench seats. It's a gorgeous boat with plenty of space.

I'm so glad that Cooper invited us to come along. I can't remember the last time I saw my big boys enjoying themselves like this, outdoors, without their heads glued to screens. I doubt their own father has ever taken them fishing. They seem to be getting on well with Cooper, too. For someone who doesn't do kids, he does a really great job at playing pretend. I think this day is exactly what they needed before starting at their new school tomorrow.

"Hey, Spence," Coop calls as he climbs from the back where he's been hanging with my boys over into the bow where I'm laying out. I had my fill of fishing after the first 30 minutes. But, God, how I've missed just being on the water, feeling the sun warm my skin. The scent of coconut sunscreen and calming sounds of nature. It's heaven.

Lowering my sunglasses back to my eyes, I prop up on my elbows to face him. I don't miss the way his eyes rove over my body in appreciation at how awesome this black two-piece makes the girls look, either. The suit was strategically chosen, of course, and judging by the lust in Coop's eyes, it was a great choice.

Cooper looks damned good himself in a pair of baby blue board shorts and his abs on full display. Those are new...I decide that I quite like this little enhancement.

"Hi, Spence," Savage mocks while wiggling out of Cooper's arms.

"Whoa, dude. Calm down," he says, setting him to his feet. "That kid is slippery, and he never stops moving. How the heck do you do this every day?" Coop looks exhausted as he sits on the bench seat across from mine as Kyle crawls around the small floor space panting like a puppy.

I let out an almost resigned laugh. "This is my life, Coop. You just get used to it."

"I don't think I could ever get used to it. I mean you literally cannot take your eyes off of him. How do you sleep?"

And there it is, another gentle reminder that Coop will never be more than a "friend." It almost knocks the breath out of me, but that's what I get for allowing myself to dream when I already knew the reality. He never promised me more than friendship. I'll just enjoy the benefits while they last, and if he befriends my kiddos, even on a part time basis...that's not a bad thing.

I force myself to smile. "He eventually runs out of steam and sleeps, too, Coop," I say with a wink while trying to swallow down the lump in my throat.

"You sick, Mommy?" Kyle asks, rubbing his baby soft hand on my cheek. "You need a nap 'cause you sick?"

I take his little hand and kiss the soft, pudgy part on the inside of his palm. "I'm not sick. I'm relaxing."

"What's dat?"

I literally laugh aloud. "I'm not really sure, baby." I scruff his hair up with my fingers. "But, it's nice." My eyes meet Cooper's and I smile in thanks.

"You're welcome," he whispers, reading my look.

"That's you booms?" Kyle asks, staring at my cleavage while pointing right at my breasts.

My cheeks flame as I look up to see the smirk on Cooper's face.

"Yes," I answer, moving his hand away. "Those are my boobs."

"Oh," my son says with such excitement that you could swear I've just given him the secret to life. "I wanna touch dat!"

Cooper fucking loses it. His body folds in half, head between the knees, and I swear the man has tears he's laughing so hard.

I sit up, tugging my sundress back over my suit. "No, sir. You will not be *touching that*."

"It's not fair, Mom!" he shouts, sticking himself in a corner with his knees pulled up and lip practically touching the floor.

"I feel your pain, little dude," Coop says, shaking his head. "But, you better get used to it."

I give Coop a little side eye and he shrugs, still chuckling.

"That kid is awesome."

"That kid," I say, glancing over to where he's still sulking, "is bad."

"Hey, you raised him," Coop taunts. "I think he's advanced—like a little man already. He curses like a sailor and wants to touch boobs. He's got it all figured out."

"I, uh…had a little *help* raising this one," I say, glaring at the twins who are fishing with headphones in their ears and the music so loud that I can hear it clearly from here.

"Speaking of help…" Coop says, motioning to my son who's now heavy-lidded and half asleep on the floor. His hand scrubs over his mouth and he rubs the scruff on his chin. His head shakes slightly. "Nah, never mind."

"You're curious about his father?"

"Just forget it, babe. I have no right. You don't owe me any explanations."

My eyes lock with his. "You're right. I don't. But, it's not like its top secret or anything."

Coop nods. "Has he ever seen him?"

My eyes well up. "Never." Shaking my head, I stare out into the water so that pitying look on his face doesn't reduce me to tears. "Well, we weren't really together when I became pregnant with Kyle." I glance at Coop's face to gauge his reaction. He shrugs.

"It happens."

"I gave him the option to be a father or to disappear." I huff, swallowing a ball of emotion. "He chose door number two. I've never heard from him again, and honestly, if he was going to be a piece of shit like the other boys' father," I whisper to make sure they don't overhear, "we're better off without him."

He looks positively pissed. "I can't imagine you doing this all on your own."

I can't help but laugh. "Coop, I can't imagine doing it any other way. It's always just been me and my boys. Sure, it's exhausting, and a lot of the time I don't know whether I'm coming or going...But, at the end of the day—" a smile spreads across my face "—they just...they love me, Coop... unconditionally...unequivocally. They're mine, and I'm theirs... and they'll never leave me."

Chapter Nine
COOPER

"Well," Momma urges, practically bouncing out of her skin, "how'd it go today at the lake?"

"It was good," I respond, slamming another bag of ice down on the brick patio to break it up and then dumping it on top of the cooler of beer.

When I raise my head, I bust out laughing at the look of annoyance on her face. Momma's lips are pursed and turned to one side, her eyes narrowed, and hands resting on her hips. "It was amazing. We had sex on the boat while the kids watched. She's pregnant, by the way. Wedding's next week."

Mom swats me in the chest with the dishtowel she's still holding in her hand from wiping down the outside tables. "Don't be smart."

I wink before leaning across the ice chest and planting a kiss on her cheek. "Some things can't be helped." Then, without another word, I cross the yard to join my father at the boiler.

"Mind purging those crawfish while I get the water going, son?" Dad looks like a textbook coonass in his denim overalls and white shit kickers. I've always admired the way the man can own a three-piece suit like nobody's business during the week and return to his Cajun roots when he clocks out for the weekend. Dad's always made a good living but has never been one to flaunt it. He values the simpler things in life. Those that really matter. Good family, food, and friends. He loves to fish, hunt, and drink his beer while listening to some good zydeco music.

"On it."

I cut the string at the top of the sack with my pocket knife and dump the crawfish into the big metal tub. After sprinkling a thick layer of salt on top, I grab the hose and begin filling it up with water.

As I watch the crawfish fight their way to the top, I'm reminded of all of the boils we had growing up. I can still picture my dad and Mr. David, Spencer's father, perfecting their craft. They must have sampled every powder and liquid seasoning combination available, trying different variations with garlic cloves, onions, oranges, lemons, and lime juice. You name it, they probably tried it, eventually settling on the method we still use today. Weekends during crawfish season were spent back here beneath the mossy oaks. Spence and I running around in swimsuits through the sprinklers. Our fathers drinking their Bud Light and arguing over football and fishing spots, and really anything and everything. If you didn't know those two ornery bastards, you'd swear they hated each other. But, Dad and David grew up on the same dead end street, and just like Spencer and me, had been best friends their entire lives. Best friends who I don't think ever agreed on anything but the best way to boil a batch of crawfish.

"You know you don't have to do that." My body tenses up, her voice pouring over me like liquid sex. She may as well have just asked me to fuck her brains out because my dick is ready to oblige. I shift my legs and discretely adjust myself. God, I am wound so tight from being with Spencer all damned day and not being able to touch her.

Twisting the nozzle to shut off the water hose, I turn around to face her. Spencer's changed into a pair of short denim shorts and fitted tee with a crawfish on it that says "Cajun Girls Suck the Heads."

I smile, running my tongue along my teeth. "Don't have to do what?"

"Why're you smilin' at me like that?" Her face blushes and I shrug, enjoying watching her squirm a little. "Uh, you don't have to purge the crawfish. They say it doesn't really do anything. You can just rinse 'em with plain ol' water."

"Sacrilege!" Pops shouts from his folding chair about ten feet away. He must be straining pretty damned hard to hear our conversation over the noise of the boiler.

Her eyes widen as she calls out, "Hey, Mr. Neal."

"Hi, sugar," he greets, walking over to welcome Spence with a tight hug. "Good to have you back."

"It's good to be home." Home. That's exactly what it feels like. This place hasn't felt much like home over the past few years. Not with Kristy or whatever girl I had with me to distract myself from Spencer and her kids. God, I'm such an idiot.

"Where're the boys? I haven't seen those little rascals in forever," Dad asks, scanning the backyard.

"They're coming with Momma. She sent me on ahead to see if y'all needed any help."

Dad shakes his head with exaggeration. "Unh unh, we don't need your kind of help. You just sit your pretty little self in a chair, kick your feet up, and let Cooper here bring you a beer. How's that sound?"

She rests a hand on my father's shoulder. "That sounds like...an old man try'na keep me outta his crawfish," she says, all dimples.

"I don't have any idea what you're talkin' about, little lady," he responds with feigned innocence. "I gotta get back to my pot. You two kids enjoy yourselves." He takes a few steps away before calling back, "Cooper, keep that girl away from our supper."

"Yes, sir." I look over at her gaping mouth and laugh.

Her finger jabs my chest. "I'm right, you know."

"Usually are," I agree, feeling my heart speed up at her nearness. "Want a beer?" I ask, already turning toward the cooler to grab one for myself.

"Sure."

No sooner than we've sat at the wrought iron table and cracked open our drinks, do her momma and kids come strolling across the yard.

"Hey, Cooper," Mrs. Elaine calls out, waving her hand wildly. "I made my crawfish dip," she singsongs. Mrs. Elaine raises the dish pointing at it with her other hand and I give her a thumbs up.

Spencer's momma makes the best dip I've ever tasted. Most everyone I know just mixes up some ketchup and mayonnaise, but hers is a mustard and mayonnaise mix with onions and spices. It's delicious. My mouth's watering just thinking about it.

Lake and Landon follow their grandmother inside the house, carrying dishes with the savage nipping at their heels.

"Thanks for today," Spence says, placing her warm hand

on top of mine. She squeezes it gently and my skin tingles beneath her touch. "The kids had such a great time."

"And you?"

"Me?" she smiles. "I'm in the clouds, Cooper James." Spencer kicks back in her chair, crossing her feet in my lap.

"Please, by all means." I laugh. "Make yourself comfortable, Princess."

Her nose scrunches as she pokes out her tongue. "Everyone's spoilin' me since I got here. I'm kinda enjoying this new life of leisure."

I rest my hands on her ankles and massage gently, enjoying the freedom of being able to touch her again. "A real life princess." I wink. "By the way, I like your shirt," I add, waggling my eyebrows.

"Hah! I thought you might."

Just then our mothers and her children file out of the house. Selfishly, I find myself wishing they'd stayed away a little while longer. It felt so good not having to share her for those few minutes. I'm supposed to be trying to get used to the idea of having her kids around, and all I want is to keep her all to myself.

"Spencer!" Momma calls out, rushing over with outstretched arms. Much to my disappointment, Spence pulls her legs from my lap and rises to greet my mother.

"Hi, Mrs. Nelly. Thanks for having us over."

"Oh, hush, child. Y'all are family." Momma rubs a few tears from her eyes, and I take that as my cue to run inside.

Placing a hand on the small of Spencer's back to get her attention, I whisper in her ear, "Be right back." She nods, never breaking eye contact with Momma, but I don't miss the way her body shivers, nor the heated look in her eyes.

With a grin I can't seem to wipe off my face, I rush inside and up to my room to change my shirt. It takes me a few minutes of rifling through drawers before I locate the one I'm looking for.

When I walk back outside, I find Spencer sitting Indian style on the edge of the brick patio. Her back is to me, hunched over as she races monster trucks with Kyle in the dirt. I stand there, feeling the stupid grin overtake my face as I listen to her rev her engine and taunt a two-year-old. A few minutes go by before she senses my presence. Her head whirls in my direction. "He..." Her greeting is lost as she looks up and snorts out the most unladylike laugh I have ever heard.

"Somethin' funny?" I ask with a straight face that's not easy to maintain.

"That's awesome." Spence laughs, pointing to my fresh shirt. It's a black tee with a single crawfish in the center that says "Suck This."

"I have to ask you a very serious question, Princess..."

"Yeah?"

"Do you consider yourself a true Cajun girl?"

She traps her bottom lip between her teeth as she stands, leaning in real close to whisper, "Guess you'll have to find out, won't ya?"

"You're killin' me, Spence."

Savage looks up from his trucks, only just realizing I'm here. "Hi, man! You here!" He jumps up and latches onto my leg. And I'll be damned if it doesn't make me feel like a million fucking bucks, even if he is bustin' my balls.

Spencer and I don't have much time together after that, the kids and our mothers commanding most of her attention. But, just having her near, hearing her voice, her laugh, seeing her smile feels good. It feels right.

When Pops calls out that it's time to grub, I fill a tray with crawfish, potatoes, and sausage, setting it down in my spot at the picnic table. Then, I walk over to the cooler to grab a fresh beer and decide to fetch one for Spence as well. I set hers down beside mine and drown a potato in Mrs. Elaine's dip before lifting it to my mouth. But, before I even take the first bite, I catch a glimpse of Spencer. She's filling trays for Lake and Landon, all the while telling little dude to hold on and she'll peel his in just a minute. Everyone else, myself included, is getting ready to stuff our faces, and she can't even eat.

I never realized before how selfless a job it is to be a mother—always just taking for granted the things my momma did for me. But, as I watch Spencer tend to all of their needs without complaint, I'm in awe of her. It's a side of Spence I've never seen, and rather than feeling jealous over the way they monopolize all of her time, I'm struck with an overwhelming urge to take care of her.

Placing my potato back on the tray, I walk over to where Lake and Landon are waiting for her to bring them their food and drinks. I may be overstepping, but, damn it...someone needs to.

"Hey, boys," I call out, standing next to them at the same wrought iron table Spence and I occupied earlier in the evening.

"Hey, Cooper," Lake says, smiling, and Landon lifts two fingers from the table in a wave.

"How old are the two of you?"

They look a little confused by the question but answer together, "Twelve."

I nod. A little younger than I'd suspected but still plenty

old enough. "Old enough to dump crawfish onto a tray and grab drinks from a cooler?"

Sounds start sputtering from both of their mouths, like the thought never crossed their minds. I'm sure it hadn't because it wouldn't have crossed mine, either. Both of their faces redden with embarrassment. They aren't bad kids. Just kids, and kids are inherently selfish.

Both boys get up from their chairs without a word, heading over to the coolers to grab their own sodas as two trays slam down onto the table simultaneously, jerking my attention back in that direction.

"Who do you think you are?" The she-devil who has invaded my princess's body once again demands.

"Your friend?" I ask hesitantly. "Hopefully still with benefits..."

"Get over here," Spencer says as the boys return to the table.

"Ooooooh," they both chant in unison as she grabs my arm, jerking me around to the side of the house.

"I didn't mean right this minute, Spence. We can wait to fool around 'til later." I laugh. She doesn't.

"You are not their father."

Whoa. "Trust me, Spence. I am very aware."

The tips of her ears turn fire red. "How dare you embarrass them like that, huh? They hardly know you. It wasn't your place to parent my children."

"I never said I wanted to parent your children."

Her face blanches, but she recovers quickly. "Mind. Your. Own. Business."

"You are my business, babe. I care about you and was just trying to help."

She scoffs. "By once again pointing out all of the ways I

suck as a parent? You are overstepping your position."

My blood is boiling. "And where exactly is my *position*, Princess? Between your thighs?"

Her hand flies out, connecting with my left cheek, and instantly her face pales. Spencer's hands cup her open mouth and her eyes well up. "Oh my God. I'm sorry."

Her hands are all over me, patting my chest, stroking my cheek as she continues to apologize. I grab both of her wrists firmly in mine and hold them down at her sides.

"This isn't about me embarrassing those boys. This is about you and your need to prove to the world that you can do everything on your own. It's about control."

She pulls her lips between her teeth, biting hard to try to stop her tears. "I foolishly thought that friends were allowed to care for one another, but I've gotten the message loud and fucking clear, Spencer. Call me when you're ready for me to assume my position. Until then, I'll back right the fuck off."

I leave her standing there and ignore the looks that our meddling parents are giving me from the table as I make my way through the front door.

She's been home two fucking days and we're already at each other's throats. I knew she'd be a little upset about my correcting her children, but I didn't expect that. How the hell am I supposed to bond with her kids and win her back if she won't let me in? If all she wants is someone to screw when the mood strikes?

"Goddamnit!" I shout, punching the frame to my bedroom door before slamming it shut.

Chapter Ten
SPENCER

What the hell just happened?

I *hit* him. I fucking *hit* him.

"Cooper, wait," I cry out, chasing after him 'til he rounds the edge of the house. He doesn't even look at me.

Throwing my hands in the air, I watch him go. *To hell with this.* I refuse to chase after him in front of my children.

Was I wrong? I mean, obviously I was wrong for hitting him, but he was wrong, too. How dare he insinuate that I'm only using him for a booty call?

But isn't that what you're doing, Spencer?

No. No, it's not. We had a great time at the lake today, and afterward, here tonight, before this...whatever *this* is.

A knot begins to form in the pit of my stomach, and I suddenly find it difficult to swallow. The wood creeks as I lean my back against the side of the house, bending at the waist with my hands on my knees. I can't breathe.

Ugh! I can't do this right now. Kyle still needs to be fed dinner, and I've got to get all of the kids cleaned up and ready for bed. My boys start their first day at a new school tomorrow, and I should be focused on that, not hiding on the side of the neighbors' house on the verge of tears because of a man. I don't have time for fights, I don't have time for feelings, and I most certainly don't have time for fucking strings. I told him that from the beginning.

Why is he doing this to me?

Retrieving my phone from my back pocket, I decide to send him a text to apologize and maybe smooth things over.

Me: I'm sorry I hit you.

I wait around for a minute to see if he'll reply, allowing time for my face to cool down, and hopefully some of the redness to leave my cheeks, but Cooper doesn't respond, and I guess I don't really expect him to.

With a heavy sigh, I come around the corner of the house, and the parents immediately stop talking, giving me worried smiles. Kyle is already eating with both Momma and Mrs. Nelly, and Mr. Neal is staring down at his food like it's the most interesting thing he's ever seen.

"Dis gooood cawfish, Mom." Kyle beams, breaking the awkward silence. He's got juice leaking down his face and arms, and his white shirt is covered in orange stains.

I force myself to smile back at my baby while trying to ignore the way my heart feels like it's been wrapped in thorns. "I'm glad you're enjoying it, bud." I can't disguise the pain in my voice.

"Go on up there and talk to him, honey. Whatever it is, y'all can fix it," Coop's mom urges.

My smile feels exactly like the lie that it is. "I'm just gonna go home and get the boys' things together for school tomorrow. Thanks for dinner, Mrs. Nelly." I place a kiss on the top of

Kyle's head, which is probably the only spot not covered in crustacean guts, and even that's iffy.

"But, you didn't even eat yet." She wipes her hands off on a napkin and starts to rise. "Here, let me make you a plate."

I hold up my hands to stop her. "I've lost my appetite. I'm fine, really. Thank you, though."

I can't handle the broken look on her face as I turn tail and head back to the house.

I keep checking my phone for a response from Cooper. Maybe an apology of his own or even a fuck you. The silence is killing me. Of course there's not one, because with the way my attention is honed in on this phone, I'd have heard it if there was.

I practically jump out of my skin as I'm setting the blow dryer down and the message alert finally sounds, but the wind is swiftly knocked out of my sails when I see that the message is from Gina and not Asshole.

Gina: You will never guess who I ran into at the club last night.

Me: You're right. Who?

Gina: Kyle's sperm donor.

Me: Did he talk to you?

My phone starts vibrating in my hand.

"Don't be mad at me, okay?" Gina asks nervously.

Oh shit. "What did you do, Gina?"

"Well, I, uh...I may have accidently told him you had a boy."

"How do you accidentally tell someone the gender of another person's child? That's not that big of a deal, but why were you talking to him about Kyle in the first place?"

"He just came up to me and asked if you were around and

I told him no…So, he asked how you were doing, and I said great."

"Okaaaay…"

"Well, then he says that he might like to see the baby sometime, and I told him to leave you and Kyle the fuck alone."

Good girl.

"But then he starts getting all googly eyed," she continues, "going on about how he has a son. And I went off and told him that he doesn't have shit because he gave up that right."

"Well, what did he say after that?" I ask as my chest tightens.

"Nothin' really. He just walked off and that was it. But, I feel really bad for even talking to him."

"I'm sure he was just drunk and feeling sentimental. Don't worry about it, Gi." But, I have this sick feeling in my gut that Alex is about to cause problems.

"You think?"

"Yeah."

"Okay, good…I can't wait to see you next week!"

The thought of seeing my best friend brings a genuine smile to my face. "I can't wait either, girl. You have no idea…"

Then I proceed to fill her in on all of the shit that's been going on with me since I arrived here yesterday morning. Just two days. I can't wait to see what the next weeks and months have in store for me.

The sound of the screen door slamming and the kids' voices lures me down the stairs. Ignoring the curious looks from my mother, I send the twins up to take turns showering and scoop Kyle into my arms, returning to my bathroom to bathe and get him ready for bed.

I spend an extra long time rocking him tonight, continuing long after he's fallen asleep. I run my finger over his face, studying his little features, which are mostly mine. His brown eyes and coloring are all he took from Alex. By the time that I lay him down, I've completely forgotten the fiasco from earlier this evening.

That is until I walk downstairs and find Momma waiting at the table with the Yahtzee game laid out and two margaritas complete with little umbrellas and limes. She greets me with a cheesy grin. *Could she be any more obvious?*

"Took him a long time to go down tonight," Momma observes, starting out with a little small talk. "Must've been over-tired from his busy day."

I decide against telling her about Gina's call, forcing a smile instead. "Must've been."

"I sent the boys to bed."

"Thanks, Ma," I say, pulling out the chair across from hers.

I must say she impresses me with her ability to wait a full ten minutes into our game before drilling me about Coop.

"So..." she drawls, leaning across the table. *Here it comes.* "You gonna tell me what happened earlier tonight?" she asks, clearly annoyed that I haven't spilled voluntarily by now.

"Not if I don't have to."

"Well, you have to. What the heck happened? I thought things were going so well."

My eyes well up, and Momma's face falls. I know it's more than just this mess with Coop that has me so emotional. It's everything compounding, and I feel like I'm falling apart. This shit with Alex is just the icing on the cake, and I don't even know for sure that there is any shit with Alex.

"We had a fight."

Momma's lips purse in annoyance. "Well, no shit, Sherlock. What about?"

I nervously click the pen in my hand repeatedly as I fill her in. "I heard him fussing at the boys and called him on it. He accused me of something that wasn't true...mostly. And I got pissed and..." *Oh God, I still can't believe I slapped him.*

"And...?"

"I, uh...I sort of hit...him"

Momma stares at me, wide-eyed, before shaking herself from a stupor. "You. Hit. Him?" she says, annunciating each syllable. "Did I just hear that right? My old ears must not be working correctly because I could swear you just told me that my thirty-three-year-old daughter just hit someone because she was angry..." Her judgy eyes scour my face. "Did I hear that right, Spencer Rose?"

"I feel bad enough without you rubbing it in."

She stands up from her seat, shoving the game back into the box with attitude. "Well, you *should* feel bad. Are you trying to push him away? Do you not want him back, Spencer? Because I'm hella confused right now."

I can't hold it in any longer as the stress of today pours out of my eyes like a raging river. "It doesn't matter what I want, Momma," I wail, rising from my seat. "The only thing that matters anymore is what's best for my boys. Why can't you understand that?"

"I do understand that, and I think you and Cooper together is it," she insists, cupping my hands in hers.

"Momma...listen to me, please?"

She nods.

"Cooper does not want kids. He left his wife because she wanted to have children. That's why they got divorced, and that's how badly he doesn't want them. I have three and their own fathers don't want them. I'm not about to get involved romantically with another man who doesn't want them. They've had more than enough disappointment in their short lives."

Momma's hands lift to my shoulders. She pulls me close, wrapping her arms around my neck, and I cry harder. "You're sup-p-p-posed to be on m-my s-side, Mom."

Her fingers comb through my hair. "I am, honey. I'm always on your side. I'm sorry. I didn't realize…" She sighs. "I'm sorry, Spence."

After our emotions settle a bit, Mom and I snuggle on the couch and watch TV before heading up for the night.

When I enter my room, my body seems to glide right over to the window where I stare across the yard at Cooper's. His light is on, but the curtains are drawn tight. It's only taken me two days to push him away, and it hurts far worse than it should. Because, no matter how many times I say that I don't want the strings, the reality is that I've been tied to Cooper since I was just a little girl.

There is a nagging pain in my chest. My heart physically aches for that man. I've picked up my phone at least a dozen times to type out another message, one that maybe he would answer. But, what do I say? I'm sorry again? No other person has ever been able to hurt me the way that Cooper can, and he doesn't even have to try. A simple unanswered text between "friends" has me tied up in knots.

When I finally collapse into bed, I crave him. It's stupid. I'm pissed at both Cooper and myself, and I'm stressed as fuck, but all I want is for him to make love to me. For him to make it all better, because I know that it would. Sex heals *everything*… well, almost. I'm fairly certain that if I summonsed him he'd come, but I don't want it like this. Not while he thinks that

that's all I want from him. Fabio doesn't even tempt me. It's finally happened. I'm broken.

I drift off to sleep both horny and frustrated.

At exactly one in the morning, a text comes in and I'm instantly wide awake as if I'd never even gone to sleep. My heart soars, beating rapidly, assuming that Coop has finally replied, and then it plummets just as quickly when a different name pops up on the screen.

Latin Lovah: Can you just send me a picture?

I can't breathe. Can. Not. Breathe. My eyes begin to burn as I screenshot his message and shoot it over to Gina, not caring about the time. I'm freaking the fuck out.

Gina: Don't answer. Are you okay, babe? Just ignore him. You don't owe him shit.

Me: Okay. I'm scared.

Gina: I'm sorry, honey. I'm so sorry.

My first thought is to message Cooper. He's a lawyer. He could help me or at least tell me what to expect. But, I can't do that because I basically told him to butt the fuck out earlier today.

With a few deep breaths, I attempt to calm my racing heart. I try to rationalize with myself. Nothing's happened. He asked for a picture. Maybe he will just go back into the hole he's been hiding in for the past three years. *As if I could be that lucky.*

Clicking back over to my messages with Cooper, I find that there's still no reply. With a lump in my throat, I send him another.

Me: This hurts.

It's the middle of the night, and I don't expect a reply, but almost immediately my phone sounds.

Asshole: Is this a summons?

Me: No. I'm just sorry. I miss you already.

Asshole: I'm sorry. That sounds like strings. Hit me up if you need to take advantage of my position. I'm always up for a good fuck.

Ouch.

Shit, does that hurt. Cooper has never ever been downright cruel to me. Even when we broke up, he did it in the gentlest way he could. I shouldn't have messaged him. I shouldn't have come back here. If it was only me, I'd leave tomorrow. But, what would I say to my children? Psych! We're going back home, kids. No. I have to stay, and hopefully he will get his own place soon and things will blow over.

Chapter Eleven
COOPER

Today sucked.

This entire week sucked. Every single day since Spence and I got into it has sucked more than the one before. But, today...today, I've reached my breaking point.

I never allow myself to become emotionally connected to my cases. Hell, I was a divorce attorney before moving home. You won't make a living in Cedar Grove as a divorce attorney. There just aren't enough of them.

Dad's firm, which will soon be mine, practices all aspects of family law, and today I got my first taste of child custody. Let's just say that it wasn't a good one. We lost. We fucking lost, and I have never questioned my career choice until today.

A huge chunk of our clientele belongs to the Department of Child Protective Services. We represent the children and the state of Louisiana. Today's case should have been cut and dry. Our client is a two-year-old little girl who's been living with her foster parents for almost a year. The biological mother has missed nearly all visitations and the next logical step would be to seek termination of parental rights and to allow her new family to adopt her.

But the mother's attorney threw us a curve ball. Apparently, when said child was removed from her mother's custody, the social workers forgot to file some paperwork. Since the paperwork had never been filed, the child technically should never have been removed from the home, and the judge did the only thing that the law allows him to do. He gave her back.

Normally, I'm a man who believes in the law, but today the law can suck my fucking dick because I will never forget the pain in those foster parents' faces or their raw, guttural cries for as long as I live.

So, here I am, pulling up to the house at two o'clock in the afternoon because Dad didn't want me back in the office. Not that I had any desire to work anymore today. I may never go in to work again considering the way I feel right now.

I park my truck and don't even bring my briefcase with me. I can't. I'm in desperate need of a mental break. Maybe I'll hit up the bar tonight.

When I walk through the door, it is with every intention of swallowing a few Advil and taking my ass straight to bed for a much-needed nap, but nothing about this day is going as planned.

I hang my keys on the key holder next to the door and toe off my shoes. "I'm home, Ma. I'm gonna go lie down and try to forget this shit day."

The voice I hear is not the one I'm expecting. "My man here! My man here, Nana!"

I won't even tell you that my heart does a fucking summersault in my chest as Savage comes running through the hall right at me because that would make me a pussy.

"Hey, little dude," I say, shocked to see him in my mother's house. *Did he just call her Nana? What the hell?*

"You have shit day, Pooper?" he asks with genuine concern.

And after one of the worst days I've had in a very long time, this little guy has me in stitches not even two minutes after walking through the door.

"Don't say shit, Kyle. You're momma's gonna kick my butt, and I don't know if you know this yet, but your mom has a hell of a swing."

"My mom kick you butt?"

"She will if you keep saying that word."

"Ohhh," he says, widening his big brown eyes. "Wanna come play wif me in duh room, Pooper?"

"Kyle?" Momma calls, her voice coming from the direction of the kitchen. Within seconds, she rounds the corner, drying her hands on the front of her apron. "Oh, there you are!" she says. "And you found a friend!" She looks up at me with sad eyes. "Sorry about court. Dad told me you're taking it hard."

"Hey," I answer, giving her a hug. "I really don't wanna talk about it," I say, shaking my head and pinching the bridge of my nose. "What's he doing here?"

"Oh, Spencer had a job interview today, and I offered to watch him for her. Elaine was gonna take a day off from teaching, but there's no sense in that, right?" She seems nervous. Like I'm going to lay into her for keeping him just because Spencer and I aren't speaking.

"It's fine, Ma. I'm sure Spence appreciates it."

Her cheeks puff up and she blows out a relieved sigh.

"You two having fun?" I ask, and Kyle smiles up at me, all teeth. "Did I hear him right? Is he calling you Nana?"

Momma's face flushes with embarrassment. "Well, uh. He can't really say Nelly. The Ls are hard for him. I asked Spencer, and she said it was okay."

Good. Let her love on Spencer's kids and maybe she'll get over the fact that I'm not giving her grandchildren. "It's cool. Just surprised me, is all." My mom is on cloud nine with this kid. How could I be upset seeing how happy he makes her.

"Yet's go play now." Kyle tugs my arm and I allow him to lead me until I see the room we're heading for.

"Oh no. We can't play in there."

"Nana say yes!"

My eyes narrow as I assess him. "Did you really ask her?"

He nods. *Hmm.*

We reach the formal living room. The one with the white carpet and antique furniture. The very same room that I've gotten my ass busted for leaving footprints in. Sure enough, there's a toy box in the corner overflowing with trucks and balls, as well as a TV on a console table that wasn't there this morning.

"Momma..."

She walks over with a big ol' smile, like nothing is untoward. "He needed a place to keep his toys."

"And you gave him *this* room?" I ask in disbelief.

"Well, I mean...it's just sitting here unused. Seems sort of silly, right?"

I scoff. "It sure didn't seem silly to you when you were beating the shit out of me for sneaking in here."

She laughs again. "Coop, don't tell me you're jealous of a two-year-old."

"I'm not jealous...Just shocked."

"Good. And stop saying the s-h-i-t word in front of Savage or that little slap Spencer gave you last weekend is gonna feel like a love tap." She pats the side of my face, smiling.

How the hell does she know about that?

"Elaine," she says in answer to my unspoken question before turning away and heading back to her kitchen.

So, Spencer told her mom...*Nice*. My parents knowing all of my fucking business is really getting old quick.

"C'mon, man. Come see my stuff."

Playtime with Kyle is exactly what I need. I can't remember the last time I sat on the floor and pushed cars around. It's impossible to be upset around this kid. He just breeds happiness. I can't even explain it.

After an hour in the forbidden room, I've got the *Hot Dog* song from Mickey Mouse on loop in my head and life feels pretty damned good.

Then suddenly Kyle gets this serious look on his face, and I think he might cry.

"Is something wrong, Savage?"

He nods and his little eyes gloss over. "My weewee hurtin'."

Maybe I misheard him. "Your what?"

"My weewee hurtin'," he says again, slapping the front of his pants.

"Uhhh, Ma?" I call out. *Help...*

She peeks her head inside. "He has a little diaper rash, Cooper. He'll be fine."

I look back over to my little buddy. "You have a rash?" I ask with a frown. "I'm sorry, little dude, I hope you feel better."

"Yeah, I have rash," he says with a pout. "You kiss it?"

Holy fucking shit. I mean...I can't even make this stuff up. This kid is hilarious.

"You kiss my owie?" he asks again.

Lord, I need to stop laughing long enough to answer him. "Kyle, I'm not kissing your weewee."

"You not nice, Pooper." His hands cross on his chest and his bottom lip hangs to the floor. He's got that pout down to a T. And, of course, right now is when Spencer decides to walk in. I can tell she wasn't expecting to see me. Her nerves are written all over her face. Our eyes lock and both of us stare without saying a word.

Kyle runs over to his mom, still pouting. "Mommy, Pooper not kiss my weewee."

"Uhhhh..." She looks around in confusion. "Good?"

"I have owie, Mommy. You kiss it!"

Light bulb.

Her cheeks flame with embarrassment as she bursts into a fit of laughter.

"He has a little rash," Momma says as she walks over to greet Spencer, who still hasn't caught her breath. "I put some butt paste on it when I changed his diaper."

When her laughter finally dies down, Spencer thanks my mother.

"How'd it go?" Momma asks, completely unfazed by Kyle's owie.

"It went well. I think I'll get it, actually. It's not really what I wanna be doing, but small towns aren't really ideal for what I do."

I laugh to myself at the way she avoids using her title with my mother.

"I understand," Momma says, not taking the discussion any further. "Well, let me know if you ever need me to keep him again. He is just the sweetest little thing."

Absorbed in her shock at seeing me when she walked in and the ridiculous conversation with her son, Spence only just realizes that her kid has taken over the forbidden room.

"You put him in here?" she asks with her eyes bugging out.

Momma rolls her eyes, like it's so not a big deal. "He needed his own space."

Spence nods. "All righty, then." She reaches out for Kyle. "Ready to go home, baby? Gramma Elaine and your brothers will be back soon."

"You not comin', Pooper?"

I hate that things are so fucking awkward between us. "Not today, buddy. Thanks for letting me play with you, though. I had fun."

"Bye, man!" he calls out as his mother heads for the door. "I miss you, man!"

Chapter Twelve
SPENCER

I couldn't get out of that house fast enough. I hadn't even seen Cooper's truck parked in his spot on the way in. I hadn't looked because he's never home this early. Most nights I don't see his truck roll up 'til six or seven. And, yes, I've watched.

My chest feels tight as I cross the yard back over to Momma's, and before I've even put the key in the door, Mom and my boys pull into the drive. I must admit that it's nice having my mother work at their school so that I don't have to worry about picking them up after football practice. She sticks around 'til they're done to complete her lesson plans.

Unlocking the door, I shove it open with my hip and set Kyle down inside, turning back around to wave hello to my boys, who are climbing out of Mom's van.

"How was practice?"

I hear them talking but am unable to focus on a word they say as my attention is stolen by the man who's just stepped out onto the neighbors' porch. He must've changed the minute Kyle and I left, trading the suit for jeans that hug his ass to perfection and a blue button down with the sleeves cuffed at the elbows. His hair is freshly styled in that just fucked look he wears so well.

"Hey, boys!" he calls out, waving at the kids as he heads in the direction of his truck.

The boys both take off toward him, and I have to force myself to turn away and join Kyle and Momma, who at some point have managed to sneak around me, inside of the house.

"How was your interview, baby?" Mom asks as she snatches an apple from the fruit bowl and begins cutting it into slices for Kyle.

"You're spoiling me," I tell her, placing a kiss on her cheek. "You may never get rid of me." I wink, resting my forearms on the counter across from her.

"I like having people to take care of again. Y'all don't have to leave. I told you that already."

"I know, Momma. We'll see." I snatch a slice of apple from the plate in front of her. "The interview was good. School counselor isn't exactly at the top of my list." I frown. "Oh my God, Principal George actually said that I'd be the perfect assistant to the nurse when it came time for sex ed because she's a big ol' prude." I laugh.

"Nuh unh. He said that?"

I finish chewing and swallow before answering. "Yep. This whole town is obsessed with my job. It's so embarrassing."

Lake and Landon finally make their way into the house, bringing with them the scent of ass. *Gag.* The whole house smells as soon as they walk inside. I don't know how Momma survives the ride home with them in the afternoons.

"Peeyew," I gripe, pinching my nose. "Showers, boys!"

"Awe," Landon whines, "can I get a snack first?"

"Dude, you smell like you've been dipped in shit. Go shower and then get a snack."

Lake hangs back, allowing Landon, who is always starving, to shower first. "Hey, Mom..."

"Yeah?"

"Are, uh...are you and Cooper still fighting?"

I'm not sure how to answer that. Of course they figured out what was going on. They aren't babies anymore. "Um, we aren't fighting."

Lake lifts his brows in disbelief. "Well, 'cause I don't want you to be mad at him because of us. He's nice, and he was right, too. He wasn't mean to us or anything. Just pointed out that there's some things we could be doing for ourselves to help you out."

"Lake, I appreciate your concern. Really, I do. But, it's more complicated than that. I don't want you worrying about it. Coop and I have been friends for a long, *long* time, and this will eventually blow over." *I hope.*

He smiles. "Sure, Mom."

"Did he say where he was off to?" I ask without thinking and immediately wish I could take the question back. I shouldn't involve my son in our shit.

Lake's face turns up in a knowing smirk. "Rough day at work. He was going to T-Boy's."

The afternoons on school days seem to fly by. There just aren't enough hours. By the time the boys and Momma get home after practice, it's nearly 5:30. The few hours before bed are spent on showers, dinner, and homework. And sometimes we can squeeze in an episode or two of *CSI Miami*. Tonight was a really good night and we were able to work in three.

After the kids and Momma have gone to bed, I take myself out to sit on the porch and soak up some fresh air. Before I realize it, I've passed out in the wooden rocker. When my phone dings, waking me, I realize that it's nearing midnight. I wonder how long I'd have slept if my phone hadn't gone off. Speaking of which, I swipe the screen to see who's messaging this late.

Latin Lovah: Don't make me take you to court, 'cause I will.

I press the power button, darkening the screen, and set the phone face down on the table, as if avoiding looking at it will make it disappear. The acid in my stomach begins to churn. I'm so scared. I should've had Alex sign something. I have no clue what rights that asshole actually has or whether or not our text messages will even hold up in court. I don't know, and I'm too afraid to find out, so I'm holding on to the hope that he will give up and vanish again.

I'm methodically rocking, gnawing off my fingernails, when Coop's truck swerves into their drive. *He's drunk.*

I fly out of my chair without giving it a second thought, meeting him at his truck before the door has even swung open, and when it does, I fly off the handle.

"What're you thinking getting behind the wheel in your condition? Huh?" I shove his chest with so much force that he has to grab the door to keep from falling over.

"Hey, Princess," he says clutching his chest where I've just pushed him. "Why you gotta be so violent? Let's make love, not war." His words are slow and drawn out.

"Stop kidding around. I'm serious. You could have killed

yourself or someone else. You have a fucking phone. Use it!"

"Would you misssss me, baby?" His hand darts out and grabs onto my hip. Coop pulls me forward to stand between his parted legs, his ass resting on the edge of the truck seat. "You s-smell so good."

"You reek."

He chuckles. "You always say the sexiest th-things, Princesss." Both of his hands slip around my waist, cupping my ass. "You have the best butt ever in the whole world, Spence..."

"You need to go inside and sleep this off." I try to move away, but his hold is really tight.

Coop's head falls forward, resting on my breasts. "I had a bad day, friend."

"I heard," I say softly, placing a hand in his hair and massaging his scalp.

"You gotta esplain how this works."

Lord, give me patience. "How what works, Coop?"

He hiccups, lifting his head. "The benefitsss. Can I cash in or do I have to wait 'til you wanna do it? 'Cause I could really, really use some right now."

Dear God, I should be pissed, but I can see the sadness in his eyes, and I know that he's not trying to insult me.

"Cooper, I don't think you could get it up tonight if you tried." I'm not being mean. I'm serious as a heart attack. Whiskey dick is real.

"Wanna bet?" he counters, emphasizing the T.

"Not especially."

"They were so sad, Spence—her parents. And when they broke down...I s-saw you."

I am so confused. "What are you talking about, Cooper?"

"The f-f-foster mom. When they took her away. I pictured

you and Savage and it hurts. It hurts, Princess. I don't wanna do it anymore."

Oh no. I remember him mentioning the hearing in passing now. "You guys lost? Did they give her back to her mother?"

He nods, and I feel warm, wet tears on my chest.

"Hey," I say, lifting his face. "I'm sorry, Coop. I'm so, so sorry." The sadness in his eyes is too much and soon I'm crying right along with him.

"I need you." *God, how I wish it were true.*

"Cooper, I'm not sleeping with you like this. You're drunk."

"I won't press charges."

How can he be stupid drunk and still so damned cute? "Coop, I'm not worried about you pressing charges," I say with a laugh. "You hate me right now." He shakes his head. "You do, and you just don't remember because you're drunk and sad and horny and you 'need me.' But, in the morning, when you've sobered up, you're going to regret it and I won't be able to handle that. So, no, you can't *cash in on benefits* tonight."

His head shakes. "You're wrong. I would never regret fucking you."

I find myself once again giggling. "You're a real Casanova tonight, let me tell you."

"What about kissing? Is that off the menu, too?" His hands flex, squeezing my ass as he nips at my nose.

"I guess that'd be all right."

He brings his lips to mine slowly and I expect his kiss to be sloppy and drunk. But Coop must not need his wits for this skill because in this kiss, I feel more connected to this man than I have ever felt in my life. And that says a lot. I don't know if it's because he's not overthinking it. It's honest and pure. I feel the emotion in my bones.

He doesn't try to take things further, content to make out like teenagers in our parents' front yards. Our connection is so powerful that it overwhelms me. I find myself crying for no explicable reason.

He feels it too and pulls his lips from mine, kissing my tears away. "Don't cry, Spencer. Fuck. I can't take it."

"I'm sorry." I sniffle, trying to dry my tears. "It's just...Wow, Coop."

"I'm a good kisser," he beams.

I chuckle. "The best."

"It feels different," he muses, "kissing you."

"Different than it used to?" I ask, searching for his meaning.

Coop shakes his head. "No, esactly the same." He takes both of his hands and tucks my hair behind my ears. "It never felt like this...with anyone else." He seems surprised by his own admission, and I'm starting to really like drunk, filterless Cooper.

"For me either," I find myself admitting.

He nods, clearing his throat. "I was wrong."

"Don't even worry about it. The kids aren't upset." I'm just so relieved we're finally hashing this out and pray that he remembers it all in the morning.

"No. I was r-right about that."

Okay, scratch that. "What were you wrong about, then?"

"I should've never let you g-go."

"No," I agree. "You shouldn't have."

Chapter Thirteen
COOPER

I wake up with a headache of mass proportions, and as I wretch into the toilet, I promise myself that I will never drink again. Of course, it's a lie. One I've told myself plenty of times before. One that, no doubt, I will tell myself again.

The door cracks open and Dad peeks his head into my room as I'm literally dragging myself across the floor to get back to bed.

"Ready for work?" he teases, to which I give him the finger.

He laughs. "Boy, when're you gonna learn that drinkin' like that never fixes anything?"

"Ugh," I groan as my stomach revolts.

"Serves you right for keepin' that poor girl up all night."

What is this man going on about?

"Huh?"

"Oh yeah. I had to come outside and pry your drunk ass off of her. Cryin' like a puss, too. Lord only knows what you said to poor Spence."

"Ah, shit."

"That's the thing with drinkin' like that, son. You may not remember, but she will. And you're gonna be in a heap of shit all over again. What part of getting drunk and crying all over the girl sounded charming to you? Huh?"

I stuff my face into the pillow. "Go away," I mumble.

"I gave you some solid advice and you just wiped your damn ass with it."

"I'm sick," I grumble.

"You're a fool's what you are," he says, shaking his head with a big ass grin. "Woo the girl, Cooper. Stop pissin' her off, and for God's sake, find your fuckin' man card before you scare her away for good this time!" he adds, slamming the door.

What the hell happened last night?

I remember going to the bar and playing a few games of pool with a couple of my old buddies. Lots of shots...*Too many shots.* I don't remember coming home, but I think I remember kissing Spence, although that could have been a dream. It's so foggy.

I grab my phone from under my pillow and there's already a message waiting from Spencer.

Princess: Hope you feel better.

Me: Sorry about last night.

Princess: Don't be. I think I like you better drunk.

Me: I think I like you better naked.

Princess: I'm a lot more agreeable, for sure. :p

Me: So, I didn't do anything stupid? I can't really remember.

Princess: I wouldn't go that far. You don't remember anything?

Me: I think maybe you kissed me?

Princess: Hey, you promised not to press charges.

Me: I what?

Princess: Nothing. You were really quite charming, actually.

Me: That's not what my Dad said.

Princess: It's fine. Don't even worry about it.

Me: I do worry about it. I'm fucking this all up, aren't I?

Princess: I don't know about you fucking it all up. I think I'm doing my fair share. I'm really sorry, Coop. I don't wanna fight with you. I'm sorry I freaked out.

Me: I'm sorry if I overstepped. I wasn't trying to make you feel like a bad mom. In fact, I think the exact opposite. I couldn't take my eyes off of you. I admire you so much, Spence. Please know that.

Princess: Thank you for saying that. I feel like a crazy person lately.

Me: Must be something in the air around here.

Princess: Hey, are you not going in to work today? Just saw your truck is still here.

Me: I don't think I'm getting out of this bed today. I could be dying.

Princess: I'm off to check out daycares with Savage. Call if you need anything. Feel better, Coop.

Me: Later, babe.

I set my phone down on the nightstand, plug it in to charge, and then slip into some sort of alcohol induced coma.
Tap. Tap. Tap.

It takes me a minute to realize that the sound is coming from my bedroom door. "Yeah?" I shout, still half asleep.

The door opens just a crack and Spencer's face appears. "Oh no. Were you asleep? I can come back later." She slinks back through the opening to leave.

That wakes me up. "No. No, come in, Spence. I need to get up. What time is it, anyway?"

"It's almost six," she says, walking into the room and placing a few Tupperware containers on the nightstand before sitting at the foot of my bed. "I brought you some gumbo. It, uh… always helps to coat my stomach after a hangover."

"You made me dinner, Princess?" A stupid grin overtakes my face.

"Well, I mean, it's not just for you. We're eating some, too. Don't get a big head or anything over it." She pokes out her tongue, and if my mouth didn't taste like ass and I didn't smell even worse, I'd have her pinned to this bed.

I smile and feel some shit starting to form in my throat again. Dad's right. I'm a pussy gettin' all emotional over a bowl of gumbo. "Were you making gumbo before you found out I wasn't feeling well?"

She smirks. "What's with the interrogation?"

"Answer the question, counselor."

"That lawyer talk is kinda hot." She smiles over at me, waggling her brows.

"Were you?" I persist.

"No." Spencer wrings her hands in her lap.

My head swells at her admission, along with my heart and my cock. "Thanks for cooking me dinner, Spence."

"You're welcome, Cooper."

Our eyes lock and the space between us becomes charged.

"You making me dinner is hot."

"That's so caveman of you. You gonna start carrying a club and dragging me around by the hair?" she teases.

"Is that an option?"

"No." She laughs, rising from the bed. "I have to get back and feed the kids. I hope you start to feel better." She places a hand in my hair and moves it down, tracing the side of my face. "Is there ever a time that you don't look absolutely gorgeous?"

I feel sick again and not from the hangover. It's because she's leaving and I don't want her to go. "Will you come back?"

"When?"

"Tonight...after you get the kids to bed. I'll shower and change the sheets and we can maybe watch a movie? If, you know...you don't have plans or anything."

She smiles. "I'd like that."

The minute she leaves, I hop up and jump into the shower. Then, I strip my bed and throw on a fresh set of sheets and blankets. I tidy up the room, and when it's cootie free, I sit and enjoy the best damned bowl of gumbo I've ever eaten.

"Coop," Mom calls out, advancing down the hall to my room. The door opens and she walks in. "Elaine said that Spence is coming over tonight. I guess that means you're feeling better." Her eyes dart around the room and she nods, looking impressed. "I was gonna ask if you wanted me to come freshen up in here, but I can see you've been busy."

"Thanks, Ma."

"You're welcome, baby." The back of her hand goes to my head to check for fever. I don't bother telling her that hangovers don't produce temperatures. She never listens, anyway. "You still don't look too good."

I shrug. "Still kinda queasy. We're just watching a movie."

"I'm happy the two of you made up. I was getting worried," she says, sitting next to me on the bed. "Elaine's worried, too."

I stare up at the ceiling, releasing a frustrated breath. "Y'all need to stop worrying and back off."

"Oh, Coop," she says, patting my cheek, "that's what mommas do. We worry. And then we step in and offer some divine intervention when our little ducklings lose their way."

There's no use arguing with this woman. She's bound and determined to mettle in my affairs. So, I try a different approach, hoping to get rid of her quicker.

"Thank you for everything. I don't know what I'd do without you."

Her eyes tear up. "You're welcome. I just want the best for you."

"I know, Momma." *Leave already...*

"Be a gentleman, Coop. I mean, I'm not gonna tell you not to have sex, because she seems to really like that sort of thing."

My eyes get huge when I spot Spencer standing in the open doorway with a finger to her lips, indicating for me to be quiet. *Oh shit.*

"Just you know," Mom continues, completely oblivious, "try to be more tender this time. Take it slow and show her how much you really care about her...that she's more than just a quick romp in a dirty bathroom."

Spencer literally spits out a laugh, and Momma's face turns beet red when she realizes her speech was overheard.

"Spencer!" Momma says nervously. "When did you get here?"

Spencer cannot stop laughing long enough to answer. Her response is broken up between guffaws. I think she says she just got here. I can't be sure.

Momma looks ready to cry with embarrassment, and, well, she should. She walks over to the door, giving Spencer a pat on the back in greeting. "Y'all have a good time, and, uh...well, holler if y'all need anything."

"You've done enough."

She clears her throat. "Right, well...I'll just leave y'all to it, then."

"Bye, Mrs. Nelly."

Spencer is still giggling when she shuts the door.

"Lock it," I tell her before she starts walking to the bed.

"Feeling a little sure of ourselves, are we?" Spence teases, doing a little shimmy as she twists the lock.

I waggle my eyebrows with exaggeration. *God, how I wish.* "Actually, I'm still not really feeling well. Just trying to keep the crazies out."

"I thought my momma was bad. Is she always like this?" Her thumb points over her shoulder toward the door that my mother just left through.

I shake my head and shrug. "Just since you came back. She's got Dad on my case, too. It's, uhh...it's been interesting, to say the least."

Her lips form a little O and her eyes get big. "Your momma just gave you permission to *fuck* me in your bed, Cooper James."

"You misunderstood. She specifically forbade me to *fuck* you in this bed. I think she used the word tender."

"It's a good thing I *like that sort of thing*, huh?"

I'm so embarrassed. "I'm really sorry, Spencer."

"Pfft." She waves her hand. "Don't be. The whole town seems to think that enjoying sex makes me a whore. It's not just her." She's saying that it doesn't bother her, but I can see the sadness in her eyes. Hear the tremor in her voice. "Funny thing is, I've only had sex with three people, Coop. *Three.* I kinda feel like if I'm gonna get labeled, I at least should have had the fun that goes along with it."

I'm ashamed to admit that I'm shocked by her confession. Not that I ever assumed she was giving it up to everyone. But that means she's only been with her kids' fathers...and me. "Well, I for one am A-okay with the fact that you missed out on all of *that* fun."

As Spence walks over to the bed, I lift the covers for her to crawl in beside me.

"I bet you are," she whispers, climbing in.

I place a kiss on her forehead as I reach across her body to the table for the remote. My heart starts pounding as her warmth and the smell of her perfume engulf me.

"Coop," she says nervously, her fingers fiddling with the button on her shirt.

"Yeah?"

Spencer takes a deep breath. "I probably shouldn't ask, and I know it's none of my business, but...Were you with a lot of girls?" Her cheeks flush as she gnaws on her thumbnail. "Never mind. It's been fifteen years. Of course you were."

I really don't want to answer. It's uncomfortable. "I don't know," I say honestly. "So, I mean, yeah. I guess there were sort of a lot. I don't remember most of them, to tell you the truth."

She nods, and I watch her throat move as she swallows.

"Before you married Tate, there was only you," I add, because I want her to know that I didn't go off to college to fuck around.

Spencer's body stiffens.

"I just wanted you to know that."

"Thank you," she whispers, her voice clogged with so much

emotion that it pierces my heart.

"Can we watch the movie now?" I ask, wanting to end this conversation before we make ourselves feel any worse.

"Yeah, what're we watching?" She moves closer, snuggling into the crook of my arm.

"You'll see." I already chose the movie and ordered it while she was away, so when I power on the TV, the title is on the screen. *Bad Moms.*

Just like I hoped, she busts out laughing. "You are too much."

"I try."

"See, the bad moms are the *cool* ones."

"That was hilarious!"

"It was. I'm glad you enjoyed it." I fish around in the blankets for the remote and click off the TV.

Spence moves to leave, and I pull her closer. "Stay with me?"

She blows out a long breath. "Coop, I have to go. I can't be sleeping over at men's houses. I have kids."

"I want you so bad," I groan. "You have no fucking idea." I can't believe that after all these years I finally have this girl in my bed and I'm too nauseous to do anything about it.

Her hand trails down beneath the blankets. "Oh, I think I have some idea."

My body jerks at her touch.

"Ooooh!" Spence pulls her hand away and flies out of the bed.

"Where're you going?"

She flips on the light switch before returning and throwing the covers back. "Do it."

She's lost her marbles. My brow furrows. "Do what? There are lots of its I could do, Princess. You'll have to be a little more specific."

"Do your trick." She is absolutely bursting with excitement. It could be the cutest thing I've ever seen.

I can't stop laughing. "You're serious right now?"

She bobs her head while staring at my crotch. "Of course I am! You said it was better without the pants. Now get 'em off," she orders, snapping her fingers. "I made you dinner." *Bribery.*

"You take 'em off."

"You think I won't?"

I smirk. "I know you will." I just want her to touch me.

Spencer straddles my legs at the knees and grips the waist of my basketball shorts and underwear. I lift my hips, and in one fell swoop, she has them down. It's a damn good thing I'm not shy because Spencer is staring like it's the first time she's ever seen a dick. Which, I know for a fact, is not true.

"Is something wrong?" I ask, amused by her reaction.

Her mouth droops, hanging open for a moment before clamping shut. She doesn't make a sound. "No," she finally whispers, shaking her head. "It's just, well...*bigger* than I remember. You think maybe it kept growing after we broke up?"

"I don't know, Spencer. I didn't keep a growth chart or anything." I laugh.

"Right. Okay." She closes her eyes, takes a deep breath, and releases it with a sigh. "I'm ready." The bed starts to shake as she bounces on her knees, rubbing her hands together with excitement.

I can't help but to shake my head at the absurdity of this moment before putting on a little show for my girl.

"That's amazing."

"I like to think so."

Spencer pokes out her tongue, scrunching her nose. Then, her eyes light like she's just gotten the most incredible idea. She leans forward while peering up at me through her long, dark lashes, and without breaking our gaze, she runs her tongue along the tip of my cock. "I think you've earned yourself a reward, Mr. Hebert."

High school Spencer refused to ever put her mouth anywhere near my dick, and I never asked her to do anything she was uncomfortable with. Apparently, grown up Spencer is a little more adventurous.

And really fucking talented. "Holy shit, Spence," I groan, fisting my hands into her hair. "Where'd you learn to..." Nah, I don't even want to go there. "Never mind. Just...don't...stop..."

And she doesn't. Not until she's sucked me dry. Spence kisses her way up my stomach, teasing my nipples, sucking my neck. She feathers her soft lips along my jaw before planting a final kiss in the center of my forehead.

I am boneless, blessedly numb. Lost in sensation. My heart beat echoes in my head as the blood whooshes in my ears. "Spence," I say, cradling her face between my hands.

"'Night, Cooper," she answers as she cups her hands over my own, pulling them down from her face. She slips out of my bed, rushing to the door before I can try to convince her to stay. "Feel better," she calls as she twists the lock and pulls it open.

"Already do."

She beams. "Ah, the healing powers of orgasms." Spence

winks at me before squeezing through the crack. When I hear her footfalls clambering down the steps, I know that she's really left.

I find myself smiling after her minutes after she's gone. A lovesick fool, more desperate than ever to win her back. Game on.

Chapter Fourteen

SPENCER

I'm in the middle of the most delicious dream starring Cooper and his massive erection when I feel little eyes staring at me. *Go away...*

"My pull-up all quishy, Mommy."

Hello, reality.

I peel my eyes open, blinking a few times to clear the fog from my vision. "Mornin', baby," I grumble.

"I all wet."

Still half asleep, I reach out, scruffing his hair.

"You not mess up my hair, Mom!" His little hands fly up, swatting mine away.

"Sorry, Savage."

After stretching my arms and legs while releasing a groan that could wake the dead, I force myself to roll out of the bed and take my son to the bathroom. I clean him up and brush his teeth then my own before carrying him down to the kitchen for breakfast.

"Mornin', Princess," I hear as I step through the doorway. "Hey there, little dude."

Cooper is seated at the table with my mother, sipping on a cup of coffee, already a few rounds into a game of Yahtzee. It's such a casual scene that for a moment it steals my breath. I drink him in, all 6'2" of his delectable frame. The Saints ball cap that's turned slightly to the left. His Brees jersey and khaki cargo shorts. The bare feet resting on the bottom rung of his chair.

Kyle squeals, squirming in my arms to be put down. "My man here, Mom!"

Screw you, Mom. Cooper's here.

I bend over, setting my son on his feet while completely forgetting that I've only just woken up and haven't gotten dressed yet. It isn't until I look up to find Cooper's eyes fixed on my breasts, which are completely visible through the gaping neckline of my sleep shirt, that I realize I'm not even wearing a bra.

Quickly, I stand, crossing my arms over my chest, feeling the heat rise in my cheeks.

Cooper winks and a sexy smirk fixes itself on his face just as my son barrels in to his lap.

"What's up, Savage?" he asks, settling him on his right leg while casually resuming his game and rolling the dice.

"Mornin', Spence," Momma greets after finishing up her turn. Thank God she was too busy tallying her scores to see me flash Cooper. That would have been infinitely more embarrassing.

"Mornin', Momma," I return, kissing her on the cheek. "I'm gonna run upstairs real quick and put some clothes on. I didn't realize we had company." I look pointedly at Cooper.

"Don't hurry on my account," Coop teases, his eyes glistening with mirth. "I'm fully on board with freeing the tatas."

"I wanna free tatas, too!" Savage announces in worship of his new idol.

Momma snorts out a laugh. "Behave, Cooper," she chastises, pointing a finger at him.

"You're ruining my kid." I narrow my eyes, trying for a serious look that just doesn't work with the smile that's plastered on my face.

"Enhancing," Coop corrects.

"Maybe try enhancing age appropriate behaviors, huh?"

Coop's brows dip toward his nose and his lips pucker in a sour face. "What fun is that?"

I shake my head while still smiling. "I'm going to get dressed," I announce, backing toward the stairs with my eyes fixed on Coop's booboo lip that could put Kyle's to shame.

I don my favorite pair of distressed jeans and my pink Saints jersey with pink chucks. While I'm running the flat iron through my hair, my phone dings.

Gina: On my way! Can't wait to see you and those boys.

Me: Same here. Drive safe!

I take my time artfully applying my makeup and styling my hair to try to redeem myself for the ratchet state I was presented in this morning. I don't know how that man hasn't gone running for the hills yet.

An hour later, I'm descending the stairs and through the screen door I find all three of my boys throwing a ball around the yard with Cooper.

My heart bursts in my chest. Just explodes. It physically hurts to feel so much all at once. It's like I'm staring at a movie of what my life—our life—could have been. It's watching my boys get the attention they're starved for from a man who doesn't owe them a damned thing. From a man who genuinely seems to enjoy their company. It's a punch in the gut, a slap in the face, a tease. It's what I want more than anything else in the world. But it's a mirage. It's only temporary.

Coop is a good man, but he's not looking to raise his own, much less anyone else's children. And something tells me especially not mine.

The door creaks open, breaking my trance. "They're having so much fun out there, Spence." Momma's smile fills her entire face. It makes me happy to see her smiling again. She's only fifty-one and has been living like an old woman. I'm glad my boys seem to be helping to pull her back from the depression that's been weighing her down.

"I can see that." I'm once again staring as I make my way down the last two steps.

Momma slips her fingers through my hair. "You look beautiful."

"Thanks, Ma."

"Now, go on out there and have some fun, huh?" She swats me on the butt to get me moving before disappearing into the house.

"Hey, Mom," Landon calls as I step out onto the porch. He's lying on the ground with Cooper and Lake piled on top of him, and Kyle screaming that it's his turn while trying to strip the ball from his hands.

The rest of the boys all turn my direction with huge smiles.

"How 'bout a little two on two?" Coop suggests, rising to his feet and dusting the fresh cut grass from his shorts.

Before I can answer, Lake bursts into laughter. "Mom doesn't run...or sweat. She probably can't even catch a ball."

Ohhhh, that little shit.

"Oh, I don't know. You're momma used to be able to keep up with us boys pretty well."

I really haven't done anything physical in so long. "It's okay. I'll just watch y'all."

The next thing I know, the ball is soaring toward my face. My hands fly up without thought, catching it before it smacks me in the forehead.

"See, she can catch," Coop says to my boys, coming to my defense. "Pick your man." His eyes stare into mine, issuing a challenge.

If only it were that damned easy, right?

I toss the ball back before lifting my hands palms out. "It's really fine. I just got dressed and fixed my hair and makeup. I haven't really played...well, probably since the last time I played with you. I'm good. Y'all play," I say, waving him off.

"When did you turn into such a priss?"

My eyes narrow as Coop taunts me from across the yard. "Fine. I'll take Landon."

"Wha? Why me? I don't wanna lose."

Ass.

"You be with Cooper. He's good. Me and Landon can be together and the teams will be more even," Lake suggests.

"No, I on Pooper team!" Kyle shouts, stomping his bare foot on the grass.

"Well, if she's that bad, I don't want her, either!" Coop rags.

I grab the pony tail holder from my wrist and knot my freshly ironed hair on top of my head. "Let's go, Coop. Me and you...and don't make me look bad in front of my boys." I eye him as I walk over to stand beside him and Kyle.

Cooper chuckles. "I'll try, Princess."

I learn real quick that there is a huge difference between an eighteen-year-old body and a thirty-three-year-old body. It doesn't move quite as fast or as gracefully. And getting tackled to the ground *hurts* way more than it used to. My boys seem to enjoy trampling over me more than they should.

"Babe," Coop whispers, helping me back to my feet as I groan and slap some of the dirt from my favorite jeans, which are now covered in grass stains. *Why did I agree to this?*

"Yeah?"

"You don't need me to make you look bad."

"Screw you," I spit back with a grin. I'm freaking exhausted and panting like I've just had hours of sex. I'm filthy and my pants are ruined. I have grass sticking out of my hair and every inch of my body hurts. But, I can't stop smiling.

Coop's brows bounce. "Anytime."

We've been playing for over an hour when Gina's red Audi pulls into our drive. Her window is down, and she's pumping the horn and screaming her hellos out before she's even stopped the car.

My boys, all three, rush to her vehicle. It's been less than two weeks since they've last seen her, but you could swear it's been years. They are closer to Gina than anyone else. She's the only one who's been around regularly since they were born.

"Whodat?!?" she yells, climbing out of the car with her hands in the air, raising the roof. She's of course all decked out in her Saints gear. This is south Louisiana, after all, and tonight we play our biggest rival, The Falcons, in a very rare Saturday night football game.

My boys give their Auntie GiGi big hugs, and Kyle pulls at her clothes, trying to climb up into her arms.

"Hey, boyfriend," she sings after greeting Lake and Landon,

swinging Kyle up onto her hip. "You been being a good boy for Auntie?"

His eyes get big as he nods his head while the twins give theirs an exaggerated shake.

"Of course you have, angel." She glares at Lake and Landon while reaching into her purse and pulling out a plastic container of mini M&Ms.

"You bring me nem-nems! Tank you, GiGi."

Gina kisses his face a few times before setting Kyle down to eat his snack. When she finally looks my way, her eyes bug out and she does a double take. "The fuck happened to you?" Gina's face screws up in disgust.

My hands automatically react to her grimace, reaching into my hair, plucking out leaves and grass. "We've been playing football."

"Well, shit...I'm sorry I missed that!"

Coop's laugh rumbles through his chest. "Hey, Gina. It's been a minute." He leans in, giving her a hug.

She returns it, patting him on the back a few times. "It's good to see you, Coop." Her voice hitches and she coughs to clear her throat.

My girl. Gina has claimed to hate Cooper for years because of the way he hurt me, but the two of them used to be really close. It was always the three of us growing up.

"You look good, Gi."

My eyes well up as I witness their reunion. There's just something about being here again with the two of them. I can't explain it, but the time we spent apart just seems to vanish.

We're once again the five-year-olds who got in trouble for eating paste in Mrs. Landry's kindergarten classroom. Ten-year-olds lost hiking in the woods that had to be rescued via search party. Lemonade stands in the summer and Friday nights at the skating rink. Nick at Night marathons and choking on pilfered cigarettes. First highs, first drunks, first dances, kisses, cars, loves. We're bonfires in the cane fields and shared limos to prom. We're so deeply woven into each other's lives that no amount of time or distance could ever sever our bond. We shared our most formative years, molded each other into the people we are today, and the three of us together will always feel like home.

My bestie dabs at her eyes. "You, too, Coop."

"Is that a tear?" Landon jeers.

"No." She huffs. "I just had an eyelash."

Coop and I share a discrete smile while my tough as nails bestie tries to save her reputation with her godson.

"I think Aunt Gigi has a feeling," he teases, pointing and laughing.

"I'm gonna show you a feeling in a minute, you little shit." She reaches out her index finger, poking Landon in the tummy repeatedly as he folds over laughing. He hates to be tickled, and it's Gina's favorite method of torture. "What's this I hear about you giving your momma a hard time, huh?" She keeps poking away.

Landon's hands go around his middle, trying to block her attack. "Stop," he whines, bending at the waist. Gina is relentless, and when he takes off into the house, she is right on his heels, tripping up the steps behind him.

"They seem pretty close," Coop observes with a smile.

I turn from the house with a grin still plastered to my face. "They are. She's like their second mother. I swear, if I could convince myself to become a vagitarian, I'd have married that bitch years ago."

Coop chokes, his face turning bright red.

"Don't worry." I wink, shifting my eyes to his crotch. "I'm a little too fond of the peen."

He shakes his head, rolling his eyes. "You're insane."

I pinch my fingers together, leaving a sliver of space. "Just a little bit."

"A lot a bit," he counters. Cooper reaches out, attempting to pull a twig from the rat's nest on top of my head, but it gets stuck.

"Ow!"

"Oh," he hisses, sucking in his breath. "Sorry, Princess." My obsession moves closer, and with both hands digs the offending trash from my hair. He works slowly. Gently.

Coop is so close. His warm breath drugs me, making me weak and wanting. My breathing changes. It's quicker, shorter, louder. My heart races. I'm dizzy.

"Got it," he whispers, running the stick along the side of my face, my neck, and over the tops of my breasts before dropping it in the grass between us. His eyes are heavy-lidded—his stare ravenous. Coop cups the side of my face.

Kiss me. Kiss me. Kiss me.

"What's a vagarian?"

Shit! I allowed myself to get so caught up in the moment with Coop that I forgot Lake and Kyle are still running around the front yard.

Coop's sigh is half chuckle as he hangs his head, taking a few steps back while I turn to my baby boy. He's staring up at me with curious brown eyes and a creased forehead.

Thinking quickly, as motherhood has trained me to do, I spit out a lie. "It's veterinarian," I say really slowly, enunciating each syllable. Out of the corner of my eye, I watch Coop's face light with the sexiest grin. "It's a doctor who takes care of animals."

"Oh, yike Doc Muffins?"

"Just like Doc Muffins," I agree, sighing with relief.

A loud guffaw bursts from Cooper's lips, and I turn on him, raising my brow.

"Oh, come on. Doc *Muffins*." He stresses the word muffins as if it explains his obnoxious laughter.

I roll my eyes. "It's a kid's show, Coop," I explain, crossing my arms on my chest. "Her name is Doc McStuffins. He can't pronounce it right. Don't you think you're a little too old to make fun of a toddler?" I don't even try to hide my annoyance with his juvenile behavior.

"Calm down, Chachi," he says as his laughter dies down. "I'm not laughing at him."

Humph.

"Seriously?" His eyes widen. "You told him a vagitarian was a veterinarian and he said like Doc Muffins." His head comes forward a little as his brows jump in a "Get it now?" gesture.

"Oh, for God's sake," Gina says, walking up behind me. "Muffin, Spence...*muffin*..." My best friend looks at me expectantly. "Muffin is eating the...uh..." Her eyes fall upon Kyle, who's still standing at my side. "Eating the *muffin*..."

"I yike eating muffins!"

Coop's mouth falls open. "Of course you do, potty mouth." He snorts.

My eyes close as I shake my head. Gina is about to piss herself, and Coop is having way too much fun with my fucking kid.

Kyle laughs because they're laughing. Always eager to put on a show, he adds, "Muffin's nummy, Pooper."

Coop composes himself...somewhat. "Muffins are *very* nummy. You should definitely be a veterinarian when you grow up so you can eat lots of muffins, Savage."

"I will!" Kyle says excitedly before running off to tell Lake.

"Did you just tell my baby that he should be a pussy eating lesbian when he grows up?"

Coop huffs, indignant, and looks at me as if I've just grown two heads. "No. I told him to be an animal doctor and eat muffins. Get your mind out of the gutter, Princess."

"Where'd Coop run off to?" Mom asks, lifting her eyes from the papers she's been grading with a panicked look on her face.

Good Lord, our parents need to stop with this crap.

Coop had to take off because he was meeting the guys to watch the game at the bar, but before I can answer, my best friend calls off the dog.

"What was that?" Gina asks sarcastically with her hand cupping her ear. "Was that an, 'Oh my God, Gina's here?'" my best friend asks, making jazz hands in the air as she sassy-walks over to my mother, who's curled up on the couch with her feet propped on the coffee table, papers resting on bent knees.

Momma tosses the papers to the side, standing to greet her "adopted" daughter with an exaggerated eye roll. "Hey, Gina," she says, enveloping her in her arms. "How was the drive?"

"It was a bitch getting out of the city. The traffic was insane with the game today, but after that, it was nice." Gina kisses Momma's cheek, loosely grabbing each of her hands with her own before backing away a little to appraise her. "You look good, Ma."

"Thanks, baby." Momma drops back into the dip of the couch that's still visible due to her always sitting in the same spot, patting the space beside her for us to join her in front of the TV. It's almost kickoff time. "So, you back for good now?" Momma asks, getting settled into position to grade more papers.

"Yeah," Gina answers, curling her feet under her thighs. "I'm renting one of the apartments behind T-Boy's. There's no way I'm moving back in with my folks." She cringes and visibly shivers.

Momma giggles. "Oh, they aren't that bad, Gina!" Her hand pats Gina's thigh.

"Hah." I snort, perching on the arm of the couch beside Momma. "Her parents are freaks, Momma."

Mom's eyes roll up again as her head shakes.

"They really are," Gina adds. "Last time I came home unannounced, they were...uh...*doing it* on the kitchen table. I will never get the image of my Daddy's wrinkly old ass out of my memory. Scarred for life." Her finger goes to the back of her throat and she gags.

Momma's face blushes. "Well...I guess you don't show up unannounced anymore, do ya?"

"Hell no. I left my key on the table that day just to make sure I'd never forget to knock. I don't think any two parents have ever been more excited about getting their house back to themselves than mine were when I moved out. And I'm not going back!"

Which reminds me..."Oh, yeah. Momma, Gina's gonna stay here for a few days 'til her apartment is ready, if that's okay?"

Like she'd ever say no.

"Of course it is." Her eyes start to well with tears.

"What's wrong?" I ask, smoothing her long, dark hair.

She sniffs, rubbing her nose on the back of her hand. "I'm just so happy to have my girls back." Tears begin dripping from her eyes as she takes a deep breath and clears her throat. "It's nice to not come home to an empty house anymore."

My heart breaks, and as much as it sucks that I lost a job I loved and had to uproot my children, as much as it is rocking my world to have Coop in such close proximity again, in this moment, I am completely at peace with my decision to come home.

I feel myself beginning to doze off when the sound of a lock clicking jerks me awake. The door to my bathroom swings open, and Gina walks out with a warm cloud of steam trailing behind. Her short, blonde hair is sticking up in all directions. She's in black booty shorts and a New Kids on the Block reunion tee she got from a concert we attended together last year. When she realizes I'm awake, my best friend pauses in the middle of the room, placing a hand on one hip and the other on the back of her head, striking a pose.

Goober.

She struts the rest of the way before flopping down beside me on my full-size bed and lacing her fingers with mine. We lay quietly staring up at the pink canopy with our legs dangling over the side of the bed.

"Why couldn't you have a dick?" I ask after a few minutes, breaking the silence.

My best friend, who is totally used to my randomness, doesn't even bat an eye at the question. "I'm sorry," she whispers. "My tits are pretty nice, though." She relinquishes my hand, cupping her boobs and lifting.

"Meh. They're all right." Gina narrows her eyes at me. "You're kinda short, too," I note.

"Yeah. That'd be weird." She turns her head to the side to face me and shrugs. "You'll have to be the man."

"But I have the better boobs," I whine.

"Look, bitch," my best friend says, propping herself on her elbow. "I can get implants and you can get a fake cock, but I can't get taller than you. We're not going to be the weirdo lesbians where the short one wears the pantsuit."

The girl does have a point..."If I get a dick, can I keep my boobs?"

"Fine, but it better be a big dick."

"You know I don't do anything half-assed. You better be able to take a foot long dong, sista," I tease, lifting my brows.

She giggles, causing the bed to shake. "I wonder how you get it up..."

"There's a button on your side...You press it and boy-yoy-yoing!"

Gina huffs. "No shit? How the hell'd you know that?"

"Google."

She nods. "Google knows all the things."

"I wonder if I'd still be able to orgasm..." I say, already reaching for my phone. I open up Safari and begin searching, as if I'm actually considering this ludicrous idea.

In the middle of reading, I feel Gina's elbow jab me in the ribs and wince. "What's it say?" she asks with the impatience of a toddler.

I ignore her until I've finished reading. "It says I get to keep my clitoris. It will be the tip of my new penis...But, only eighty-five percent of patients who have the surgery are able to orgasm after."

"Well, those are good odds."

I snort. "For whom? That's a fifteen percent chance I never orgasm again. Fuck that shit. Can you even imagine how miserable I'd be?"

Gina and I share the mindset that orgasms are vital to a happy life and are not above telling each other when we could stand to go rub one out.

"You're right. I wouldn't want to live with your bitch ass."

"Me either," I agree. "Guess that kills that wonderful idea."

"I'm convinced God created that miraculous appendage to make up for how horrible men are." The disgusted look on Gina's face makes me grin.

"Without a doubt," I agree. "They've got us all hypnotized with those damned things."

"Think that's why all the princesses and fairies carry wands?"

"What the hell are you talking about?"

"You know...so they could have a magic stick of their own. I bet old Walt was feeling sorry for us when he designed *the wand*." She holds an imaginary scepter in her fingers and swirls it around the air above us.

"You know..." I yawn, feeling sleep threaten to take me. "You may be on to somethin', bestie."

"Course I am," Gina says through a yawn of her own. "Why do you think they call dildos wands?"

Well, I'll be damned. "Never really gave it much thought," I answer, silently noting to Google that shit tomorrow.

Gina and I right ourselves in the bed, and before dozing

off, I shoot a quick text to Cooper.

Me: You win. I'm not getting a dick. :(

Asshole: Have you been drinking, Princess?

Me: Googling.

Asshole: I see. Did fabulous Fabio die or something?

Me: No, dummy. A real one. But, if I get a dick installed...there's a 15% chance I'll never orgasm again.

Asshole: I don't know what to say, Spencer. I may be too drunk for this conversation.

Me: Don't worry. I'm not doing it. It's too risky.

Asshole: I'm glad to hear that. Why exactly are you wanting a sex change?

Me: So I could marry Gina. She loves me and my kids. They love her. It would be perfect, right? Stupid wands...

Asshole: Are you high?

Me: Just tired. 'Night, Coop.

Asshole: 'Night, beautiful.

Chapter Fifteen
COOPER

B*eep.* "Cooper, you have a call on line one," my secretary's nasally voice blares through the intercom.

"I'm really busy right now, Jill. Can you take a message?" I'm actually on pace to finish up early today, and the last thing I need is to get caught up on the phone. I've stayed late all week, and I'm really hoping to catch up with Spence and possibly even fool around a bit this evening.

"It's a daycare..." she says nervously. "They said they've been trying to reach Kyle's mother and can't get ahold of her."

"I'll take it." I jab the button for line one, lifting the receiver to my ear. "Hello?"

"Hi, Mr. Hebert...We hate to bother you at work, but we've called Ms. LeBlanc and her mother's phones. They aren't answering. We really need someone to come and pick up Kyle."

"What about Gina?"

An annoyed sigh comes through the phone. "She didn't answer, either."

Shit. "Is he sick?"

"No, sir. He's...suspended."

"Suspended!" I shout. Since when do toddlers get suspended from preschool?

"Yes, sir."

"What the hell could he have...No, you know what? I'm on my way." What the hell kind of place did Spencer leave her kid at?

Slamming the phone down, I begin shoving files into my briefcase like a madman. As I storm out of my office, I pause at Jill's desk to inform her that I'll be out for the remainder of the day and then poke my head into my father's office, wrapping my knuckles on the doorframe to get his attention.

Dad peers up over his glasses, which are sitting low on his nose without raising his head. "Yeah, son?"

"I'm leaving for the day. I just got a call from Kyle's daycare... They need me to go and get him."

Dad's forehead crinkles with concern and he removes his glasses, setting them on top of the stack of papers he's been working on. "Is he okay?"

"Suspended."

His jaw drops. "What?"

"Yeah, I don't know what the hell is going on over there, but they can't get in touch with anyone else, so I'm going to pick him up."

"Do you even have a car seat?" Dad asks.

My face falls. *Damn it.* I hadn't even thought of that. I guess when Spence asked if she could add me to his list of contacts that I should've gotten one just in case. But, I never thought I'd actually have to go get him.

"I keep one for my grandson in my car, Cooper," Jill offers, walking up behind me. "Come on." She waves her arm, brushing past me toward the door. "You can give it back tomorrow. I'll go install it in your truck right quick."

By the time I pull up to the red building designed to model an old schoolhouse, my blood is boiling. And when I walk inside to find Kyle on a chair in the front office crying, I'm ready to make some fucking heads roll.

"What's wrong with him?" I ask, walking over to where he's seated.

At the sound of my voice, his face turns in my direction. My chest squeezes when I see the relief in his little face the moment he recognizes me. Kyle's brown eyes are bloodshot. His lips quivering. "M-my m-man h-h-here," he snivels.

Fuckin' right, his man's here.

"I'm sorry, sir," the secretary says, stepping in front of Kyle. "We need to see your ID before you can touch him."

"Are you shitting me right now?"

She clears her throat loudly. "No, sir. I assure you I am not, and I would appreciate it greatly if you would not speak that way. That language is highly inappropriate." Her eyes dart around the room, reminding me of where I am.

Whoops. "Sorry," I say, and I mean it. I usually conduct myself in a more professional manner, but seeing Kyle this upset has me all out of sorts. "Clearly, he knows me."

"Your identification, please?" she asks once more, holding her hand out palm up.

Pulling my wallet from my inside coat pocket, I dig out my license. Every second that Kyle is reaching for me and I can't comfort him pisses me off more.

The tiny blonde bouncer studies it for a ridiculous amount of time before finally nodding and removing herself from between us.

Kyle practically leaps into my arms. "I miss you, Pooper."

I wipe away his tears and smile. "I missed you, too, little dude. What happened?"

"I in shrouble, Pooper. Wady not nice!" He looks over at her with some pretty impressive mean eyes.

I turn my head to face the woman in question. "Sir, Kyle bit another student today. We have to take these things very seriously, as I'm sure you understand."

"What did the other kid do to him?" I ask, automatically wanting to defend him.

"Well, sir...I don't know that he did anything, but that's irrelevant. Kyle left teeth marks on another student."

"It's not irrelevant, ma'am. Kyle wouldn't bite someone for no reason. He's a good kid."

I can practically hear the snort she's fighting to contain. I have never wanted to hit a woman, but I'd really like to smack that smug look off of her face right about now.

Who am I and when did I become so attached to the enemy?

"This isn't his first offense, Mr. Hebert. Kyle's mother has been warned about his *colorful* language. He's had quite a few warnings, and this is something we can't just ignore."

"With all due respect, Ms.—" I glance at her name tag, finding it odd that there's actually someone in this town that I don't know "—Ashley. No one is asking you to ignore anything. I'm simply asking if you've investigated the matter to determine what caused Kyle to feel the need to defend himself."

"Mr. Hebert, no matter the cause, biting is an automatic

three day suspension."

I can see that I'm not getting anywhere with her. "Kyle, why did you bite?" I ask, using my finger to tilt his face up to mine.

"I bad, Pooper." His bottom lip pokes out.

Hell if my heart doesn't squeeze at the sight of his pitiful face. "You aren't bad," I assure him before clearing my throat. "Why'd you bite that boy? You can tell me. I promise that I won't get mad."

"Him not gettin' off me. Boy sittin' on me. Him hit me wif a shruck on my head!" Tears drip from his big brown eyes as he reaches up to the spot that is obviously still hurting him.

I feel his head where he's rubbing, and there's a huge knot. "So, you're telling me that this big ass knot on the back of this baby's head is irrelevant?"

Ashley's face turns white and she starts sputtering. "Well, I...uh." She walks over to inspect Kyle's injury and visibly blanches. Ashley straightens her face quickly, trying to recover, but she is noticeably flustered. "We didn't realize he'd been hurt. He-he didn't tell us."

I shake my head and laugh. "Are you seriously blaming a two-year-old for the fact that you didn't do your job?"

Red splotches appear on her cheeks and quickly spread to her chest. "Mr. Hebert, I assure you that we will have a talk with the other child and his parents. But, even still, that doesn't change the fact that Kyle has to be suspended for biting. It's policy..."

"You can tear up that paperwork," I add, pointing to the clipboard clutched beneath her arm. "We won't be signing it..." Her mouth opens, but no sound comes out. "As a matter of fact, go ahead and get me all of his things. Kyle won't be returning."

"Mr. Hebert, you can't withdraw someone else's child from daycare."

Watch me. "His things?"

Ashley scurries off, gathering Savage's belongings, returning with three bags full of stuff. "Have Spencer come by and let us know what she wants to do about his enrollment. She has to give at least a thirty days' notice if she wants to withdraw him."

"How about you waive that thirty day notice and I'll consider not pressing charges on this negligent establishment?"

"That won't be necessary, sir. We will be happy to waive the thirty day notice if Ms. LeBlanc does, in fact, advise us that she wishes to withdraw *her* child."

The way she says *"her child"* reminds me of the fact that Kyle belongs to another man and *my* fucking woman, and it pisses me off even more. Shifting Kyle into one arm, I grab his bags, storm through the building, and then back out to the parking lot.

"I sowwy, Pooper." I feel Kyle's hand cup my clenched jaw and instantly deflate. The fearful look on his face makes me feel like a complete asshole.

"You have nothing to be sorry for, Kyle. I'm not mad," I assure him as I unlock the truck and toss his bags inside.

"I ridin' in your shruck?"

"Sure are, buddy. Hop up in your seat so we can blow this joint."

Before leaving the parking lot, I try Spencer's number again to let her know I've picked up Kyle, but it goes straight to voicemail. "Hey, Spence, it's—"

"Hi, Mommy!" Kyle shouts from behind me, causing me to laugh into the phone.

"Yeah, so I have Kyle. The daycare couldn't get in touch

with you and he needed to be picked up. I'll fill you in on the details later...just wanted to let you know he's with me and we're gonna go have some guy time before heading home. Don't worry, I've got this." *I think...* "Tell Mommy bye, Kyle."

"Bye, Mommy!"

"All right, Savage...let's go have some fun."

I decide to take him to The Cool Spot for snowballs. Spence and I spent many hot summer days slurping down flavored ice on the picnic tables by the lake. It's winter now, but the place is open year-round, and I'm feeling the urge to share that connection with Kyle. He chooses blue bubblegum with ice cream in the middle and gummy bears on top. I get a very boring in comparison but delicious cherry.

"Dis nummy, Pooper," Savage says with blue syrup dripping from his chin.

"Are you actually getting any of that into your mouth?" I ask, wondering how the hell I'm going to get this sticky mess of a kid back into my truck. Maybe snowballs weren't my greatest idea.

"Uh oh..." Kyle's eyes get big and his forehead creases.

I do not like the sound of that uh oh. "What's wrong?"

"I shit myself, Pooper."

I choke, spitting red snowball down the front of my white oxford. "Kyle, you can't say that word."

"I sowwy...I need a biper shange."

Son of a...I have never changed a diaper in my life. "Please tell me you are joking," I beg.

A shit-eating grin spreads across his blue face. "I for real, Pooper."

We toss the remainder of our snacks into the trashcan and head toward the parking lot. I'm practically sweating over the mess I've gotten myself into. When we arrive at my truck, I place Kyle in the truck bed so that I can safely dig around in his bags for some wet wipes and a diaper and praise God there is a change of clean clothes.

"Okay, Savage...you're gonna have to help Cooper out here. I've never changed a diaper before."

Kyle's eyes get big. "I never shange a biper before, eider." His little shoulders lift and fall in a shrug.

"Come here," I tell him, waving him over while laughing at the little smart ass. He's so advanced. I feel myself swelling with pride, as if I had anything to do with it.

I feel like an idiot when he's standing before me, and I can't decide where to start. He is sticky from head to toe, and judging by the smell, he's packing a pretty nasty mess in his Pamper. I actually glance around, spotting a hose, before realizing that it's barely sixty degrees out and I can't spray the kid down.

I decide starting with the top and working my way down to be the best course of action. "Stand still," I say to Kyle as I try to scrub the blue from his lips, cheeks, and chin.

"Dat hurts!" His head is swerving around while he tries to dodge the wet wipes.

"It does not hurt. Keep still."

Once I've cleaned his face, I begin working on his neck and arms. By the time I've gotten his hands cleaned, I've used most of the package of wet wipes. "Hopefully, the shit comes off easier than the syrup or we'll be in a heap of trouble."

"You say dat bad word, Pooper."

Crap. I didn't mean to say that out loud. "I'm sorry, Kyle... Don't tell Mommy, okay? It can be our little secret." He smirks. *This kid is so ratting me out.* "Lift up your arms for me, bud." I swap out his shirt quickly, so he doesn't get too cold, and am back at a standstill. "All right...now what do we do?"

"You gotta wipe my butt, Pooper." He spreads out his own blanket, lying down on top of it with his feet toward me. The little turd even lifts his own legs into the air.

"Kyle, you are too big to be pooping on yourself. You need to start using the toilet."

He shakes his head. "Tah-tye in the toiwette."

"There is no monster in the toilet." I remove his shoes and pants then discover that greenish yellow mush is coming out of the back and sides of his diaper. I gag. It's all over the inside of his pants. I set them off to the other side of the tailgate and begin wiping at the shit on his legs with the wet wipes and tossing them over on top of the pants. The mountain of poop covered wipes keeps growing as the bag of clean ones is damned near empty, and we haven't even gotten to what's inside of the diaper yet.

"I freezin'," Kyle stammers. The poor little guy is shaking. I finally work up the nerve to unfasten his diaper, and when I pull it open, I can't...I just...can't. I lean over to the side and puke until tears stream from my eyes. I have never felt more helpless in my life. Brought down by a dirty diaper.

Suddenly, I feel a little hand on my back and a voice that I have become very familiar with coos, "Aw, you sick, Pooper?" *No*...I turn my head to find that Kyle has gotten up. His diaper is upside down and poop is smeared from one end of the truck bed to the other.

Fuck it. Grabbing Kyle beneath his arms, I extend my own out to hold him as far away from my body as possible and make a run for the water hose. "Don't move, Kyle," I instruct as I uncoil the hose and turn on the water. "The water is gonna be cold. I'm so sorry, but we have to get you cleaned up. We'll be *super* fast."

Kyle stands as still as a statue while I spray the rest of the poop off of his bottom. The water bounces off of his body, flying back at me. A drop of shit water lands on my bottom lip, and I'm puking all over again. The entire situation is so ridiculous that it would be hysterical if it weren't happening to me.

I unbutton and slip off my shirt, wrapping Kyle's trembling body in it and head back to my defiled truck. My stomach is roiling. Savages teeth are chattering, and his one clean shirt is now soaked from the hose due to me not removing it beforehand. After lying Kyle on the back seat of my truck, I slide a fresh training diaper up his legs. Even that is an act of congress. With no other choice but to give him my undershirt, I pull it over my head and onto him. "There. That wasn't so bad, now was it?" I ask, looking for a confidence boost.

"You suck at shanging bipers, Pooper. My mommy gonna kick you butt."

"You're probably right, Savage. Now, get in that car seat so I can take you back home. I don't think my truck can handle another explosion."

Chapter Sixteen

SPENCER

I'm curled up, hugging my knees on the front porch swing, when Coop's truck comes rolling into the drive. Jumping to my feet, I shift the flannel throw blanket from my legs to my shoulders, cocooning myself inside. Yesterday, we were in shorts and flip flops, today Uggs and sweaters. Louisiana, as usual, you are drunk.

When I'm about halfway to the truck, Cooper steps out... shirtless. My feet grow roots and I stare. It doesn't even strike me as odd at first that he's riding around half naked in the dead of winter because I'm far too busy admiring the view. I feel my lady bits clench tight as my mouth begins to fill with saliva. When he disappears around the side of his truck, I shake myself out of a daze, remembering that he has my kid.

"Hey, Cooper!" I call out, shuffling my feet in quick baby steps. They are all I can manage with the burrito I've wrapped myself in. "What hap—"

My words are lost when he comes back into view, toting my toddler—my *blue* toddler who happens to be wearing a man's shirt and nothing else.

"Hey, Mommy!" Kyle shouts, reaching out for me with his teeth chattering.

Cooper passes him over, and I wrap his little body in my throw blanket. "Hey, baby. What's all over your face? And why are you wearing Cooper's shirt and not your own clothes?" I ask, looking up at the deflated man before me.

"Hey, Spence," Coop offers, attempting a smile. He looks nervous. *What did he do?*

My eyes roam from his disheveled hair to the resigned look on his face. They wander over his chest and stomach, and from this close, I can see something splattered in the trail of hair leading from his bellybutton into his slacks. I sniff, feeling my brows dip inward at the pungent smell. "My God, you two reek!" I gag, pinching my nose. "What the hell happened? Where are his clothes? Where are the rest of your clothes? Did you two fall into a freaking sewer? Cooper, are you going to answer me?"

That maddening, lopsided smirk appears on his face. "I was letting you finish, Momma Bear."

I move my hand in little circles toward him in a "carry on" gesture.

Coop swallows hard. *What is it about that tiny movement of his Adam's apple that gives me the urge to run my tongue along his throat?*

"Can we continue this inside, Princess? It's a bit nippley."

"I ha-have nipples," Kyle stutters. "Pooper have hair on him nipples. Dat's siwwy, right, Mommy?"

Giggling, I turn to stare at Cooper's chiseled chest and his nipples that I find anything but silly.

Coop laughs. "When you're a man, Savage, you'll get hair on your nipples, too...and on your butt!"

Kyle scrunches up his nose. "No, tanks. I don't want hair on my butt."

"Let's get inside before you freeze your hairy ass off," I say, winking at Cooper.

Coop takes a few steps to follow and then stops. "Actually, why don't you go and get him cleaned up. I could use a shower myself, and I *really* need to brush my teeth."

Did he just gag? "Uh, yeah. Can you hurry, though? I've been kinda freaking out not knowing what's going on." *And after this...infinitely more so.*

"Is your mom back?"

"Not yet."

"Why don't you come over to my house when you're done and Mom can keep an eye on Savage while we chat?"

"Kyle!" Mrs. Nelly exclaims, all animated, when she opens the front door.

"Hi, Nana. You make me some cookies?" my son asks as she grabs him from my arms and smothers his face in kisses. Kyle squirms, pretending not to like it, but he's giggling so hard he can't catch his breath.

"Of course, child. Let's go in the kitchen and see what goodies Nana has for her favorite little guy today."

"I thought I was your favorite little guy," an indignant voice calls down the stairs just before Coop's body comes into view with my favorite little guy pitching a tent in his joggers.

"Looks like you've been replaced," I taunt when his mother doesn't answer.

He smiles, pressing a hand on the doorframe above my

head and leaning in close. "Appears so."

I take a deep breath, inhaling the scent of his cologne, and just as I'm about to forget myself and lean in for a kiss, Coop reaches around me, twisting the doorknob, almost knocking me off my feet. "Sit with me out on the porch?"

"Sure," I say, clearing my throat as he grabs ahold of my arm, steadying me. "What happened at the daycare today? I've been so worried," I say as we walk over to sit on the porch swing.

Cooper follows, plopping down beside me with his body angled toward mine. "They never got ahold of you?"

"No. I forgot my phone on the kitchen counter, and by the time I noticed, it was too late to go back and get it. I was in offsite meetings most of the day, and the school couldn't reach me without my phone. When I returned to school, I went to the office, and they told me the daycare had been trying to contact me, so I borrowed their phone to check the voicemail on my cell. I had a few from the daycare asking me to call them and then your message...so I knew Kyle was okay because he was with you."

Coop gives me a lopsided grin as I continue. "I called the daycare and got their voicemail. They haven't called me back yet, but its dismissal time, so it will probably be a while before I hear from them."

Cooper rolls his eyes. "Oh, trust me. You'll be hearing from them."

"What happened?"

"We quit," he answers, matter of fact.

"You quit what?"

"Savage and I quit preschool today." Cooper smiles, puffing up his chest with pride. He looks entirely too pleased with himself. He's so convincing that I catch myself wanting to thank him before realizing that he's just made my life an even bigger disaster.

"You did what?" I ask, jumping up from the swing, causing the chains to rattle.

"They tried to suspend him, Spence...Can you believe that shit? Who suspends a two-year-old?"

My eyes bug out. "Oh God. What did he do?" Both hands dig into my hair, and I pull in frustration as I begin pacing the porch.

Coop shakes his head, leveling me with a look that can only be described as disappointment. "That's your response? What'd *he* do?" He laughs beneath his breath, but it lacks any humor. "He bit some little asshole for hitting him in the head with a truck. He was defending himself. You should be proud of him. No one else there was gonna do it."

"Is he o—"

"Kyle's fine. He just has a bump on his head."

Shit. What the hell am I going to do now? "Coop...you...you can't just quit his preschool. It was the only one in town with openings. I'll have a talk with them. I'm sure I can clear it all up."

Coop scoffs. "They don't appreciate him. Hell, I don't even think they like him. Those people are going to break his spirit." Cooper purses his lips, shaking his head. "Nope. He can't go back."

My head falls into my hands and I massage my temples. "Coop, I'm sure it was some sort of misunderstanding. I..." Cooper's arms cross on his chest and his eyes narrow. *How dare he judge me?* "I have to work, Cooper!" *Damn him for making me feel like the bad guy here.*

"I don't think you should bring him back there."

Stubborn fucking ass. "I have to—"

"I already told him he didn't have to go." Coop shrugs like the fact that he told a two-year-old he doesn't have to go trumps my need to support my family.

My mouth falls open and snaps shut. "Great. Well, the two of you should have a lot of fun in your new office. I hope your secretary doesn't mind looking after a toddler in addition to her other duties when you're on a call or in court! And I sure as shit hope she knows how to change a fucking diaper. Lord knows you don't have a freaking clue!"

Coop's face blanches at the diaper comment. He looks mortified as he whispers, "He can't come to work with me."

"No?" I cross my arms on my chest. "Well, where do you think he's going to go while I'm at work all day now that you've *quit* his daycare?"

The squeaking sound of a window lifting behind me causes me to spin around just as Nelly's head peaks out. "I don't mean to eavesdrop, but y'all two are so damned loud you could wake the dead. I just wanted to offer that he could stay here with me. I would love to have him. No need to send him to a germ-filled cesspool."

"There," Coop says, rising from the swing. He walks over to stand behind me, rubbing his hands up and down my upper arms to relax me. "Problem solved. He'll come here."

My head is spinning. I'm not used to having other people make decisions for me where my children are concerned, and my natural inclination is to fight it. But, Kyle loves Nelly, and I know that she loves him, too. I suck my teeth, look over my shoulder, and narrow my eyes at Cooper when I answer, "If you're sure you don't mind, Mrs. Nelly, I'd love it if you'd babysit Kyle."

Her face lights up. "I don't mind at all, sugar! Now you two carry on. Coop, watch your face. You have court in a few days." She winks. "I'm gonna go tell Savage the news!"

"Why the sour puss face? This is great." Coop spins me around to face him.

I was unaware, but now that he's said something, I can feel my resting bitch face. As annoyed as I am that he made such an important decision for my son, I learned my lesson with the crawfish boil about overreacting and force myself to smile. "It is. Your mom is great with him."

Coop smiles and reaches out, grabbing my hand. He tugs, pulling my body against his and wrapping me in his arms. "I've missed you," he mumbles into my hair. I'm not sure whether he intended for me to hear it or not, so I just snuggle closer and let the heat of his body encapsulate me. To repeat those words back would definitely be creating strings, and we're not going there. The fact that he said it, though, has me all warm and tingly and my heart beats fast. I need distance and pull away.

"I can't believe you hosed my kid off. I keep picturing that scene from the movie *Three Men and a Baby* when they're changing their first diaper and cracking up, but it's really not funny, Coop. He must've been freezing. I hope he doesn't get sick."

His brows dip inward in a look of concern. "Oh, trust me. I know it isn't funny. I felt like shit…smelled like it, too, and have you seen my truck?" he asks with a grimace.

"I haven't, but I'm sure as shit going now." I wink, taking off down the porch steps, careful not to trip on the loose board at the bottom. Coop follows closely behind. When I get there,

I can't help it...I double over laughing. It's a shit massacre. There's shit *everywhere*. What I wouldn't give to have been able to see this scene unfold. "Oh God." I wrap my hands around my waist and try to stop laughing to take a jibe at him.

"It's not that funny, Spence." The fish lips he's sporting tells me he's trying his best not to burst out laughing himself.

"Karma's a motherfucker, isn't it?" I have tears dripping down my cheeks from laughing so hard.

"It's ruined." Coop frowns.

And I'm giggling again. "It's poop, Cooper. It washes off."

Coop sticks the fingers of his right hand under my nose. "Smell that?" he asks with a look of disgust. "The smell..." He gags. "It won't come out. My truck is going to smell like crap."

"Ew." I shove his hand away. "Get your poopy hands out of my face."

"I don't get it. How do you always smell so good? One fucking dirty diaper and I'm stained."

"Well, I tend to get the shit on the wet wipes, not myself. And, if I do get it on my fingers, which happens to the even the best of us, there are methods to remove the scent."

Coop's eyes get big and his whole face brightens. "Oh thank God. How do I get it off."

"That's *not* what she said," I tease.

Coop smiles. "Cute. So how do we get rid of the smell?"

Oh, this could be fun. "Wouldn't you like to know?"

Coop runs his bottom lip through his teeth and nods.

"How much is this little bit of information worth?" I ask him with the devil in my eyes.

"Whatever you want."

A smile splits my face as I turn back toward his momma's house. "Follow me."

Chapter Seventeen
COOPER

Spence leads me Up the steps, through my bedroom, and into my bathroom, then pats the lid of the toilet. "Sit."

I watch her rifle around in the cabinet beneath the sink, coming up with a can of shaving cream. "Spread 'em," she orders.

I have no idea what this girl is up to, but those two words have my cock stirring in my pants as I open my legs wide.

Spencer bursts out laughing. I swear that I would be the butt of every joke just to see those dimples and that shimmer in her eyes. "Your fingers, idiot."

"I knew that," I lie. "I was just messing around."

"Uh huh."

She squirts a mound of cream into each of my palms and takes turns working on them individually with both of hers. I never realized before how much smaller her hands are than my own. I grow harder still as she passes her delicate fingers over and in between mine. There is nothing at all sexual in her method, yet somehow it's very sensual and sexy, and I begin to imagine those hands wrapped around my dick, lavishing it with the same treatment. The way her breasts are rising and falling heavily coupled with the breathiness in her voice makes me grateful for my decision to forgo any underwear after my shower. There is no way to disguise the raging hard-on in my sweats, and Spence has definitely taken notice.

"Now," she rasps, releasing my hands and straddling my legs, "you need to let it sit for a minute." Spencer crosses her shaving cream laden hands behind my neck, careful not to touch me as she squirms, causing her skirt to ride up. She wiggles her way further up my legs, not stopping until her heat is pressing against my cock. "Don't get any of that on me," she whispers into my ear before trailing her tongue along my jaw line and then mumbling against my lips. "Your mom will lose her shit."

It is nearly impossible not to put my hands on her as she begins grinding against my erection while thrusting her tongue into my mouth. Crossing my hands behind the small of her back, I use my forearms to guide her movements. My dick throbs—screaming for release. It takes every ounce of willpower I possess not to come like a fucking schoolboy in my pants.

"So wet," she mutters.

Fuck. I need to touch her.

"Time to rinse this off yet?" I groan as her head falls back and I begin sucking on her throat.

"Yes," she moans. "Oh God, yes."

I am unsure whether she's answering me or about to come. Either option has me sliding her off of my legs and rushing over to the sink. She's not finishing without me—not 'til I'm buried deep inside her.

When I've finished rinsing the shaving cream off and she's done the same, Spence lunges at me, cupping my face between her hands and pulling at my neck until my lips meet hers. The feel of her tongue warring with mine with such urgency leaves me with little control. I begin ripping at her clothes as Spencer's hands trail down my chest, slipping into the back of my waistband. She cups my ass and squeezes, and when the tiniest of moans slips from her lips, I'm gone.

With one swoop, I clear the counter then grip the back of Spencer's thighs, thrusting her up on the edge.

"Cooper." Her head falls back and her lips part.

"Yeah, Princess," I breathe out into the crook of her neck as my hands slip beneath her shirt, trailing up her spine. After making quick work with the clasp of her bra, I run my hands along her ribs, hiking it up. My mouth waters as those perfect tits spring free.

"Yes," she whimpers as I take her left breast into my mouth, curling my tongue around the nipple. "I need this...Oh God, I need this so bad."

I need this, not I need you. Her choice of words shouldn't bother me, but it does.

"What do you need, Princess?" I say, pulling myself out and wrapping her hand around my girth. "Say it."

Spencer moans, sliding forward until my cock is seated at her entrance. "You," she whispers. "I need you, Coop." Her hips jerk forward, and I slip inside her warm, wet sex.

"Give it to me, Princess." I grab hold of her hair, pulling until her face turns up. With my mouth on her neck, I pound into her mercilessly. Spencer's nails dig into my back, breaking skin. The sound of her moans and our bodies slapping together fills the small space. Just when I think I can't hold off a moment longer, I feel her tighten around my shaft, and the sweet sound of Spencer's release is my undoing. I pull out just in time, realizing that with all of the excitement, I forgot to wrap it. *I never forget.*

"You're on the pill, right?" It's definitely not the most romantic thing to say at this moment, but I'm still unjustly angry, and what the hell? We are just screwing around.

"Mirena," she snaps, sliding off the counter before reaching around to refasten her bra.

My brows dip inward.

"It's an IUD."

She might as well be speaking Mandarin.

"A little piece of plastic my OB shoved up into my uterus to prevent pregnancy." She pinches her fingers together, making a hooking motion with her hand. "It's over 99% effective. No worries, Coop." Spencer winks at me before she finishes redressing.

Huh. "I didn't feel anything in there."

"It's in my uterus, Casanova, not vagina." She huffs out a laugh. "You're gifted, but come on…"

I chuckle, pretending to understand while making a mental note to Google the female anatomy tonight.

"How was that for payment?" I ask, waggling my eyebrows and giving her my best panty-melting smile.

"Did you just call me a hooker?"

"Uhhhh…no?"

"No?" she asks, staring at me with those sexy as fuck momma eyes, just daring me to give the wrong answer.

I shake my head.

"Oh, good. 'Cause I thought you just tried to pay me with sex…"

"What?" I gasp in mock horror, lifting my hand to my chest in a "Who me?" gesture. "I'd never."

"That's good," Spence replies, leaning in and placing a kiss on my cheek. She trails her tongue along my jaw to my ear, whispering, "'Cause you'll be paying me with a week's worth of dishes."

"Kyle, are you ready to go? It's almost time for Gramma and the boys to get back from school," Spencer asks as we enter the kitchen.

"I not yeavin' yet." His arms cross on his chest as those tiny lips curve downward into the perfect U shape.

Spence sighs as she walks over and begins wrestling with him, trying to pry him from the chair. "Come on. You're coming back to Nana's tomorrow."

God, she's hot when she's frustrated. Her face reddens immediately, the blood still warm from our workout. Her hair is a mess, her clothes covered in wrinkles. There is no mistaking what just happened in that bathroom, but I'll let her believe she's getting away with it.

"Go on, Kyle," Momma encourages, squatting down before him. "You have to listen to your mommy. Nana's gonna have your favorite chocolate chip pancakes waiting for you tomorrow morning if you're a good boy tonight."

And just like that, the struggle ends. "Thank you," Spencer mouths to Momma as she grabs Kyle's things and heads for the door. She's almost shut it when her head peers back inside. "Coop?" she calls out.

"Yeah?"

"I'll see you at seven."

The door clicks shut, and I stand there staring with a lovesick smile on my face. Spencer makes me feel like a hormonal teenager.

Suddenly, the view changes, and I'm no longer staring at the door, but my mother's emotionless face. Her hands are resting on her hips, and that sassy slipper-clad foot tapping on the floor.

"Can I help you?" I ask, because she's obviously waiting to be acknowledged.

Her eyes assess me for a moment. "What the hell is it with you two and friggin' bathrooms?" She throws her hands in the air and stalks off, muttering something beneath her breath.

That woman's meddling will be the death of me.

Chapter Eighteen
COOPER

For a week, I've Shown up at Spencer's house at seven sharp and washed more dishes than I've washed in my entire life. I'm going to have to go chop some fucking trees or something to regain my man card. The skin on my hands has never been so soft, thanks to the lotion in their dish soap.

Tonight is the last night of my sentence, and there's a heaviness in my chest because I will no longer have an excuse to see her every night. Hell, I've even enjoyed hanging out with her kids. Hearing about their football practice and laughing at the insane shit that flies out of that little one's mouth.

Like every other night this week, I'm relaxing in front of the TV, sneaking in an extra episode of *CSI* while she gets her kids to bed. This damned show is addicting. I'd never seen it before coming here, but it's all they watch.

"All paid up," I hear in my favorite voice. Shutting off the television, I look up, finding Spencer with her hands crossed lightly on her chest and her back leaning on the doorframe. Her lips are curled slightly in a welcoming smile.

"Hey, Princess." I rise from the sofa, stretching my arms above my head. "Take a walk with me?" I ask, dipping my head toward the door.

"Sure."

Spence slips into a pair of flip flops and a hoody. It's a chilly night, in the fifties, but it doesn't matter the temperature. If she's not going anywhere, Spencer is in flip flops.

I make a face at her shoe choice, and she glares at me. "I'm fine."

As we walk out to the driveway, Spence starts talking, filling me in on every detail of her horrific day. How much she hates her job. How horrible she feels for some of the children she meets with each day. Some of their situations are truly heartbreaking, but they aren't the reason she hates her job. It's the other kids. The ones who pick on them. The assholes disrespecting their teachers and defacing school property. Kids fighting in the halls and throwing food in the cafeteria. Pissing on bathroom floors. "I feel like I'm in a zoo filled with wild animals," she whines. "They're barbaric. I'd kick my kids' asses for behaving that way."

"And that's exactly why your kids *don't* behave that way."

"I've learned something about myself since working there."

"Oh yeah?" I ask, stopping to look at her. "What's that?"

"I don't like kids. I mean, I like mine *sometimes* and a few others, but in general…I really, really don't like being around children all day."

She has this guilty look on her face, like she's just confessed to some cardinal sin. "It's okay," I answer, leaning in to whisper into her ear. "I don't really care for them, either."

She laughs, shoving my chest playfully. "Yeah, well, everyone knows you don't like kids and you don't have to. You aren't a parent."

"I like some kids," I counter, shocking myself with my own admission.

"You do?" she asks, doubtful.

I grasp her chin in my thumb and forefinger, tilting her face up so that her eyes meet with mine. "I like three."

"You do?" Spence whispers knowingly, her voice thick with emotion.

"I do," I breathe out against her lips before drawing them in for a long, tender kiss. Tears drip down Spencer's cheeks, sneaking in between our lips. The salt, the warmth, the hunger, it makes me crazy with want...for something more.

I pull back, wiping the remaining tears from her face. "I want to take you somewhere, but I'm afraid you're going to turn me down."

She sniffles, wiping her nose on the sleeve of her sweater. "Where?"

"Anywhere...You name it. To dinner, a movie, out dancing, a cruise, or a fucking deserted island. I just want to take you out on a real date, Spence. I don't want to just fuck you anymore. I want more than this. I want you back. I want us back."

Her head shakes rapidly back and forth. "Cooper," she says weakly. Her tears start up again, but they're bigger, falling faster, and more painful. "I-I can't...I can't give you more than this." She reaches a hand up to caress my cheek. "I wish I could."

And she's gone.

Chapter Nineteen
SPENCER

"This better be good, Spencer Rose. Joel and I were just about to get busy when you started blowing up my phone," Gina snaps into my ear.

"I'm sorry, bestie," I say, gasping for breath. "He messaged me again and I-I needed someone to talk to."

"Who? Cooper? Shame on him for not doing it sooner. He knew the game when he decided to play. Now can I get back to my booty call? Joel has a really nice dingdong. It's thick and—"

"Ew. Stop! I don't want to hear about Joel's dick."

Gina huffs. "You're no fun anymore."

"It wasn't Cooper. I still haven't heard from him, and I don't expect to. That was my fault...I'm the one who ran off."

"Whatevs...Who was it then?"

"Alex..."

"Shit."

"Yeah, shit. He says he got a lawyer and I should be served tomorrow. He wants joint custody and immediate visitation." I pause, sobbing into the phone. "Kyle doesn't even know him,

Gina. Hell, I don't even know him...He expects to waltz into our lives now and I'm just supposed to hand over my baby to a virtual stranger. I can't...I can't do it."

"Oh, babe. I'm sorry. You have to call Cooper. You know you do. Show him the text messages. They have to mean something. The fact that he told you he didn't want to be his father has to mean something, Spencer."

At the mention of his name, a knot forms in my stomach. "I can't call Coop."

"Why the hell not? If you don't, I will. I'm not fucking around," my best friend threatens.

"You will NOT call him. I fucking ran out on him a week ago and haven't spoken a word to him since. I can't just call him up for legal advice now. I won't use him like that."

"So go *make up* and then tell him."

I roll my eyes. Yet another problem sex can't fix. "I'll figure it out. Go enjoy your date...or whatever. I'm sorry for interrupting."

"Don't be crazy. It was important, and now I have one more reason to hate Alex, I just lost my fucking hard-on."

I giggle through tears. "Freak."

"Whore."

"Love your face, Gi."

"Love you more. Call if you need me. I'm getting rid of Joel."

Chapter Twenty
COOPER

I pull up to the house just after seven. This shit with Spence is bugging me so much that I've been submerging myself in work to keep my mind busy—to avoid going over there and making a complete fool of myself. She's not ready and maybe she never will be, but I won't stop trying. I'll be patient if it kills me. I can just see it now. *Cooper Hebert died of blue balls and a broken heart.*

As I'm gathering my things to go inside, there is a knock on the passenger side window. It's already dark out and I have to squint to see the face pressed up against the glass. To my dismay, it isn't Spencer. I press the button, unlocking the door and Landon climbs inside. Alarms begin to go off immediately. His face is red and splotchy and his breathing erratic. "Hey, bud. What's wrong?" My pulse is racing. Shit. It has to be bad. Landon doesn't cry...

He opens his mouth to speak and begins to sob instead.

"Hey. It's okay. Tell me what's going on. Is someone hurt?"

Landon shakes his head. "I don't know who else to talk to... my-my mom is gonna k-kill me, but she needs you. We need your help."

A lump lodges in my throat, and I attempt to clear it away before speaking. "What happened?"

After a few deep breaths, he regains some semblance of control. "Umm...I just got back from my dad's house and went upstairs to tell Mom that I was home, but I heard her...I heard her on the phone with Aunt Gina..."

"Okay..."

"I was about to walk in, but it sounded important so I stood there and I-I listened."

He gets quiet for a moment. He's angry. His fists clench in his lap and his jaw ticks from side to side. "She said that Kyle's dad is taking her to court...He wants custody, Coop. You can't let that happen. Please. Please don't let him take Kyle away from us."

Landon completely breaks down. I get out of the truck and walk around to his side, opening the door and pulling him to my chest. I rest a hand on the back of his head, smoothing down his unruly, blond curls. "Shhh. It's okay. It's gonna be okay, Landon. You did the right thing." He nods into my chest and I tuck my finger under his chin, lifting his face so he can see the sincerity in my eyes when I tell him, "No one...No. One. Is taking that baby away. Do you hear me?"

He nods. "Mom's gonna be so mad. She told Aunt Gina she didn't want to tell you because she wasn't talking to you and you would think she was using you...But, I think she's... she's wrong. She's wrong, right?" He stares at me, completely vulnerable with so much trust and hope in his eyes. *Son of a bitch.* I don't know when it happened, but it isn't just Spencer I've fallen in love with...I've gone and fallen for the whole damned bunch.

"Yes," I assure him, feeling a tightening in my chest. "She's wrong."

Chapter Twenty-One
SPENCER

It's a quarter to eight, and I've been crying for almost an hour, no closer to a solution. My heart hurts. The pain is worse than any I've ever experienced. *My baby.* Not my baby. Heaving sobs wrack my body.

A cough draws my attention toward the door, which I never even heard open.

"Cooper?" I call out, squinting my eyes through the dark room at the magnificent figure looming in the doorway. My heart pounds. For a brief moment, I'm filled with hope, allowing myself to believe that he's here to rescue us. My white knight come to chase the bad guy away. But, only briefly. It takes just a split second for me to remember that my life couldn't be further from anything even slightly resembling a fairytale. He's probably horny and tired of waiting. He knows better than anyone how stubborn I can be. "Coop, I can't do this right now. I'm sorry. I'm sorry for running out on you the other night, but I'm really not feeling well."

Cooper doesn't retreat but instead steps into the room, shutting the door behind him and twisting the lock. *Is he seriously doing this right now?*

"Please go."

"You are a lot of things, Princess, but I didn't take you for a liar." His voice is fire dipped in ice. Both soothing and scathing all at once.

"Excuse me?" I gulp.

Cooper kneels at the side of my bed. His face just inches from mine. So close that his warm breath makes my skin tingle when he exhales. "Why are you crying?" Cooper's hand reaches out, brushing damp hair from my cheeks. *He knows.* It's in the tone of his voice, the softness of his touch. He's both angry and hurt. He wants to lash out but his need to soothe my pain takes precedence.

"Gina," I choke out.

Coop's brow furrows. "What?"

"She called you."

His head shakes. "I assure you, she did not."

"Then who?"

Cooper clenches his jaw and sighs. "For God's sake, woman, will you fucking talk to me?"

Feeling a little too vulnerable in this position, I sit up, and Cooper rises from the floor, perching himself beside me on the edge of my bed. When I remain silent, he releases a frustrated growl, conceding with a deep sigh. "Landon heard you on the phone with Gina and freaked out. He was waiting for me in the driveway when I got home from work and told me everything."

My hand cups my mouth and I gasp. "Oh God. Oh my God." *My poor baby.*

"He was scared that you'd be angry at him, but he had enough sense to ask me for help because he knew that you needed it..." Coop shakes his head. "I only wish you trusted me enough to do the same."

"I'm sorry, Coop," I cry, reaching for his hand. I just want to crawl into his arms and hide from the mess unfolding around me. "I know I...I have no right to ask, especially after the other night, but do you think you could just...Would you just hold me for a while? I'm so scared, Cooper," I sob. "I promise to tell you everything later."

Cooper lifts my hand to his mouth, kissing each of my fingers as he toes off his shoes. Then he crawls into the bed, pulling me down to lay beside him. Coop presses kisses along the side of my face while holding me close. He doesn't pester me for answers, sensing my need for silence...for solace. And just as I'm beginning to drift off to sleep, I feel his soft lips on my cheek as he whispers the four words I've longed to hear for fifteen years. "I love you, Princess."

The sun hasn't yet risen when I feel someone staring at me. I must've rolled over during the night, because when my eyes flutter open, it is Cooper's big brown orbs I find gazing into mine. "Hey," I croak. "What time is it?"

"A little after two."

"Have you been awake this whole time?"

Coop smiles lazily, rubbing his hand up and down my arm. "I dozed off for a bit, I think. Are you feeling better?"

"A little. Thanks for staying with me."

"My pleasure...Ready to give me some answers now?" he asks, and I nod my head. "Start from the beginning. I need to know everything if we're gonna find a way to nail this asshole."

Chapter Twenty-Two
COOPER

I'm on the phone with the PI when Spencer comes barreling through the door with a stack of papers in her hand. "I came straight over after I got them, just like you said."

I hold the finger of one hand to my lips while tucking the phone under my chin to wave her inside with the other. "That all sounds great. Call me the minute you find anything of use." I glance at the date on the papers Spence just placed in my hand. "Our court date is set for March 1st. That's in just two weeks. Work fast."

"Who was that?" Spencer asks before I've even returned the phone to its cradle.

"That was the best damned private investigator New Orleans has to offer."

"You think we have a shot?" she asks with nervous excitement. It was a huge blow when I told her that without having him sign papers relinquishing his paternal rights she doesn't have a valid reason to prevent Alex from being in Kyle's life. The text messages won't do more than *possibly* taint the judge's opinion of him. They may go hard on him, limiting his visitation to supervised, especially at first. But, the courts are always in favor of a child having both parents in their life whenever possible.

"We *always* have a shot, Princess. We've just got to be smart and maybe a little creative."

"Where do we start?" She's full of fire and ready to fight. In full Momma Bear mode this morning. It's fucking sexy as hell. I vow to myself that one day soon, when this is all over, I'm going to make love to this beautiful woman right here on this desk.

"Coop?"

Shit. "Sorry, I was lost in thought for a minute there. What was the question?"

"The plan...What's the plan?"

Right. "I'm going to type up a response to this petition, refusing immediate visitation due to the fact that he has willingly never been involved in Kyle's life, and file a counterclaim for full legal and physical custody. That will hold us over 'til we get to court. In the meantime, we hire a PI, which I've just done. If there is any dirt to be dug up on Alex, he will find it. If he finds it, we use it. If there's none..."

"We make it up?"

"Cute..." I shake my head and smile. "If there's none, then we have the peace of mind knowing that Kyle is not going to be with anyone dangerous. Due to his lack of involvement in Kyle's life, we can request and should be granted brief, supervised visitations at first where you will be present. By the time Kyle is left alone with him, he will already have a relationship with Alex and we will have had time to feel him out."

Her eyes rim with tears. "We?"

"I will be with you through every step of this, Spencer. I won't let you go through it alone."

"We have to find something," she whispers, unable to come to grips with the idea of having to share Kyle with that piece of shit. I can't pretend to understand what she's going through, but I get it on some level. The thought of another man coming into Kyle's life has me sick with jealousy. *I'm* his man. I don't care that he doesn't share my fucking DNA. That kid laid claim to my heart and there's no getting it back.

"I promise, Spencer, that I will do everything in my power to make this go away."

She nods, sucking her lips between her teeth and widening her eyes to fight back tears. "Thanks, Coop."

The next few days are spent with my head buried in various law books and on the phone consulting colleagues. I've completely devoted myself to Spencer's case, letting the rest of our workload fall on Dad's shoulders. He's been more than supportive, happily taking on the extra load so I can be there for Spencer.

All we've managed to dig up on Mr. Alex Hernandez are a couple of old drug charges and one recent simple assault charge for a barroom fight. Neither is enough.

A week has passed, and each day that I have to report that the PI has not found anything that will stick sets Spencer a little more on edge. So, today when she walks in, I'm happy to throw her a little bone.

"How was work?" I ask when she comes trudging into my

office and collapses into the chair in front of my desk. "That good, huh?"

"Please tell me he found something?"

"It's not much…"

She perks up, sitting a little straighter. "Tell me."

"Stephen has been hanging out at the club he frequents, and apparently, Alex is engaged to some rich oilfield princess. The night he ran in to Gina, Alex got stupid drunk and spilled the beans about Kyle to his new fiancée. They got into a huge argument over his keeping it from her. Apparently his future wife is unable to bear children and sees Kyle as her shot at motherhood."

Spencer's eyes narrow. "That bitch."

"According to Stephen, she's good people."

Spencer glares at me. "Don't…She wants my baby. Fuck her."

I bite my lip and laugh.

"What else?" she asks eagerly.

"That's it for now."

Spencer huffs. "That's nothing we can use, Cooper. How does this help us?"

"It gives us motive, Princess. She's his kryptonite."

"Court is in five days and we have shit, Cooper," Spencer cries when she shows up after work. Her hair is a wreck and she looks like she hasn't slept in days. "Do we have anything else. Is there any other way to keep him out of Kyle's life?"

"It's a long shot." *She is never going to go for this.*

"Lay it on me."

Reaching across the table, I take both of her hands into mine and look her straight in the eyes. "Marry me." No two words have ever felt better or more right than the two I've just spoken. My heart races and bile rises in my throat as the nerves consume me.

Spencer stares, mouth gaping, like I've grown two heads. It's as if she's waiting for the punch line. When it finally becomes clear to her that this isn't a joke, her eyes begin to dart around the room, looking anywhere but at me. Finally, she laughs it off, attempting to pull her hands from mine, but I just hold them tighter. "Cooper, stop messing around." Her voice shakes.

"I'm completely serious."

Spencer's cheeks flush crimson and she crosses and uncrosses her legs...twice. "Why?" she sputters. "Why are you doing this?"

"The fact that you're engaged to be married will show the judge that you have a stable home for Kyle with two parents who love him. If there is a father figure in the picture, a judge is more likely to terminate rights. We'll still need something substantial on Alex, but it will strengthen your case drastically."

"You would do that for me?" Silent tears drip from endless blue oceans. She's shaking.

God, this girl really is clueless. "Spencer, I've already told you that I would do whatever it takes to help you. Yes, I would do this for you and for your boys." *And for myself,* I add silently. I can't let her see this as more than a strategic move. The mere thought of a real date had her running for the hills.

She's quiet for a long moment. I can see the wheels turning in that gorgeous head of hers. Finally, she pulls her hands away, shaking her head at me. "I can't ask this of you, Cooper.

It's too much."

My heart plummets to my toes and my mouth goes dry. "You didn't ask, I offered, and the offer stands."

"Can I have some time to think about it?"

"You have four days, Princess."

She rises from her chair, backing toward the door. Her head bobs, and she thanks me again as she disappears the way she entered only minutes ago.

Chapter Twenty-Three
SPENCER

I barely make it back to my car without collapsing. I have spent my entire life dreaming of the day that Cooper would ask me to marry him, and I can honestly say I never imagined it to be like this. I'm a ball of conflicting emotions. But, above all else, shitty fake proposal and all, I love that man with every fiber of my being. More now than ever.

That he would sacrifice his own future to save mine is the most selfless thing anyone has ever done for me. *Coop loves me.* His words confirmed what I think I've always known deep down when he whispered them into my ear a week and a half ago. I still believe wholeheartedly that Cooper and I are soul mates. The problem, however, has never been a lack of love for each other. Even when Cooper broke up with me, I knew that he loved me.

But, since that day there has always been something standing in our way. Today that something is my children. They are the reason I can't just say yes when every cell in my body wants to be his wife. I care about his and my boys' happiness too much. Cooper may like my kids. But, like and love are two entirely different things. It would not be fair to expect him to take on the role of doting dad to three children he never asked for, and for my boys, I would expect nothing less.

Where's a paper bag when you need one? It feels like my throat is closing up and my heart is beating way too fast. This can't be normal. I think I must be hyperventilating. I lean my head against the headrest, breathing in through my nose and out through my mouth slowly until it no longer feels like I'm drowning.

While still idling in the parking lot, I text Gina.

Me: Cooper just proposed.

Gina: What??? What did you say? You said YES, right?

Me: Not exactly. I told him I'd think about it.

My phone starts buzzing in my hand and I answer it.

"What the hell do you mean you told him you'd think about it? Sometimes I swear I don't know you at all. This is what you've wanted your entire life." Gina starts in on me before I can even get out the word "Hello."

God, my head hurts. "It wasn't like a *romantic* proposal, Gi. It was more of a business proposal."

"'Splain, Lucy."

"If Coop and I are engaged, or if I'm engaged, period, it will strengthen our chances of getting Alex's rights terminated. Apparently judges like kids to have fathers and step ones will do…"

"You're stupid. First of all, I need for you to know that."

"Uhhh, thanks?"

"That is the most romantic thing I've ever heard. What could possibly be more romantic than the man of your dreams swooping in like a white knight? This is your fucking fairytale, bitch, and you're about to let it slip away..." Gina growls in frustration. "Listen, I know your stubborn ass is used to doing everything alone, but for once will you just play the role of damsel in dis-fucking-stress and allow the man to swoop in and save your ass?"

Wow. "I'm not sure I know how to damsel."

The line goes silent for a few seconds. Gina must not know how to damsel, either. When she doesn't answer, I begin laughing. "Hello, pot."

"Shut up. Watch some Disney movies tonight and take notes. I think you have to talk like you've just swallowed helium and faint and shit," she teases.

"I almost accomplished the fainting part."

"See, you're a natural. You've totally got this."

"Totally."

"Just say yes, Spencer. It's that simple."

It's that simple...and it's that fucking hard.

The next day, as I'm packing up to leave school, a text comes in.

My Knight: We've got him. Get your sexy ass over here, Princess.

I stare down at the message in disbelief. My hand begins shaking so hard that the phone falls to the table. *Oh my God.* I don't know what exactly we've got yet, and I don't care, because Cooper wouldn't have messaged me if it wasn't something solid.

Me: On my way!

Screw the butterflies, humming birds are zipping around in my stomach by the time I walk through the door to Cooper's office. *I'm floating.*

Coop bounds out of his chair, rushing over to greet me at the door. Lifting me into his arms, he spins me around the room, kissing every square inch of my face.

His excitement is contagious, and I'm giggling like a little girl. "Well, hello there, *fiancé*."

"Fian..." He pauses, searching my eyes as a slow smile moves across his face. His eyes sparkle. "Does that mean what I think it means?"

A slow trickle of tears stream down my cheeks as I nod my head. "Yes, Cooper. I will marry you...if you'll still have me." My heart is racing. "Unless you've had second thoughts," I rush out, feeling my cheeks warm. "I will never be able to repay you for this."

"You just did, Princess."

God, the way he's looking at me almost makes me feel like this is real. Like he's marrying me because he can't imagine living any other way, rather than martyring himself. Oh, I know it isn't that bad, but there's still a huge part of me that feels guilty for allowing him to do this. *Selfish.* I feel selfish for using him this way. In a few years or hell, even months, when this is all just a bad memory and Alex is no longer a threat...if he's not happy, I'll set him free.

"I love you, Cooper Hebert, and I know love isn't everything, but it's something, right? We can do this. We can be happy..." I swallow the lump in my throat, searching his face for reassurance.

"I love you, too, Spence, and we *will* be happy."

Wrapping my arms around his neck, I give Coop another toe-curling kiss before disentangling myself and walking over to sit in my chair. Cooper follows suit, taking his seat across the cluttered desk.

"Whatcha got?" I ask eagerly, rocking in my seat.

Cooper steeples his hands beneath his chin, leaning forward. "Before moving to New Orleans, Mr. Hernandez lived in Little Rock, Arkansas, where he worked as a bouncer for a local night club. Club Rouge. It was a known hot spot for pill poppers...namely ecstasy." Cooper lifts his brow and smirks. "Alex was allegedly their main supplier."

My hands clutch the arms of the chair as I drum my feet on the floor with excitement. "A drug dealer! Coop. This is great."

He chuckles, then quickly frowns. "It gets worse. A seventeen-year-old girl snuck in with a fake ID and ODed... died, right there on the dance floor."

My heart sinks.

"Several other people were hospitalized from the bad batch of drugs that they also alleged to have purchased from Alex."

I cup my hands over my open mouth. Stunned doesn't begin to describe how I'm feeling. "This makes no sense. How is he not in jail?"

"I said alleged. Alex was accused but never charged. He must've had some friends in pretty high places...but his reputation was tarnished."

"So he moved to New Orleans and it all just went away," I add, finishing his thought.

"Bingo," Coop says, pointing at me with a wink. "Except nothing ever really goes away, does it?"

I guess not. "So if there is no record, then how can this help our case?"

"Character witnesses." Cooper crosses his arms on his chest, leaning back in his chair. "Five of the people who were hospitalized are willing to come forth and testify that they purchased their drugs from Alex Hernandez that night."

My heart starts racing, and I can feel myself beaming. "So it's done, then? There's no way we can lose?"

Coop's head shakes. "I didn't say that...but, it looks good. We've got a shot, Spence, and that's a hell of a lot more than we had when we woke up this morning."

Chapter Twenty-Four
COOPER

I thought that learning of ALex's past would afford Spence a little comfort, but it's done the exact opposite. She is completely losing it. She's been sick as a dog and won't hardly eat a thing. Spencer hasn't been to work in three days. It was hard enough when she thought that Alex was just a deadbeat, but after learning about his past, she is positively terrified of Kyle having a relationship with this man.

I don't think she will be able to handle it if we lose, and we still *could* lose. I have to do something, and I've come up with a plan. One that isn't exactly legal but just might work.

"Dad, I need to go take care of something. I've got to go out of town, but I'll be back before morning," I call out, walking past his office.

My father comes sprinting out to the lobby. "Just where in the hell do you think you're going, son? You've got court tomorrow damned morning."

I grab my suit jacket from the closet and drape it over my arm. "Exactly," I answer, giving Dad's shoulder an affectionate squeeze before continuing toward the door.

"That girl's gonna lose her shit if you take off right now," he threatens, rubbing at the back of his neck.

My mouth twitches into a half smile. "I'm pretty sure she's already lost it, Dad. I'm doing this for her. Don't worry about Spencer. I'll call her on the way out."

"Don't go gettin' yourself in any troub—"

The door closes behind me, cutting him off mid-sentence. On the way to my truck, I pull out my cell to give Spence a ring. The last thing I want is to have her worrying about me on top of everything else.

"Hello." *Fuck.* She's been crying.

"Hey, babe," I say, holding the phone to my ear with my shoulder and setting my things down on the back seat. "I just wanted to let you know I've got some things to take care of for court tomorrow and I have to go out of town."

"Is something wrong?" she asks with a tremor in her voice.

"No, no...nothing like that. I'll be back really late, or maybe even early in the morning, and I don't want you to worry about a thing, okay?"

She scoffs. "Yeah, okay," she says mockingly.

"I have a good feeling about this, Princess. Try to relax and I'll see you first thing in the morning."

My heart knots when I hear her sniffling through the phone. "I'll try."

After hanging up with Spencer, I punch the address Stephen gave me earlier this morning into the GPS and begin making my way to New Orleans.

I've been parked outside Alex's townhouse for almost three hours when his black jeep rolls in, parking in the spot right next to mine. I wait until he's gotten inside before leaving my vehicle and walking over to knock on his door. I don't want to risk a public confrontation in the parking lot. The conversation we need to have will be between just us two.

"Can I help you?" he asks politely upon opening the door. Alex is about my height with dark skin and hair. His eyes are brownish-black and scrutinizing. Aside from the eyes and dark skin, Kyle doesn't look a thing like his sperm donor.

"Hi...Alex Hernandez?" I ask to be sure I'm speaking with the right person.

He nods. "And you are?"

"My name's Cooper Hebert. I'm Spencer's fiancé. I was hoping that we could have a few words."

Alex starts to shut the door in my face. "Not interested, buddy."

I wedge my foot into the doorway to prevent it from closing. "I really think you'll want to hear what I have to say."

His eyes become menacing. "I said I'm not interested."

"What if I told you I know about Lisa Chedwick? Would that change your mind?"

His face pales and all of his features droop. It's as if he's seen a ghost. Without another word, Alex glances around the parking lot before opening the door wider and allowing me inside.

"Excellent choice," I say, giving him a triumphant wink.

"What do you want?"

I look him dead in the eye. "I want you to withdraw your claim and sign papers officially relinquishing your parental rights to Kyle."

"No." He stares me down, but I can see the nervousness in his posture by the way he's suddenly shifting his weight from one foot to the other.

"No?" I huff. "You went through an awful lot of trouble

reinventing yourself to throw it all away now, especially over a kid you've never even bothered to see…Moved to a new state. Got a respectable job. A beautiful, wealthy, *revered* fiancée… How do you think she's going to handle it in court tomorrow when she learns that the man she's about to marry is a liar? A drug dealer? A murderer?"

Alex is seething. His jaw clenched tight.

I scrunch my nose up, shaking my head. "Probably not too well, am I right?"

"He's my son."

At that I laugh. "That boy doesn't know you from a stranger on the streets. He already has a family who loves him. He's happy and well cared for. Do what's in the best interest of Kyle and leave him the hell alone."

"And if I don't?" he asks, moving half a step closer in an attempt to intimidate me with his size. We're similar in height, but he's got a much bigger build.

"Then I guess we'll see you in court, along with statements from five of your former clients that say you sold them bad ecstasy that night. The night they all ended up in the emergency room and their friend died of an overdose from drugs she too obtained from you."

Alex reaches for the knob, pulling the door open. "Get out of my house, Mr. Hebert."

I nod, having said all I came here to say. I only hope it was enough.

Chapter Twenty-Five
SPENCER

"How'd your errand go last Night?" I ask when Cooper shows up, ready to escort me to the courthouse.

He rests his soft lips on my forehead, allowing them to linger as he rubs a hand up and down my back in soothing strokes. Coop's breath is warm against my skin. "It was fine," he answers curtly as he reaches for my hand. "Ready?"

No. "Sure," I lie, forcing a weak smile. Something's off with him this morning, and I find myself trying to be stronger than I feel to counteract whatever's going on in his head. Cooper was so confident yesterday. Maybe it's just a case of nerves, or it could all be in my head. Lord knows I've been a complete basket case the past few days.

We arrive a full twenty minutes early and find Gina already there waiting on us. The moment she spots me, her face lights up as she runs over in her ridiculously high heels, her arms flailing at her sides.

"You didn't tell me you were coming," I whisper, hugging my best friend close.

Gina tsks. "Where else would I be?"

"Thanks for being here, Gi."

She waves me off just as an important looking man in a suit approaches our little group.

"Are you here for the custody case?" he asks to no one in particular.

Cooper offers his hand. "I'm Ms. LeBlanc's attorney, Cooper Hebert."

The two men shake hands. "My name is William Smith, and I represent Mr. Hernandez. I'm afraid there've been some last minute changes and I was hoping that we could speak privately before the hearing?"

My stomach begins to churn, but when I look up at Cooper, he offers me a confident smile and nods, setting me at ease. The three of us follow the flustered man into a small conference room and seat ourselves at one end of the oval table which encompasses nearly the entire space.

"What's going on?" Cooper asks with an almost smug look. *He knows something...*

"I met with my client this morning, and it appears he's had a change of heart."

A sly smirk forms on Coop's face, disappearing almost as quickly as it appeared.

What did you do, Cooper Hebert?

"What's that mean?" I ask, not wanting to assume anything, but my pulse starts racing with excitement. *A change of heart...* This must mean—

"We've received your counterclaim for full physical and legal custody, Ms. LeBlanc, and my client has decided that he too feels that that would be in Kyle's best interest. When I return to the city this afternoon, we'll be meeting to sign papers relinquishing Mr. Hernandez's parental rights."

"Are you serious?" I ask as my lips and hands begin to shake uncontrollably.

The attorney, whose name I've already forgotten, smiles at me affectionately. "Yes, ma'am. Congratulations." To Cooper he adds, "I'll take care of cancelling the hearing."

Coop nods his head and the two shake hands again before Alex's lawyer leaves the room.

After weeks of constant worry, this all just feels too good to be true. "S-so that's it?" My eyes well up as I turn to face Cooper. "It's over?"

"That's it, Princess." His lips turn up in a radiant smile, and I want to run to him, but it's taking me a moment to process what's just happened here.

"Fuck yeah!" Gina shouts, jumping up from her chair beside me, earning herself a glare from my sexy as fuck attorney.

"I do still work here regularly, Gina...If you could not make that completely humiliating for me, that'd be great." He winks, unable to wipe the smile from his face.

We won.

"Oh, right. Sorry, Coop...but, oh my God, you did it!" My favorite little pixie launches herself at him, wrapping her arms around Coop's neck and planting big wet smooches on each of his cheeks.

I watch the excitement unfolding around me in a daze. I haven't yet moved from my seat because I don't trust my feet not to fall out from underneath me. Apparently, I'm better at this damsel thing than I thought. Once Cooper pries Gina off of him, he returns to kneel before me. Cooper holds my face in his hands, wiping tears away with the pads of his thumbs and then pulling me into his chest. "You didn't do anything illegal, did you?" I ask staring into the most beautiful brown eyes I've ever seen.

"Let's go home." Cooper places a tender kiss on my forehead, causing my whole body to shiver. He takes my hand into his own. The way he avoids answering my question doesn't miss my attention as he gently tugs, leading me in the direction of the door. I narrow my eyes at him, making sure that he knows it, and follow Coop out of the court house with every intention of revisiting this conversation later.

Gina and I have a moment in the parking lot, holding each other and bawling our eyes out, while Coop looks on affectionately from the truck.

"Still think fairytales don't exist?" she asks in my ear.

I look at the ring on my left finger—the one that signifies the engagement fabricated to solidify our case—and frown. "Oh, they exist." My heart is filled with dread. "Just not for me."

"What are you talking about?"

"There's no reason to continue the charade, Gina," I answer quietly. "We don't have to get married now."

As if it just dawns on her as well, my best friend's face falls. "Well, it still could happen."

Not likely. "I'm too happy to be sad right now, Gina. Can we not talk about this?"

"You're right. Let's mourn next week." She gives my hands a gentle squeeze. "Don't keep the man waiting." Gina kisses my cheek. "I'll talk to you later." She motions her head to the truck where Cooper's waiting patiently. "So freaking happy for you, babe," Gina says before swatting me on the ass and heading off in the direction of her car.

I climb up into Cooper's truck, which is already nice and toasty. He's listening to some thuggy rap music, and it makes me smile because I know it's not a coincidence. He's fully aware of how much I can't stand it.

As soon as I've buckled my seatbelt, I reach out to power off the radio. Coop's eyes dart to the side momentarily and he smiles knowingly.

"Where'd you go last night, Cooper?" I try again, staring at his profile.

He coughs, never taking his eyes from the road. "I told you. I had some last minute details to work out."

"Did your trip have anything to do with what happened today?"

Cooper flicks the left blinker on then makes the turn onto our street. I keep staring expectantly as he pulls into his parents' driveway and parks the truck. "Maybe, a little," he finally admits, turning to look at me.

"What'd you do, beat him up?"

He chokes on a laugh. "No..."

"Ugh," I growl. "Will you just tell me?"

"Can't you just thank me and leave it alone?" *He's really not going to tell me.*

"I did thank you."

Coop's eyebrows waggle. "I could think of a few other ways you could thank me."

I gasp in mock horror. "Really, Cooper?"

"Hey, I'm not as opposed to hooking as you seem to be." He shrugs. "I will happily accept payment in sexual favors."

What the hell? Why not?

"What'd you have in mind?" I ask, already unbuckling his belt.

"That's a fantastic start." Coop groans, his body jerking as I pull the zipper down, slipping my hand into the opening of his boxers and fisting it around his shaft.

"Start?" I quirk my brow.

"Mmhmm." Cooper's mouth slowly curves into a sexy smile as he begins thrusting gently into my palm. "I'm sure we can work out an installment plan of some sort." His voice is strained as I begin working my hand up and down his length, feeling him harden and swell in my palm.

My tongue darts out to moisten my lips before dropping my head into Cooper's lap and sealing them around the head of his erection. His hands grip my hair, and I take him as deep as I can manage, working the base with my fingers.

The throaty sound of his moans and the way his back arches, pushing him deeper into my mouth spurs me on. Swirling my tongue around his length, I hollow out my cheeks as I work him slow and deliberately.

Giving head is not something I've ever particularly enjoyed, but with Cooper, I find it incredibly arousing. The sexy noises he makes and the way he completely loses control. It takes immense restraint not to reach between my legs and rub out the ache that's building in my core. My panties are soaked, but this isn't for me. This is all about him.

"Fuck, Princess. Oh God. Don't stop...Don't stop, baby." His hands tighten in my hair to the point that it's almost painful as he guides my head up and down his cock, reaching for his release. His entire body jerks as it sprays down the back of my throat. I continue sucking until his body goes slack, taking every last drop.

When I raise my head from his lap, Coop's eyes are still closed. His breathing labored. Smiling triumphantly to myself, I wipe at my mouth then turn to find Mr. Neal standing right outside of Cooper's window. He's staring off to the side, but from the way he's specifically avoiding looking into the truck,

I'm positive that he's just gotten a fucking eyeful of his son's dick in my mouth.

I elbow Cooper in the chest hard and he jumps. "What the hell'd you do that for?" His hand comes up, rubbing at the spot where I've just hit him.

My throat goes dry and I break out in a cold sweat. I feel like I'm going to be sick and am seconds away from releasing Niagara Falls in his truck. "I'm about ninety-nine percent sure your father just saw us." I motion with my head to the window where Mr. Neal is still staring out into space.

Coop gets an evil gleam in his eye as he tucks his dick back into his slacks and begins rolling the window down. "Hey, Pops. You need something?"

"Huh?" his dad answers, jumping. "Oh no, I was, uh...just watching a squirrel in that tree over there trying to get a nut."

I literally choke on my saliva so badly that Coop has to beat on my back.

"All right. Just checkin' on ya. Spence and I are going to finish our *conversation* and then we'll be right in."

"Oh. Okay...that sounds good, son." Mr. Neal never turns his head in our direction throughout the entire interaction. Whatever tiny glint of hope I'd had that he hadn't witnessed what just went down in this truck is smashed.

"So, you should probably go inside the house and let mom know that we'll be inside in just a minute," Coop urges, trying to contain his laughter.

"Right," Mr. Neal says, finally turning around. "You two, uh, have fu—"

"See you in a few minutes, Dad," Coop says, cutting off his old man.

After rolling up the window, Cooper bursts into a fit of

hysterics.

"It's not funny, ass."

"Oh my God," Coop howls, wiping at the tears dripping from his eyes. "Why aren't you laughing?"

"Ummm, probably because I'm the one who just got caught with a mouth full of cock. I will never be able to look your father in the eye again." Acid churns in my stomach. "You really need your own place, Coop."

"I agree. We need our own place. Start searching online for a few you like and we can go have a look together…Maybe even this weekend."

Suddenly, the cab of this truck feels really, really small. "About that," I say, slipping his grandmother's borrowed diamond from my finger.

"Don't," Coop objects, his face panicked as he slides it back on. "Don't do that. I heard what you said to Gina and you're wrong."

Shit. "What am I wrong about?"

"We should still get married, Spence. I love you." His voice cracks. "And you love me." I nod. "We've been in love with each other since before we were even old enough to know the meaning of the word. This court fiasco just helped to speed things up a bit, but I had every intention of asking you to marry me eventually…whenever I thought that there was a chance you might actually not turn me down."

How did things suddenly become so serious?

"Cooper, the timing won't ever be right." I stare down at my lap, unable to handle the broken look on his face, and methodically spin the ring around my finger. "I will always be a mother. My children…they will *always* come first, and you…you don't want to be a father."

"You're wrong," he counters, cupping my face in his hands. "I didn't want to be a father with Kristy...or any other woman, for that matter. Those ties...those ties are forever, and I never wanted to be connected to any other person so permanently. Forever was always meant for you and me, Spence."

Holy fucking shit.

"B-but, my kids..."

"Are amazing just like their mother, and if you'll give me the chance, I'd be honored to help you raise them." His big brown eyes stare deep into mine. I've never seen him so vulnerable—so scared.

I am now a full-blown, sobbing mess. "You're serious?"

"I'll admit that at first I wasn't too keen on the idea. I couldn't handle that you'd had children with anyone who wasn't me. I just...I could never bring myself to want anyone else in that way." Cooper pauses to clear his throat. "They were supposed to be ours and I resented them," he admits, his face flushing with embarrassment. "I looked at them and I-I saw souvenirs of a life you lived without me. Little trophies you'd flaunt in my face just to show me that you'd moved on." He shakes his head. "I was a fool."

"Coop, it was never like that."

"I know that." He reaches up, loosening the knot in his tie. "But it was easier for me to be angry with you than to admit to myself that every bit of this was my fault."

"I-I don't know what to say."

Cooper takes both of my hands back into his own. "Say you'll still marry me," he begs. "For the first time since I was stupid enough to let you go, there is nothing but fear standing in our way. Be brave with me, Spence."

My throat is caving in. I need to get out of this truck. I

can't think. I can't breathe. "You have no idea how much I want to say yes," I whisper.

"Then say it," he urges.

I can physically feel the ache in my chest where my heart is being ripped in two. "I can't marry you, Cooper, but you have to know that it's not because I don't love you or because I don't want to." I pause to catch my breath, squeezing his hand. "It's not fair to you or to my boys. You-you hardly know each other...You can't even change a diaper, Cooper." I sniff through a sad smile. "You don't even know what you're asking for—not really." He starts to speak and I press my finger to his lips. "There's no way for me to say this without sounding like I was using you, but the only reason I agreed to marry you was because you made it sound like a business proposition, and I would have done anything to keep my child." Fuck. I hate that no matter how I say this it comes off sounding terrible. "Cooper, I would have given our marriage my all. I selfishly would have allowed you to risk your future and risk making my children unhappy to save Kyle, but I would have done everything in my power to make you happy." Cooper sucks in his lips, biting down. His nostrils flare in and out slowly as his eyes begin to shine with unshed tears. "But at the first sign that you weren't, I would have let you go...and it would have k-killed me. I don't want to risk that. I can't...I won't risk that."

"Babe, I would never have left. I won't ever leave you." There's so much desperation in his voice. Cooper looks as heartbroken as I feel.

"There was a time that I believed that with every beat of my heart, Cooper James, but that ship has sailed, and I'm not trying to hurt you or to make you feel guilty. I'm only trying to protect my heart. To protect your happiness and my children's..."

I can see the resignation in his face as Coop pulls me into his lap. "It's okay, baby. Don't cry." He dries my eyes and kisses my swollen lips. "If you need time...I can give you that. I'm not going anywhere. Even if you never give me more than this...I'm yours because you are all I need, Spencer."

Time...I don't have the heart to tell him that not even time will be enough to fix the mess we've allowed ourselves to become.

Chapter Twenty-Six
COOPER

"Are we okay?" Spencer asks nervously, wringing her hands as we're walking up to the house.

I wrap my arm around her shoulders, pulling her close. "We're perfect," I assure her, placing a kiss on her temple. "It's my dad you should be worried about." I give her a little nudge with my elbow, trying to lighten the mood, and earn myself another jab to the ribs.

"Can you just go get Kyle and bring him to me next door?" She steeples her hands together, poking out her bottom lip, looking so much like Savage.

I chuckle. "Not a chance, hoover."

Spence glares at me, opening her mouth to speak, but before she can even make a sound, the front door swings open.

"There you two are," Momma says, assessing us both. "I was about to send out a search party." She ushers us inside, closing the door behind us. "I called your momma and told her about court, Spencer Rose, since you didn't see fit to do so yourself."

Ouch.

Spencer bites her bottom lip. "Thank you, Mrs. Nelly. I

guess I was just so preoccupied with all that was going on, I just forgot to call."

Mom huffs, glaring at Spence and me. "Yeah, I heard all about how you two were keeping yourselves *occupied*."

Spencer's jaw drops to the floor.

"Mom, that's enough," I warn, giving her a stern look.

"No, Coop, I don't think it is. Your father shouldn't have to come home to that foolishness in his own damned yard. You two are acting like some goddamn horny teenagers."

"Ignore her," I mumble to Spence when I feel her hand start shaking in mine.

"You roll them eyes at me again and you'll be picking teeth up off the floor, you understand me, son? Can you imagine if it would have been Lake or Landon who walked up and caught you two like that? I mean, for God's sake, you had your mouth on his genitals outside in broad daylight!" Momma shouts, throwing her hands into the air.

I look over at poor Spence, who's now as white as a sheet. "I-I'm so sorry, Mrs. Nelly. It won't happen again."

Whaaaat? The hell it won't. "Pssh," I huff, and Spencer gives me the evil eye.

"You see that it doesn't." Momma shakes her head. "I mean, honestly, you're better than that, Spencer. That type of behavior is reserved for truck stop hookers, not respectable ladies. I would never stoop so low."

I snort. It's a knee-jerk reaction and one that only pisses my mother off further. Spencer sucks in her lips, biting down hard to contain hers.

"I'll be sure to give my condolences to Dad." And that does it. Spence folds over, laughing. The look on my mother's face is priceless. I've decided that if they're going to insist on being all up in our business, I'm not going to make it easy for them.

"Cooper, stop it," Spence grits out between her teeth, her nails digging into the palm of my hand.

"I really wish you'd stop being so disrespectful, Coop."

I have had enough. "And I really wish you would stay out of our business. We're adults, and you need to back off, Mom."

Momma lifts her hand, pointing a finger in my direction, and sucking in enough breath for an epic tongue lashing, but instead blows the breath back out in a long sigh. She jerks her hand back to her side and trudges off to the kitchen, grumbling the entire way.

"Your mother was right, you know?" Spence says quietly.

I scoff. "She most certainly was not. Do not listen to that crazy woman. I find blow jobs to be highly respectable. In fact, I can't think of many things I respect more than your lips around my cock."

Spencer sucks in a sharp breath. "Not about that," she says, giggling. "I meant she was right about the boys. We didn't even consider that we were out in the front yard and anyone could have just walked up on us."

"Well, banning blow jobs is *not* the answer."

Her brows lift and the corners of her mouth curve into a curious smile. "No?"

"Definitely not," I say with the shake of my head.

"What do you propose we do, then?" She crosses her arms on her chest, cocking a hip out to the side.

"It's simple. We need our own place."

Chapter Twenty-Seven
SPENCER

Over the last month or so, it Has become the new routine for Gina and Coop to join us at Momma's for dinner on Tuesday nights. Today, I was able to duck out a little early from work to swing by the store and grab all of the fixings for Taco Tuesday. It's not even four o'clock yet and I've already picked up Savage and have almost finished cooking.

Tuesdays are my new favorite day. I mean, they already freaking rocked, because...tacos! Add in a little quality time with my B.F.F. and Cooper and I'm on top of the freaking world.

As I'm dancing around the kitchen, belting out the lyrics to *This Girl is on Fire* by Alicia Keys, I see Mom and the twins pull up to the house.

"You not on fiya, Mom," Kyle says, making a face at my screeching. "I not yike dis song." He crosses his arms and pouts.

"Alexa," I say while glaring at my toddler, "play the song *You're a Jerk*." Like magic, the song comes on. I still can't get over how amazing the Amazon Echo is. Just about any song you can imagine available on voice command. What will they come up with next?

I laugh as Kyle starts singing along at the table, bobbing his head from side to side with the beat. He really is such a savage.

"What's a dildo?" Landon asks, barging into the kitchen and tossing his twenty-pound backpack to the floor.

Hello. "Ummm," I mumble, glancing at Kyle, who is sitting at the kitchen table coloring. "Give me a sec."

I amble over to the living room and ask my mother to keep an eye on Kyle so that I can speak to the twins privately and then usher them up the stairs to my bedroom, locking the door behind us. "Why do you want to know what a *dildo* is?"

"The kids here say that a lot," Lake replies, staring down at his feet while cracking his knuckles one by one. My shoulders tense at the sound. "We laugh because everyone else does," he continues, "but we don't know what it means."

Holy crap. I'm not ready. "What do they say exactly?" I pry, not wanting to unwittingly provide any more information than absolutely necessary. *Why the hell are twelve-year-old boys talking about dildos?*

"I dunno," Lake says with a nervous smile. "They just say things like 'Go suck a dildo' and stuff."

Reaching over to the bedside table, I grab a small stack of paper and begin fanning myself. I feel like I'm going to vomit. "They say that, do they?" I ask, stalling for time.

Landon nods.

I can't do it... "Actually, guys, I think you're a little...or a lot too young for this stuff right now. Can we just revisit the question in like—" I glance down at my wrist at the watch I'm not wearing "—three years?" I plead.

Landon's eyes roll up in his head. "Told you she wouldn't tell us."

Inhaling a deep breath, I take a seat on the edge of my bed. "A dildo is a fake penis," I blurt out, feeling my cheeks flame.

The twins "oh" and "ahh" in understanding. Their world makes sense once again, which is lovely, because mine is tilting on its axis.

If I were smart, I would just drop it and send them on their merry way, but because I am a glutton for punishment, I can't let it go. "Why are you boys telling each other to suck penises, real or otherwise, anyway? What kind of kids are you hanging around with?"

Lake sighs. "Mom...it's *everyone*. Landon and I are so babyfied compared to the other kids here. They even watch Pornhub." *The fuck?*

"Yeah, Jake said he watches it on his phone at night when he goes to sleep. I Googled it while we were at Dad's—" he gives me a guilty look "—and found out it was people with webcams having sex," Landon adds with a shrug.

I blanch. Oh my God. I am really going to be sick. The last time we had the sex talk was less than a year ago and they still thought it meant kissing in bed with your clothes off, under the covers. I didn't tell them better, wanting to keep my boys innocent for as long as possible. Something tells me they aren't quite so innocent anymore. "Do you two know what sex is?" I ask, looking around the room, anywhere but at their eyes. Trust me I know how ridiculous it must seem that I can't make eye contact with my children when I've made my career discussing sex. But, talking about sex with adult strangers is completely different from talking about it with your baby boys.

"It's when a boy puts his penis in a vagina," Lake mutters

beneath his breath.

Landon bursts into a fit of hysterics. "You are so freaking stupid," he says, pointing at his brother. "You don't put it *in* a vagina. You put it on *top*." *Noooo. He did not just say that.*

It's my turn to laugh. I try holding it in, but he's so sure of himself, and he's so *wrong*. When I calm down enough, I correct him. "Lake was right. You do put it inside," I say, coughing. "But not 'til you are *much* older," I add.

"But, gay people put it in a butt, right, Mom?" Lake adds, staring as he waits for confirmation.

Oh, sweet baby Jesus. What is even happening right now? "Yes," I squeak. "Gay men have sex by sticking their penis in another man's butt."

Lake nods and his brows dip inward. I can actually see another question forming in his head, and I'm a bit terrified. "But, how do gay women have sex if neither of them has a penis?"

Dead silence. My mouth opens and closes. Everything I think to say sounds worse than the last. I'm not about to explain clitoral stimulation to my twelve-year-olds.

"Ohhhh!" Landon says, his eyes lighting up. "Is that what the dildos are for? Lesbian sex?" *Thank you, son.*

"Yes. That is exactly what they are for." *Please let this be the end of it.*

"Okay, well, what about truffle butter? Is that real?" Landon inquires. Wow. Okay, this conversation just took a complete one-eighty. I breathe out a sigh of relief. Food is a good change of subject. I can handle food.

"I guess so...I think they use truffle butter in fancy restaurants on steaks."

"Ewwww," Lake and Landon both groan simultaneously.

Oookay... "Why? What do *you* think truffle butter is?"

Lake's face turns beet red and Landon begins choking on his saliva.

"I told you guys that you could tell me anything. I meant it."

"You can't yell at us," Lake warns, eyeing me.

I roll my eyes, crossing my arms on my chest. *How bad could it possibly be?* "I will not yell." I mean, it can't be worse than butt sex.

"Ryan told us that it's when you stick your penis in a butt and then in a vagina and when you pull it out, it makes a buttery substance called truffle butter," Landon answers, scrunching his nose in disgust. "Is that true?" Okay, so I was wrong. This is worse.

I stand there with my mouth agape, once again speechless. I'm fucking speechless. After sputtering wordlessly for a moment, I finally manage to screech out, "Who the hell is Ryan and where did he hear that?"

"Ryan is Dad's neighbor's son. He comes over to play basketball sometimes. It's lyrics from a Nicki Minaj song. He looked it up, and that's what it said," Lake explains.

Landon nods. "It's true. He showed us the Urban Dictionary on his phone. He said they make it into bars and sell it." He gags, no doubt imagining the steak houses buying that shit up and slathering it on his filet.

What the fuck is wrong with children these days? "Your friend Ryan is a fucking idiot," I say, seething. "The only thing you are going to get if you stick your penis in someone's ass is a di—penis covered in *shit,*" I yell, feeling the burn in my cheeks, as I begin pacing back and forth in my old bedroom. "And you'll give the girl a nasty infection...and probably yourself, too."

The boys go silent for a moment before Landon asks, "So putting your penis in a butt is gay, right?"

"Yes."

Once again I can see the hamster wheel in his brain turning. "But, what if it's a girl butt?"

I don't even know how to respond to this. My kid is a fucking freak! I didn't realize the back door was even an option until I was in college and I damn near killed Tate when he tried. No one's dick will be going anywhere near my no-no hole. "Why are you so fascinated with putting your penis in a butt, Landon? Most people don't ever do that...And, anyway, you aren't even old enough to be thinking of sex. Sex is for adults. Grown-ups. People in *love.*" And he's done it...sent me off on a tirade. "And," I add, opening Safari on my phone, "sex causes diseases. You can get puss-filled blisters and pee blood and, come here," I say, motioning them both over to look at the blue waffles I've just pulled up on my phone.

The boys study the picture for a moment before they both start retching and move away. "Oh, Mom." *Gag.* "That's disgusting," Landon moans.

"What the hell is that?" Lake asks.

"That is what can happen if you have sex when you aren't mature or responsible enough to do so. You want your penises to look like that?" I ask, staring them down.

Both of their heads shake rapidly.

"Keep those things in your pants, boys, and for God's sake, stop listening to stupid kids that don't know what the hell they're talking about!" I shout, opening the door. I storm out, mumbling the words "truffle butter" and shaking my head when I run right into Gina.

"Good song," she says, straightening her top. "When'd you

start listening to rap?"

"I don't listen to that shit. Can you believe some kid told the boys that truffle butter is when you put your penis in a butt and then a vagina and it makes butter? What the hell is going on at this school?"

Gina busts out laughing as she pulls out her phone and begins pecking at it rapidly. After finding whatever it is she's looking for, Gina holds it up to my face. The Urban Dictionary.

"Well, I'll be damned. Those little shits just taught me something."

"Oh, Spence. You make me laugh..." my best friend chimes, patting me on the back.

"I just can't believe little kids are talking about this stuff, Gina. I'm going to have to monitor their music better..."

"And you'll make them prime meat for all the little asshole kids at that school. You can't shelter them here, Momma. You aren't dealing with that snooty little catholic school anymore. Just be open and honest with them as much as you can. Lake and Landon are good kids. Don't put a target on their backs."

Gulping, I nod. She's right. "It's okay. I don't think they'll be thinking about sex any time soon."

Gina glares at me. "What'd you do?"

I smile innocently at my best friend. "I just showed them what could happen to their penises if they have sex before they're supposed to." I shrug.

Her mouth falls open. "You didn't?" She covers her mouth with both hands.

I nod. "You bet your ass I did."

"Blue waff—" Gina can't even finish the word waffles before she's gagging.

"Yup. I'm thinking about framing a picture and hanging it

up in their bathroom over the toilet as a reminder."

"But, that's a made up disease."

"So...?"

She nods. "Let's wallpaper their bathroom in it."

Me: Have you ever heard of truffle butter?

My Knight: Been listening to Nicki, have you? I knew there was a little gangsta in you somewhere, Spence. Probably in that big ol' booty. :P

Me: Ha ha. You're so funny. No, not Nicki...My kids.

My Knight: Did they ask you what it means?

Me: More like they've just educated me. I told them it was the fucking butter restaurants put on your steaks.

My Knight: You didn't? lol

Me: Then they asked me all these questions about butt sex. It was horrible.

My Knight: God, I wish I could have seen your face. What did you tell them?

Me: I told them that most people don't do that.

My Knight: What about you? Are you most people, Princess?

Me: What about me??? Are you asking if you can stick it in my ass?

My Knight: No, of course not. I mean, unless you are down for that kind of thing.

Me: Oh God, you're all disgusting. The whole fucking lot of you.

My Knight: So, just to clarify...That was a no?

Me: Let me put it to you in words you'll understand. I'll chop your fucking dick off and feed it to you for dinner if you even think of putting that monster in my no-no hole.

My Knight: Understood.

Me: Good. So, what time are you coming over?

My Knight: I'm a little afraid of you right now...

Me: Stop. You are not.

My Knight: Leaving the office now. See you soon, Princess. And no worries...The virtue of your no-no hole is safe with me ;) I'll treat it like my dick depends on it.

"Cooper's here," Lake calls from the living room.

I leave Gina chopping tomatoes and grab Coop a beer from the fridge on my way to greet him.

"Hey now," Coop says, pulling me in for a hug. "A man could get used to this!" He takes the Bud Light from my hand, kissing my forehead. "Thanks, Spence."

"You're welcome," I answer, narrowing my eyes at his chauvinism.

Cooper glances around the room, making sure the coast is clear, before his hand lowers from my waist to my ass. He cups the right cheek, squeezing hard. "If you ever change your mind..." He trails off, chuckling as I punch him in the chest.

After dinner, Gina and I clean the kitchen while Cooper and the boys play Madden on the PlayStation. I catch myself smiling, not paying attention to a word of Gina's gossip, as I strain to hear Cooper and my boys ragging on each other over the game. I can't help wishing that things could be different. Cooper would have been an incredible father.

"You didn't hear a word I just said, did you?" Gina asks, shoving my shoulder.

I frown guiltily. "Sorry, I was daydreaming."

"About a cute little house on the lake with a white picket fence, a certain ring back on your finger, and Cooper's cum pop between your legs every night?"

The plate I'm washing slips from my hands into the sink as I stare at her, open-mouthed.

"'Cause you can have all of that, you know?" she reminds me with a wink.

"You're so gross."

"I'm so right."

"What about you?" I ask, tossing the question back into her court. "What about your fairytale and white picket fence? For someone with so much advice…"

Gina gets quiet and goes back to drying the dishes. "We're not talking about me," she eventually grumbles.

"We're never talking about you because we're always talking about me."

She shrugs.

I sigh. "Are you ever going to settle down, Gi? You'd be the best mother."

Gina rests her hands on the edge of the counter, hanging her head. I'm not sure what's happening 'til I see the slight shuddering of her shoulders.

"Gina," I whisper, placing a soapy hand at her back. "Gi, are you *crying*?" My heart sinks.

My best friend takes the towel in her hand and uses it to mop the tears from her face. Her sad green eyes look up through wet lashes, connecting with mine. "I can't have kids," she whispers, her lips flattening into a straight line. "And besides, that title already belongs to you." She tries to blow off the fact that she's just dropped a confession the equivalent of an atomic bomb in this kitchen.

Now, when I tell you this girl is my best friend, I mean she is my person—the other half to my B.F.F. heart. We know everything about each other—have shared every single moment of our lives from the time we were in kindergarten. For her to keep something this huge from me…I'm stunned. I experience a vast array of emotions all at once, starting with shock, betrayal, and everything in between, before finally settling on sheer devastation. "Gina?" I say, feeling my heart sink. There's no way I'm just dropping this.

"I've known for years. The, umm…" She sniffs, wiping her nose. "The endometriosis is too bad. There's virtually no chance, but I'm okay. I've come to terms with it."

I swallow and swallow but can't seem to remove the lump in my throat. "I can see that," I say, watching the girl who has always been my rock fall to pieces before me.

She blows air upward, trying to dry her eyes. "I really am. I mean, as okay as a person can be with that kind of news. I have your kids, Spence, and they mean everything to me."

"Why didn't you tell me?" My voice cracks.

Gina shrugs. "I don't know. I didn't want you feeling sorry for me. You had a lot going on with the boys and their piece of shit fathers. It's just something I felt like I needed to deal with on my own."

The guilt I feel threatens to swallow me whole. I can't believe Gina's been dealing with this all on her own for years because my life is such a big clusterfuck that she felt like she'd be imposing. "So this is why you haven't taken any of the guys you've dated seriously? Because you can't have children?"

Gina nods. "I can't do it, Spence," she whispers. "I can't allow a man to fall in love with me knowing that I could never give him a family—a baby."

The tears just keep falling from my eyes. I want to tell her it's okay, that any man would be lucky to have her, that they wouldn't need anything more, but I understand how she feels. I get it, because if I were to marry Coop, that's exactly what I'd be doing—thrusting three children he never wanted into his life and preventing him from ever finding someone who could give him the family I can't. Sure he says he doesn't want kids now, but that could change. So I swallow the words that are on the tip of my tongue, because Gina and I keep things real. I wrap my arms around her, pulling her close. "Now you see why I can't marry Coop."

Chapter Twenty-Eight
COOPER

"Boom!" I jump up from my seat, throwing the controller down onto the couch and beating my fists against my chest like King Kong. "Still got it, boys."

Landon huffs. "You got lucky, old man."

"All right, you two, it's almost ten and y'all have school in the morning. Time for bed," Mrs. Elaine says, setting her grade book down on the coffee table as she pushes up from her usual corner on the worn couch.

"Come onnn, Grandma Elaine, I didn't get a chance to play yet," Lake gripes.

"Nope, get movin'. You can play with Coop tomorrow." Elaine winks at me as she says it, and I smile at her not so subtle invitation as she leads them off to bed.

After the room has cleared out, I realize that I haven't seen the girls for a while. The sound of hushed voices leads me back to the kitchen.

"That's not the same thing, Spencer. Cooper doesn't even want kids, and if he ever decided he wanted to have children, you could give him that. I can't," Gina argues. Her hands are resting on Spencer's shoulders and both women are dripping in tears. I hang back just outside the door, eavesdropping on the rest of their conversation.

"I'm not having any more children, Gina." The breath whooshes out of me like I've been punched in the gut. I'm surprised by how much that hurts to hear.

"But if you were with Cooper, things would be different. It wouldn't be so hard, and could you just picture him with a little baby? God, I think my fucking useless ovaries would explode!" Her hands come off Spencer's shoulders, making fireworks in the air.

Listen to Gina. She's smart.

Spencer laughs, and I feel it right in the chest. "I can imagine it," my girl answers, wiping her tears on the sleeve of her sweater. "He deserves a family—his *own* family."

"Well, I think you're screwing with fate. I'd love to have another baby Spencer running around, and since I can't make my own baby, you have to do it."

I watch from behind the doorframe as Spencer glares at Gina. "That's really low, Gi."

Gina shrugs. "I fight dirty. You know this."

"What's up, ladies?" I ask, walking into the room as if I haven't been snooping for the last five minutes. "You're looking at the reigning champ!" I beat my chest again.

"So, you won?" Spencer asks, laughing.

"Whooped Landon's ass!" I hold out my hand and Spence high fives me.

Gina keeps her face turned away from mine as she excuses herself to the bathroom.

"I'm so proud of you," Spence mocks, running her hands up my chest and around my neck.

"Why do you look like you've been crying?"

Spence shrugs. "It's a little warm in here."

She's caught by surprise when I lick the side of her face, eliciting a loud squeal. "What the hell are you doing?" she giggles, attempting to squirm her way out of my embrace.

"Collecting evidence."

"Evidence?"

"Yes, evidence. After sampling the crime scene, I can confirm with one hundred percent certainty that you have indeed been crying."

"Is that so?" she asks, pulling in her lips between her teeth in an attempt to hide her smile.

I nod, pushing her hair behind her shoulders. "The temperature of your skin coupled with the traces of salt proves that tears have recently touched this beautiful face." I trail the back of my hand down her cheek and she melts into me. "The question is, why are you lying, Ms. LeBlanc?"

"This is all so very *CSI* of you, Mr. Hebert. I must admit, it's kinda turnin' me on." Her brows waggle as she presses her breasts against my chest, causing my dick to strain against the fabric of my jeans. My heart begins to race, and just as I'm about to lean in and kiss her…Gina comes blazing through the kitchen with a hand shielding her eyes.

"All right, lovebirds, that's my cue to get outta here." She nabs her purse off the counter with the hand that isn't covering her face and calls back from the living room, "Talk to you tomorrow, Spence! Bye, Coop!"

"Who set her ass on fire?" I ask after the door slams shut.

"Maybe she had a hot date?"

It takes everything in me not to laugh at the guilty look on her face. Even if I hadn't just heard their conversation, I'd know she was lying. "Speaking of dates...can I take you somewhere?"

"What...? Right now?" she asks, glancing at the clock above the door.

Cupping her ass in both hands, I pull her body closer, lining up our centers. "Yes," I whisper against her ear. "Now."

Her hand trails down my front until she's cupping my hardening dick. Spencer smirks and her breathing changes. Her eyes are bedroom heavy as she rolls her tongue over her bottom lip, nodding up at me without a word.

"I can't believe you brought us here," Spence offers, looking around in wonderment as I help her down from the truck. Judging by the smile on her face, you'd swear she was looking at anything but the miles and miles of empty cane field surrounding us.

"Brings back memories, right?" I ask, inhaling the cool night air.

"So many," Spencer whispers, reaching for my hand and lacing her fingers in mine as we walk around to the bed of my truck. "It's so quiet out here."

"It is," I agree with a smile.

"It's kinda creepy, actually," she adds. A chill moves through her body. "And cold."

"Come on. I'll keep you warm."

When we arrive, I let the tailgate down, retrieving the wood that I packed earlier this evening, and build us a small fire.

"Sit with me?" I grab Spencer's hand, as she slips down from the tailgate and lead her to the blanket I've already laid out for us. I plop myself on the ground first then position her between my legs with her back to my chest. Her windblown hair tickles my nose. "I want to talk to you about something."

Spencer's face appears over her shoulder, her lips turned down in an exaggerated frown.

"Why the sad face?"

"When you said you'd keep me warm, I kinda thought that meant you were cashin' in." Spencer tilts her head to the side, fluttering her long lashes.

Laughter rumbles through my chest. "Don't worry...we'll get to that." I place a kiss on the tip of her ice-cold nose.

Spence shimmies her ass into my crotch, making it almost impossible to concentrate. "Well, hurry up...before I decide to take care of myself."

It would totally be worth the blue balls... "I'd pay top dollar to see that."

Oomph. Her elbow flies back, jabbing me in the ribs. "Why're you always beatin' me up?"

"Why do you keep trying to turn me into a hooker?"

"Why are you trying to marry me off to another woman?"

"Wha—" Spence turns in my arms to face me. "What are you talking about?"

"I heard you and Gina in the kitchen tonight..." Crickets. Literally, all I hear are crickets chirping and wood popping.

Spencer's face falls and she tries to move away, but I tighten my grip. "Don't pull away from me, babe."

She stops struggling but won't meet my eyes. "What exactly did you hear?"

"Enough."

"You were spying on us," Spence whispers accusingly.

"I didn't want to interrupt, and then when I heard my

name..."

Her lips purse as she continues to stare down into her lap.

"I didn't bring you here to try to pressure you into anything you aren't ready for, Princess. I told you that I'd accept whatever you have to offer, and I still mean that."

Tear filled eyes glisten in the firelight. She's so fucking beautiful that it hurts to look at her, but it's an ache I hope to feel for as long as I live, because the pain of losing her again... that I don't think I'd survive.

"I mean that forever," I add, feeling my heart tighten in my chest. "There's no one else I want." Tucking my finger beneath her chin, I turn Spencer's face until I'm staring into her hypnotic blue eyes. "No one," I stress.

"You don't know that, Cooper."

Taking her tiny hand into both of mine, I lift it to my chest, placing it right over my racing heart. "You feel that?" I rasp, swallowing hard. Her head bobs. "That's yours. It's always been. So, the next time you try to convince yourself that you know what's best for me, I want you to remember what you feel when we're together." I touch the pads of my first two fingers to her neck, feeling her pulse flutter against my skin. "I feel it, too."

Spencer raises her hands to cradle the sides of my face. "I'll remember," she whispers, blinking away tears.

"There is no getting over this, Spencer."

Frightened lips begin to tremble as the tears freely fall from her eyes. "We said no—"

"No strings," I finish for her before placing a kiss on her temple. It's so hard to be understanding—not to allow my frustration to show. Somehow, I've got to find a way to make her trust me again. "I'll take stolen kisses and trysts in the cane fields for as long as I live over a life without you in it."

Her lips turn down into a sad smile. "I'm so sorry, Cooper."

Shaking my head, I wipe the tears from her cheeks with the pads of my thumbs. "None of that. I made my own bed."

"I just wish..." she whispers, trailing off.

"You wish what?"

"I wish that I could give you more..."

"There is one thing I want."

"What's that?" she asks breathily.

"Forget our deal for tonight. Not another word about the fucking strings," I say, tucking a lock of hair behind her ear. "Give me this, Spence."

She gulps and her lips part.

"I want to make love to you. Not a quick fuck in a bathroom or in the woods behind our parents' houses..."

"Okay," she whispers, pulling my face until her lips brush mine.

I hear her answer, but for some reason, it doesn't register. "Let's pretend just for a few hours...Let me show you how good we could be."

"I said okay." At that, her lips crash into mine.

Spencer crawls into my lap, wrapping her jean-clad legs around my waist and crossing her ankles at the small of my back. Her tongue delves into my mouth, thrusting ravenously. It's always this way between the two of us—this desperation. The overwhelming urge I have to touch her everywhere all at once. As hard as it is to control myself...I want tonight to be different. It has to be special. Time never seems to be on our side, but tonight I'm determined to take advantage of every last second. It'll be a night she won't forget—a game changer.

"Slow," I groan into her mouth, setting the pace with softer, longer, strokes.

I feel the vibration of Spencer's moan against my lips as her nails dig into the skin of my back. She moves closer, grinding into my erection, her hips circling in the same unhurried pace. Her breath is warm on my neck, her nipples hard against my chest. The mewling sounds coming from her lips are the fucking sexiest thing I've ever heard.

If we don't switch places, this will all be over far too soon.

Gripping Spencer's legs beneath her thighs, I lay her on the ground, hovering above her. We undress each other slowly...layer by layer until there is nothing left between us. By the time I'm done with her, there won't be a spot on her body I haven't touched.

Chapter Twenty-Nine

SPENCER

"Mommy, you back!" Kyle calls out the moment I step through the door of Nelly and Neal's house. The familiar smell of fresh baked cookies assaults my nose as the sound of his bare feet slapping on the wood floor bounces off the walls. My baby rounds the corner at full speed in a pair of Superman boxer briefs, a red cape, and nothing else.

"Hey, Savage. What're you wearing?" I know it probably should have, but the thought of potty training him really hasn't even crossed my mind yet, so the sight of him in anything but a diaper is a bit shocking. My heart lurches. He looks like such a big boy.

"Pooper gived me unawares," he explains, beaming from ear to ear while shaking his little tush.

"Pooper, huh?"

"Yeah, him give me dem for a puhprise."

Out of the corner of my eye, I watch a shadow move across the floor drawing my eyes up to find the man in question lurking in the doorway to Kyle's playroom. His arms are extended above his head, clutching the doorframe. *Hot damn.* "Well, that was really nice of, Cooper." My voice sounds higher even to my own ears as my eyes connect with his. A cocky smirk graces his face.

It's been a few weeks since court, and despite my turning his marriage proposal down, I can't remember ever feeling closer to Cooper. The way my body comes alive whenever he's near...There is no other feeling in the world like it. My heart is already beating triple time at the mere sight of him.

"Yeah, him give me nem-nems if I peepee in the toiwette."

"Well, that was really nice of him. Have you been using the potty?"

Kyle nods at the same time that Cooper mouths the word no, shaking his head. "I not gonna pee on myself again, Mom."

Coop chuckles, ambling over, looking edible in his mussed suit. He's ditched the tie and undone the top two buttons of his oxford, which is only half tucked into his dress slacks. My mouth goes dry. I want to rip the rest of those buttons open and climb him like a monkey in a banana tree. *Oh God, what I would do with his banana...*

"It's been a rough one," he offers, skimming his nose up the curve of my neck, which does little to calm the clenching going on between my thighs.

Chills ripple through my body. "Has it?" I ask breathily. "What, umm...What made you decide to potty train Kyle?" A month or so ago, I'd have taken it as an insult and reamed his ass, but I've learned that his help is well-intended. Coop isn't trying to undermine me, and it feels good to know that he cares.

Cooper shrugs. "Just thought I'd like to start taking him

places, and, well, diapers, and I..." He cringes. "We don't really mesh," Coop says, chewing his bottom lip.

He still turns red in the face any time I mention the poop incident. So, of course, I do it at every opportunity. "I'll never forget waking up the next morning and finding you lathering the bed of that truck in shaving cream."

Coop's eyes roll upward and he points a finger at me, a silent order to behave. He clears his throat. "He's gone to the toilet five times in the hour I've been home just to get M&Ms, but he hasn't actually gotten anything in there. He has however blessed the white carpet," Coop's brows raise. "And the bathroom floor." He holds out two fingers. "Twice."

"Oh God, what did your mom say?"

He gives me a look that says *"What the hell do you think?"*

"She cleaned it up and told Kyle what a great job he's doing and that he'll have it in no time."

"Who is this woman and what has she done with the one who used to tan our asses with a—"

"It a wittle bit quishy," Kyle interrupts, pulling on the bottom of my skirt.

"What's squishy, Kyle?"

"My weewee. It a wittle bit quishy, Mommy." Choking, I look down to find him pinching his penis through the front of his underwear.

Oh dear God. I'm feeling feverish as Cooper's loud laughter booms through the foyer.

"Stop touching it." I swat his hand away and he brings it right back. "Don't touch that, Kyle."

"But it's quishy."

"Yes, I know. Just *please* leave it alone." Tilting my head, I widen my eyes at Cooper, begging for a little assistance. After all, he is the one who started this.

Coop squats before my son, a fist at his mouth, trying to stymie his laughter. "Savage, you only get to touch it when you go peepee. That's part of the fun."

"Cooper!" Shaking my head to myself, I cup my hands over my mouth, trying to hide my laughter. Coop flashes those pearly whites, shrugging his shoulders. He's so fucking unconventionally perfect. I don't know whether I want to kick him in the balls or lick his face. I'm momentarily distracted by the slight scruff on his jaw, imagining the way it would feel between my thighs—

"*Ohhh.*" Kyle nods in understanding, his eyes huge with wonderment. It's adorable the way he hangs on Cooper's every word. He freaking idolizes him. I'm not sure if that's entirely a good thing, but it could definitely be worse.

Suddenly, Coop spits out a laugh, obviously remembering something. "Oh my God. You have to see this."

"See what?"

"Kyle, show Mom your pocket."

Kyle looks down, pulling the little flap on the front of his underwear open and shoving his other hand inside.

I nearly fall over. "Did you show him that?"

"Figured it out all on his own," Coop answers like a proud poppa. "He keeps shoving his little cellphone in there."

"That's not cute. It's gross. Don't let him do that."

"The inside is sewn shut. He can't actually get in-*in* there."

Rolling my eyes, I kneel down yanking Kyle's hand out of his underwear. "That's not a pocket."

He tilts his little head, creasing his forehead at me. "Yah, it am."

"No...it's really not."

Cooper's hand wraps around my upper arm, lifting me back to my feet. "Calm your tits," he rasps into my ear. "He's only two. It's funny." What's not funny is the way my body is such a whore for this man. I'm pretty sure I need new panties.

My head falls back, resting on his shoulder. The heat of his breath on my neck warms my blood, muddying my thoughts. *Fucker.* He always manages to make me swoon when I want to freaking deck him. "Please, Coop," I pant. "He's bad enough. People are going to think I'm the worst mom ever."

"Well, I think you're the best mom ever, and my opinion's the one that counts."

I start to say something smart, but hearing his mom's footsteps, I hurry to straighten myself up before she arrives.

"Who's ready to peepee in the potty?" Nelly singsongs as she approaches.

Kyle starts bouncing up and down. "Me...and I get nemnems, right, Nana?"

"Of course. Nana's so proud of her little man." Nelly smiles at me and winks as she leads Kyle down the hall to the restroom with his little baby hand tucked neatly into hers. The same one that was just in the "pocket" of his underpants. *Gross.*

"She really loves him," I say to myself in awe. Nelly shows it constantly in a million ways, and it still amazes me how she's adopted my child right into her heart and home.

"It's almost sickening how much," Coop teases, making me realize I've just said that loud enough for him to hear.

"Jealous?" I smooth my hand over his collar.

"Abso-fucking-lutely."

His large hands grip my waist, pulling until my chest presses into his. "God, I've missed you," he growls, burying his face into the bend of my neck. He runs a finger along the V of my navy silk blouse.

"You saw me this morning," I say, giggling. It tickles, but at the same time feels so damn good. I'm pretty sure my nipples could cut glass.

"I've missed touching you." His lips ghost across mine and he squeezes my ass in both hands.

Feathering kisses along his jaw, I whisper back, "I miss you, too, Coop." My hands fist into his hair, and I give the strands a gentle pull. "But, Kyle could be back any moment." He blows out a long breath as I force myself to pull away, going against every natural urge I possess. It just keeps getting harder and harder to control myself with this man.

Cooper scrubs at his face in frustration before glancing at the clock on the wall. "What time are you leaving to meet Tate? Do you want me to come with you?"

My whole body tenses at the mention of that asshole. "I'm not. He cancelled...again."

Cooper's nostrils flare and he shakes his head. "Do the boys know yet?" I don't miss the way his hands ball up at his sides. He's angry, and it's oddly satisfying.

My lips press into a flat line. "No. He sent a message a few hours ago while they were in school and they aren't home yet."

"Mind if I take them?" He runs a hand lightly up and down my arm while pleading with his puppy dog eyes. "They wanted to go to that game so bad, and it's kind of a guy thing, you know?"

My heart smiles, mimicking the one on my face. "Is that your way of uninviting me?" Of course I'm only pretending to be upset. I can't fucking stand baseball, and the fact that he cares so much about making my kids happy is *everything*.

Cooper taps my nose with his pointer finger. "You're a

smart one, you know that?"

"Can you even get tickets this late?"

"Can I—?" He scoffs, giving me a stupid look. "Don't you know by now that I make shit happen?"

My eyes roll. "I'm sorry. What was I thinking?"

"Is that a yes?" He really wants to do this. *He cares*...truly cares for my children. I've never had anyone besides Gina and my parents who I could depend on with my boys, not even their own fathers. My eyes well up as I squish his face between my hands, planting a big wet one on his lips. "That's a hell yes!" A tear slips down my cheek. "Thank you, Cooper. You have no idea how much this means to me—what it will mean to them."

Cooper kisses the tear from my cheek. "None of that, Princess. We'll have to leave as soon as the boys get back if we're going to make it in time. I need to make some calls to secure those tickets and change out of my work clothes. Send 'em with an overnight bag."

Overnight? I gulp. My throat feels tight. Coop notices the panic on my face.

"Don't look at me like that. You can trust me, Spence."

I nod. It's not about whether I trust him or not, but giving up that control isn't easy for me.

"The game's gonna end late and it's almost three hours away. We're going to get a room and have beignets at Café Du Monde in the morning...maybe hang out in the Quarter for a bit before we make our way back."

What the hell am I freaking out about? This is Cooper. I should be happy that they're going with him instead of Tate, not getting all weird about it. "Okay."

Coop runs a hand through my hair, soothing me. "Call Gina and have a girls' night or something. Don't worry about us."

Lake and Landon left with Cooper a few hours ago, and I'm in the bathroom getting ready to meet Gina at T-Boy's when I see my momma through the mirror, standing in the doorway behind me. She's sporting a shit-eating grin and looking at me funny.

"What?"

"You let him take the boys overnight. Does that mean you're ready to give him a real shot?"

I turn my head for a moment to look at her. "Nothing's changed, Momma. We're good like we are."

"Y'all are bangin' like bunnies. He's..."

Ouch. My eye begins to water due to the fact that I've just stabbed it with the mascara wand.

"...potty training your baby, and picking up the slack for that deadbeat ex-husband of yours," Momma continues. "What's it gonna take, Spencer?"

Great, now I'll have to wash my face and start over. I look like a fucking raccoon. "Not this again," I grumble, reaching for the makeup wipes.

"I'm just sayin', baby. I don't know what else that man can do to prove himself to you. Open your eyes before you lose him."

I glare at my mother. "I won't lose him, because he isn't mine."

Momma reaches out, clutching my shoulder affectionately. "You don't believe that lie any more than I do. That boy has always been yours." She takes my wrist, lowering my hand from my face so I'll pay attention to her. "You're all losing every day that you keep this up." My momma's eyes well with tears. "I know you're scared, Spencer, but you can't let this fear run your life, baby. Happiness is right there for the taking. You only need to reach back."

Bracing my hands on the bathroom counter, I stare at my mother. *How can I make her understand?* "You know that saying, 'Don't try to fix what ain't broken?' We're doing so good right now, Momma, and I don't want to rock the boat."

"Don't you want to go to sleep and wake up in his arms, Spence?" She hugs herself, getting a dreamy look in her eyes. "To snuggle up on the couch watching movies at night after the kids have gone to bed? You could give those boys the father figure they deserve...Raise 'em in a home with parents who love each other. They need that more than they need to be sheltered."

"But what if it doesn't work out?" My lip begins to tremble. "I wouldn't survive that, Momma. Not again." I shake my head. "My boys have had enough disappointment in their lives."

"You think you're protecting yourself from getting hurt by playing it safe?" She shakes her head. "I just wish I could make you see that by risking nothing, you risk everything." Momma places a gentle kiss on my cheek. "Really think about it, Spence."

The thing is, I am thinking about it. In fact, it's practically all I think about. If it was just me, I'd dive in head first, but the thought of having another man abandon my children is too much to risk. "I will, Momma," I assure her before turning back to the mirror to fix my now splotchy face.

"Hey. Psst...Hey." *Nudge.* "Princess, wake up."

I strain to open my eyes, but the light is like laser beams aimed right at my eyeballs. Oh my God, and the room...The room is spinning. *Why is Cooper waking me up?*

The sound of his laughter is infuriating. It feels like there are jackhammers going off inside of my head. "I'm going to punch you if you don't go away," I warn, rubbing my knuckles into my eyes.

"Damn, babe, how much did you drink last night?" Could he possibly be any louder?

Swatting blindly, I connect with a leg—I think—before stuffing a pillow over my head. "Go away, Coop. I'm sick."

Cooper snatches the pillow, flinging it across the room. "I see that." The sting of his hand connecting with my ass finally jolts me awake.

"Asshole," I mumble, wiping the drool from my mouth with my sheet. *Such a lady, right?* Propping up on the elbow of one arm, I shield my eyes with my other hand.

"It's past lunchtime...Have you eaten anything?"

The mere mention of food has me ready to hurl. My face screws up in disgust. "Stop smiling like that. You're pissing me off." And turning me on. *Fuck me.* No, really...please.

His smile widens. "You need food. Go get a shower and let me feed you."

Reaching out, I pat the bed beside me, searching for Gina, but come up empty. "Where is she?"

Gentle fingers begin to massage my scalp. I think maybe I just purred. "Downstairs playing video games with the kids."

"Lay with me?" I ask, patting the bed behind me.

"As tempting as that offer is, you need to get up and get some food in you, Spence. You'll feel better, I promise."

I have a better idea. "How 'bout you take this Cajun injector here," I say, gripping the steel rod in his shorts, "and give me a shot of protein instead." I remove the hand that's shielding my eyes so he can see me waggle my brows—seductively, I hope.

"Then you'll get up?" he asks, as if he's in any position to bargain. A few strokes and he's at full mast.

"I promise."

Coop doesn't put up a fight, climbing over me and sliding beneath the blankets within seconds. He pulls my body backward, molding it to his. The back of his hand brushes the side of my face as Coop pushes my hair out of the way and starts to nibble on the nape of my neck.

He's getting a little too close to my drunken morning breath for comfort. Squirming, I move his mouth away. "Stay away from my face and fuck me, Coop. I'm nasty."

He snorts into my hair. "Do you have any idea how fucking sexy you are right now?" Coop teases, sliding my pajama shorts down to my knees. Before I can respond, he's sliding his dick along my entrance, and I lose sight of all rational thought. His fingers ghost along the sensitive flesh on my inner thigh, and I'm ready to crawl out of my skin. Bucking against him, he slips inside, filling me so completely.

With a hand tugging my hair and the other squeezing my breast, he pumps into me relentlessly. "Fuck, yes," I moan, feeling better already. That orgasm, girls. I'm telling you, it works every time.

"You like that, Prin—"

The door to my room swings open. Cooper and I both freeze as my mother comes barging into the room.

Son of a bitch.

Coop's hand brushes my nipple when he pulls it away, and

I have to bite down on my lip to keep from squealing.

"Told you she was a mess, Cooper James. I tried to get her lazy bones up three or four times this morning…"

She's still rambling on when she sits on the bed just inches from where Cooper is still buried deep inside me. All I can do is pray that she doesn't lift the blankets.

"Right, Spence?" Momma asks, and I have no fucking clue what I'm agreeing to. "Uh, yeah, Momma. Sure."

Cooper moves his hips just marginally, but it's enough. Oh my God, I'm going to come with my mother in the bed if he doesn't keep still.

"This room reeks of alcohol, Spencer." Her nose crinkles. "Go get in the—"

Her hand grips the blanket to throw it off of me, and I grip it like my life depends on it. *Holy fucking shit.*

Cooper's body starts shaking with laughter behind me, which is movement…and, yeah, I can't speak. I can't breathe. I shove my face into the pillow, on the verge of orgasm. Trying to hold it in only makes my impending climax more intense. I'm white knuckled, ready to explode.

"I almost had her, Mrs. Elaine. Give us a few minutes. I'll get her into the shower." How can he speak to my mother as if nothing's going on?

Cooper trails a finger up the back of my leg deliberately slow. Every touch is heightened by the fear of being caught. *I'm going to kill him.*

"What in the hell is wrong with you, Spencer?" Momma asks, her voice getting further away as she takes a few steps back. Oh, thank God. Go. *Go, go, go.*

I grumble, but it sounds like a moan.

"She's about to blow, Elaine," Coop warns, shifting his hips.

I gasp, biting down on the pillow.

Well, aren't we quite the fucking comedian this morning?

"Do you need some Emetrol or ibuprofen?" my concerned mother's voice calls from the doorway.

"No," I growl before the door slams shut and that infuriating man behind me gives me the best damned orgasm of my life with just a few strokes.

There's something to be said for delayed gratification. *Holy shit.*

Chapter Thirty
COOPER

I retrieve the folder of documents I've so carefully prepared from my briefcase, placing them on the desk, as I await Spencer's arrival. My hands are tingling, my forehead blanketed in a light sheen of sweat. By nature, I'm not usually a nervous person, but this woman...She's always been different. To be honest, I'm accustomed to having the upper hand where women are concerned, but Spencer LeBlanc holds all the cards, and I'm just hoping she'll deal me in.

The bell chimes as the door swings open and Spencer rushes in. Her hair is wild and windblown. The apples of her cheeks and the tip of her nose red from the cold.

Spence drops her purse to the floor before shrugging out of her heavy coat, revealing a simple red tunic style dress with black leggings. Simple but beautiful. I can't take my eyes away.

"Coop...Coop!" she snaps her fingers in front of my face. "Cooper!"

I shake myself out of a stupor. "Wha—Oh, sorry, babe. I was thinking."

She chuckles. "Don't hurt yourself. What's so important?"

My heart is racing. *What if she says no?* "I, uh, I wanted to see if you would look over some proposals for me."

She screws up her face. "Um...okay, but I don't know if I can be of much help." Confusion is replaced with a slow smile. "Is this really what you called me out here for or are you just trying to disguise a booty call?" She laughs, placing her palms on my desk and leaning forward. Her tits are all up in my face, but I will not be deterred. I'm a man on a mission. "'Cause you know, I'd have come without the charade."

Ignoring her attempt at seduction isn't easy. I cough, turning my head before asking, "Can you have a seat for a sec, Princess?"

"Sureee." She falls back into *her* chair, looking almost as nervous as I feel.

I hold the folder out to her across the desk. "I want you to look these over and tell me what you think."

She nods, looking a little dejected. As she cracks the file open, bile begins to burn in the back of my throat.

Spencer's lips move silently as she reads. Her mouth falls open and then closes. It opens again and remains until she's finished reading. Her bottom lip begins to quiver and tears unabashedly roll down her cheeks. "We agreed no strings, Coop..."

"Yeah, well...that doesn't really work for me."

She pulls in her lips, swallowing hard.

Rising up from my chair, I walk over to kneel at her feet. "I want the strings. I want the ball and fucking chain. I want to be so tied to you that you can't ever slip away from me again." Loud sobs wrack her frame. "Spencer, I've tried doing life without you. For fifteen years, I've been dead inside, and in just a few months you've reminded me what it feels like to be alive."

"These are adoption papers," she says with disbelief, holding them out to show me.

"They are..."

"Y-your name is on them."

I nod, getting choked up. "It is."

She takes a few deep breaths. "You want t-to ad-dopt my baby?"

"More than anything."

"He l-loves you so m-much." She nods, squeezing my hand tight.

"I love him, too."

"You're not just doing this for me? You really want him? Because, this is forever, Cooper. Do you realize wh-what you're asking for? Even if you ever decided to leave me...you-you couldn't just abandon him. So, if you're not ready to make a lifetime commitment to that baby..."

"I'm ready...for him. For you. For us. But, I understand what you're saying and I swear to you that I want to be that boy's father for no other reason than I love him."

"Coop..." Her chest heaves with sobs. I grab the box of tissues from the desk behind me, pulling a few out and sopping up some of her tears.

She reaches her hand out and cups the back of my head, gently rubbing her fingers through the hair at the nape of my neck.

Slowly she nods, and my heart lodges in my throat. "I can't believe I'm agreeing to share him...Cooper, you have no idea what you mean to me—to him. I'm trusting you to love him, to put him first..."

"I know how hard this is for you. I won't let you or those

boys down. I swear it." I grab her other hand in mine, kissing each of her fingers as a tear drips from my eye. "I know that I've hurt you, and I, along with every other man in your life, have let you down. I know that I probably don't deserve another chance, but I want it more than anything else in this world. Our life was meant to be lived together. If our time apart has convinced me of anything, it's that you were made for me. And that kid may not carry my DNA, but by God, I don't care. I love that little shit like my own and I want to be his daddy."

Her head bobs, slightly. "Let's do it," she whispers, looking up at me through tear soaked lashes.

"Well, you do know that there are two proposals in that folder, and I'm gonna need for you to clarify here a little Princess."

She begins to laugh through her tears. "Oh, Coop—"

Reaching into my inside coat pocket, I pull out the little velvet box, and she freezes. The color drains from her face as if she's finally realizing that this is real. I remove the Verragio engagement ring that I spent a ridiculous amount of time agonizing over. It had to be perfect. I wanted her to love it. It's a square cut diamond set high in an intricate setting—elegant without being gaudy. Just like my girl.

Her hand trembles as I slide it onto her finger. "Spence, I feel like my entire life has been leading up to this moment." I look deep into her eyes. "I got off track for a while, but I would love nothing more than to spend the rest of my life as your husband. I promise to you that I will never take this second chance for granted. I love you. God, I love you so much. Be my wife, Princess. Marry me?"

Her face is torn. She wants to say yes. I can see the words

on the tip of her tongue, and I came prepared. "Before you give me your answer, you should know that Lake and Landon have given us their blessing."

She's taken aback. "They've what? You spoke to them about this?"

"The night of the baseball game…I asked them how they'd feel if I asked you to marry me."

"You did that?" Her hand traces the side of my face.

"I also told them I wanted to adopt Kyle and that I wouldn't do so without their support. I didn't want them to feel like I was leaving them out, because, babe, I would adopt them too if I could. You have to know that. I wanted for them to know that."

She nods, unable to speak.

"They understood. They really did. They have a father, and Kyle doesn't. They want him to have that, Spence. They are fucking amazing kids. I may not be able to legally make them mine, but I will be a father to them in every way that they'll allow it."

"Yes," she whispers so low that I'm not sure I hear her correctly.

I clear my throat. "Say that…say that again for me, baby."

"Yes!" she shouts, tackling me to the floor. "Yes, I'll marry you, Cooper James."

"You have no idea how long I've dreamt of bending you over that desk like that, Princess."

I feel a sharp pain as she answers by biting my nipple before resting her cheek on my bare chest.

"Ouch." I reach for her boob to retaliate, but she's too fast. Spence jumps up, running naked across my office. I'm too busy watching that ass to get up and chase her. Rolling over onto my stomach, I prop myself up on my elbows to ogle her as she begins to dress.

"You just gonna lay around the office naked?" she asks, flustered.

"I'm just enjoying the view for a minute."

"Well, stop it. You're embarrassing me." She hurriedly pulls her dress on before her pants, covering up all the fun bits.

Without a lick of embarrassment, I stand in all my naked glory to join her across the room. "Don't ever hide from me, Spence. You have nothing to ever be ashamed of. I love every inch of your body, and I plan to stare at it often, so get used to it."

She nods, wrapping her arms around my neck and leaning in for a kiss. Just before our lips connect, I exact my revenge.

"You motherfucker!" she yells, grabbing her tit.

I wink before strolling across the room to put on my clothes. "Hurry up, babe. There's something else I want to show you."

Chapter Thirty-One
SPENCER

Cooper grabs another folder from his desk and a set of keys before leading me outside to the empty office space next door.

"Go in," he says, pulling the door open and ushering me inside.

The space is identical to his but vacant. There's a reception area with a large mahogany desk and a small hall leading to two offices, which are directly across from each other. At the end of the hallway is a bathroom.

"What do you think?" he asks with a huge grin splitting his face.

"Um...I'm not sure. Are you thinking of expanding and hiring more attorneys?"

"Not exactly," he hedges, handing me the folder. "Now what do you think?"

He's rocking back and forth on his heels while watching me open it. It's a bit distracting, but my pulse begins to race with excitement. His excitement is contagious.

Just when I think I can't possibly love this man more. "It's a contract. You got this for me?"

He nods. "It's yours if you want it, Spence. All you have to do is sign on the dotted line. Consider it your wedding gift from me."

"You're serious?"

He crinkles his brow. "Of course I am."

"You got me a business as a wedding present?"

Cooper's tongue darts out, wetting his lips. "You're unhappy at the school, and this is our chance to get it right. I want to get everything right. You're quitting at the end of the month when school ends, either way."

I can't help that my eyes narrow at his authoritative tone.

He smirks. "I want to make you happy, baby."

"You do make me happy, Cooper. You make me so fucking happy." I look around the room, imagining it with furniture, fresh paint, and décor. "But, this is a lot…Are you sure?"

"I'm sure that I want to make you happy a lot." Coop walks over, hugging me from behind. He rests his chin on my shoulder, and the scruff on his face tickles my neck. His warm breath makes me shiver.

"I don't deserve you," I whisper, layering my hands over his, which are resting on my stomach.

Cooper places a soft kiss on my collarbone. "You're wrong."

Spinning around in his arms, I lift up on my toes and kiss him with everything in me. "I love you so much, Coop," I whisper against his velvety lips. "Thank you."

"I can't believe we open in three weeks," Gina says, lugging another box into her office across from mine.

When Coop gave me this place, I knew it wouldn't be the same without my girl. Gina was eager to go into business together, this time on our own. No penises allowed. We had to get a bit creative. This little town is extremely conservative. Instead of sexual health, we've gone under the blanket of family therapy, specializing in marriage counseling. It sure as shit beats working at the school.

"I know. I can't believe it's all come together so quickly." In just a few short weeks, on top of finishing out the school year, we've managed to get this place together. Actually, Gina did most of the work, due to her having yet to find a job. She even held interviews and hired a secretary. She's completely thrown herself into creating the perfect atmosphere. "You did such a great job, Gi."

She beams. "I did, didn't I?"

Gina was a little bummed at first that we aren't opening an actual sexual health clinic. She thinks it's bullshit that we have to cater to the hicks in this town. Her words, not mine. Sex therapy and marriage counseling are actually very similar. That elusive orgasm is usually the key. When I explained to her that we were really getting one over on 'em, she finally came around. Gina's like a fourth child sometimes, high maintenance little brat that she is, but I know that I couldn't survive without her.

Oh, and our wedding is in a week. Yeah, we wasted no time, figuring we've already done enough of that. In just seven days, we fly out to Cabo, along with the boys, our parents, and Gina, and I will finally become Mrs. Hebert. I pinch myself daily. How is this even my life?

"You ready to go?" Coop asks, ducking his head into my office.

Him. That's how.

I glace over to the clock. "Is it that time already?"

He smiles. "We meet the realtor in twenty minutes." Coop snaps his fingers. "Chop chop."

"Get outta here," Gina yells from across the hall. "I'll lock up."

On the drive over, I get butterflies. "This one's it, Coop. I can feel it."

"You've said that about the last three houses we've looked at," he says, giving me the side eye.

Yeah, so we've been really busy. But it's the best kind of busy. "I know, but it has everything we want…the lake, the fenced in yard, five bedrooms. It's a Victorian with a wraparound porch and fully remodeled."

"And let's not forget it's almost a hundred grand over our initial budget." Coop shakes his head, running his tongue over his teeth.

"Are you mad?" I bite down on my lip as we turn onto the winding road leading to the strip of houses along Magnolia Lake.

"Princess, I'm just so ready to have a house and a bed and a fucking room that belongs to the two of us," he laughs. "Without the parents," Coop adds, raising his brow. "If this is what you want, it's yours, so *please* want it."

The house comes into view and it literally steals my breath away. It's a creamy yellow color with stained glass in a few of the windows. The porch is huge with the most adorable rocking chairs and a swing. I reach out my hand, squeezing Cooper's arm. I literally have tears in my eyes. "I told you."

I throw my door open before he's even shifted the truck into park. "Isn't it beautiful?" I ask as Cooper walks up beside me.

"You're beautiful," he says, kissing my temple. "I guess the house ain't bad, either."

"Come on." I grab his hand and lead him around back to scope out the yard while we wait for the realtor to arrive. It's enormous and backs up to the lake with a private pier. "For your boat," I say, shaking his hand and looking at him expectantly.

"This is pretty bad ass," he admits as our realtor, Jennie, walks up behind us.

"Wait 'til you see the inside."

She takes us through each room one by one, and with every room, I fall more in love with the house. I wanted our home to have character. This one has it in spades with the turrets and bay windows. The attention to detail. I mean, the woodwork is just incredible.

"There's a fireplace in our bedroom," I squeal, jumping into Cooper's arms. "Imagine the hot sex we could have in front of that," I announce, forgetting the poor woman in the room with us.

"Sold!" Coop shouts as my face heats.

"I'm so sorry," I mouth to Jennie.

She winks, shaking her head. "Don't worry about it, hon."

"Let's do it," Coop says. "This one is definitely it."

Chapter Thirty-Two
COOPER

"Her's comin' now?" Kyle asks, tugging on my arm.

"Almost, buddy." I clasp his little hand in mine to comfort him as my own pulse races wildly with anticipation. Within seconds, the wedding march starts up. "Now," I say, looking down at him with a smile before turning back to watch for my princess. My heart is beating out of my chest.

"My feet is burning," Kyle whines, hopping from foot to foot. It's a little warm, but not overly so. Savage just can't stand for anyone else to have the attention, not even his mother.

Gina shushes him, quickly scrambling over and lifting Kyle into her arms.

The sun begins to set, casting an orange glow behind Spencer as she makes her way down the petal-lined path. Her dress is a simple ivory lacy thing that hits at her ankles. She's barefoot with bright red toes, carrying a small bouquet of white and yellow lilies. My heart is in my throat. I'm not even sure I'm breathing. Spencer truly is the most beautiful woman I've ever set eyes on.

Flanked on either side with their arms laced into hers are Lake and Landon, wearing white linen button downs paired with khakis, identical to mine and Kyle's.

My eyes meet with each of theirs and the smiles on their faces fill my chest with pride. Today, I'm not only marrying Spencer but these children as well. The symbolism of them handing their mother over to me means more than they will ever know.

"Who gives this woman to be married to this man?"

The boys each lean in, kissing their mother on opposite cheeks. Her sparkling blue eyes shimmer as they fill with tears. "We do," they answer in unison.

Lake reaches for my hand, the way we practiced at rehearsal last night, but I pull him in for a hug and tears begin to prick the backs of my eyes. "Thank you, son," I whisper, my voice catching on the last word. I kiss the side of his head and he nods, too emotional to speak before moving to the side to take his position as groomsman.

It's Landon's turn, but he freezes, a little unsure after watching the display between his brother and me. I take the initiative to walk over to him, extending my arms, and to be honest, I'm sweating a little, because this one just might leave me hanging. But then the slightest grin finds his face and he opens his arms wide, hugging me back. "Thank you, son," I repeat what I've just said to his brother. The meaning of that little word is so powerful. I want them to know that we are a family, the five of us.

Elaine lets out a loud wail from her seat behind us followed by an apology.

"Why my gramma cryin', Pooper. Why Mommy, cryin', too?"

"Shhh," Gina says, trying to quiet him, but he's too little to understand that sometimes tears can be happy.

"It's okay, buddy," I call over my shoulder, trying to settle him.

"You cryin', too. Everybody cryin'," he whines, touching a tear on his Auntie Gi's cheek.

"If you be really quiet 'til Mommy and Cooper finish, I'll buy you all the M&Ms," I hear in whispered negotiations behind me.

The officiant chuckles, giving Gina the thumbs up.

When Landon has moved to stand beside Lake, I reach out for my bride. Her hand is warm and soft. She smells of flowers and mint, and her beautiful face is red and splotchy with tears. You'd think we were attending a funeral with all of the crying going on out here, and we're only getting started.

"I love you so much," she whispers, throwing her arms around my neck. I envelop her tiny frame in my arms, getting so caught up in the emotion of the moment that I forget where we are and our purpose for being here. I set her on her feet and lean in, kissing her slow and deep, tasting the salt from her tears.

"Ahem," the minister sounds, vying for our attention.

Guiltily, we look up.

"We haven't gotten to that part yet."

"Sorry," Spence whispers, rubbing a thumb over her kiss-swollen lips.

"It's quite all right. I believe you've each written your own vows? Is that correct?"

"Yes, sir," I answer, squeezing Spencer's hand in mine.

"I'm supposed to tell you to join hands, but seeing as you're already doing that, Cooper, you're up first."

I close my eyes, taking a long breath before opening them and looking deep into Spencer's.

"This feels right, doesn't it?" I ask, tears welling in my eyes.

Spencer nods, sniffling.

"For as long as I can remember, I've been comforted by these baby blues. I didn't realize how much until they were no longer there. Whether it was standing in front of class to give a speech or lost at night in the woods, they've been my compass. You," I say, tugging her hands. "You are my compass, Spencer. For fifteen years, I've been lost, more lost I think than I ever realized. But this...this right here is my home. Like a fool, I threw what we had away, and I realize that not everyone finds their way back to each other. Second chances aren't guaranteed, but you...you've let me come home." My voice cracks, and I clear my throat as I gear up to recite my vows. "I, Cooper, graciously take you, Spencer, as my wife. It is my promise to you that I will never lose my way again. I could promise to love you, but that for me isn't a choice. What I can promise is to love you better. I will always put you and our boys first, and let you think you're right, even when I know you're wrong." I wink as Spence scoffs, rolling her eyes. "I will probably suck at the politically correct parenting, but I vow to be the perfect example of a loving husband and doting father. I promise to never take you for granted and to crack inappropriate jokes just to see you smile. I will do everything in my power, Spencer, to make sure that you never regret allowing me to share this crazy life with you."

I look to the minister, nodding my head, an indication that I've finished as Spencer and I share a smile.

"Spencer," he says, motioning to her with his hand. "You may now recite your vows."

She shakes my hands side to side, blowing out a long breath as she rolls her neck. "Cooper James..." She sighs. "I can't remember a time in my life when I didn't love you. There was a time when I didn't want to, but there you were—so deeply engrained in my heart that I couldn't wish or will or cry you away." She shrugs, darting her tongue out to wet her lips. "I believe in soul mates. I believe that some people are fated to be together, and I believe wholeheartedly that you are that person for me...We all make mistakes," Spence says, rubbing her thumbs over my knuckles. She then turns, looking to each of her children individually. "But there is a reason for everything. Who knows what would have happened if things had played out differently? We are who we are today because of the choices we've made, and it wasn't easy, but, Cooper, I forgive you."

I had no idea just how badly I needed to hear those words. Nodding, I mouth the words *"Thank you"* as the floodgates swing open.

"Sharing my children with others has never come easy, but it's because I was trying to do it with the wrong people. Your love for my boys, your dedication and passion for their happiness and their well-being means more to me than you will ever know. I am honored, Cooper." She releases one of my hands, clutching it to her chest. "And so very thankful that I have the privilege of sharing them with you." She pauses for a moment, which we both use to collect ourselves after her heartfelt declaration.

"So, without further ado, Mr. Hebert, these are my promises to you...That was pretty good, right?" Spence whispers with a wink, to which I shake my head and try not to roll my eyes. "I, Spencer, *finally* take you, Cooper, as my husband. I promise to keep on loving you, through the good times and the bad, in sickness and in health, and even during the times when you act like a chauvinistic pig." I snort. "I will do my best to be less controlling, and I promise to never go to bed angry, even if it means arguing half the night...That only means we have the other half to spend making up."

"Ew," Landon says, screwing up his face.

I glance around at the parents who are oblivious and take note of the hidden smirks on the twins, Gina, and even the minister's faces. "What am I going to do with you?" I whisper.

Her eyebrows waggle. "I can think of a few things," she mumbles low enough for only the two of us to hear.

The minister clears his throat and a blush appears on my girl's cheeks. *Guess he heard, too.*

"I promise that I will always try to be the wife that you deserve and that I'll do everything in my power to make you as happy as you make me. I probably will never obey but will worship and adore you all the days of my life." Spencer releases my hands for a moment to wipe the tears from her cheeks, doing that little eye roll up thing and patting beneath her eyes in an attempt not to smear the mascara that's already beyond ruined. "This is it, Coop," she says, grabbing my hands. "This is forever."

After exchanging rings, the officiant gets a Cheshire cat grin on his face. "By the power vested in me, I now pronounce you, husband and wife. *Now*...you may kiss the bride."

I briefly hear the giggles around us, but they are quickly drowned out when my lips connect with hers. The overwhelming sense of relief that I feel in this moment is beyond compare. *She's mine.* It's as if someone's just removed two tons of bricks that have been weighing on my chest for years. I raise my hands to cradle her head, digging my fingers into raven curls and deepen our kiss.

"Mmm," Spencer moans into my mouth, placing her palms on my chest and pulling away. "Cooper..." Her hand lifts to wipe her mouth and I begin to hear the applause and laughter from our family once again.

"May I present to you, for the first time ever, Mr. and Mrs. Cooper Hebert!"

"It's about fuckin' time!" Gina shouts, earning a glare from our poor minister, who I'm sure we've now scarred for life, and my *wife*. "What?" she says, shrugging with our two-year-old still clutched in her arms. "We're not in church."

"Sometimes I swear there is not enough alcohol on earth to deal with you, Gi," Spence says with a resigned laugh before apologizing profusely to the minister.

"Speaking of alcohol, this is a party now, right?" Gina asks, setting Kyle back on his feet.

"Not yet," I say, motioning for everyone to sit back down. "Spencer, the boys, and I have a surprise for all of you."

"She's pregnant," my mother says to Elaine, bouncing to her feet. "I knew it!"

"For God's sake, Mother." I shake my head. "Spencer is *not* pregnant." *Although I have plans to rectify that immediately*, I think to myself. "Spencer, Lake, and Landon...and, of course, the little dude himself have agreed to allow me to adopt Kyle." My voice shakes and I widen my eyes, trying to hold fresh tears at bay.

"Oh my God," Mrs. Elaine's shocked voice calls from behind and she and my mother embrace in hysterics.

"We signed the papers at the court house the day before leaving to come here, but we wanted to hold off on telling all of you until today—the day the five of us officially become a family." I feel Spencer's hand rubbing my back and glance over to the twins' dimpled smiles. Then I look down at Savage, who is digging in the sand near my feet without a care in the world, and I lift him into my arms. "I present to you, my son, Kyle Jude Hebert." Extending my arms, I hold him out like the cub from *The Lion King*.

He squirms, wiggling like a worm on a hook. "Put me down, Pooper."

I pull him into my chest for a squeeze before releasing him. God, *I can't wait for the day when he finally calls me Dad.*

As everyone else joins in our celebration with tears and hugs, I look over to Gina and add, "Now it's a party."

Epilogue
SPENCER

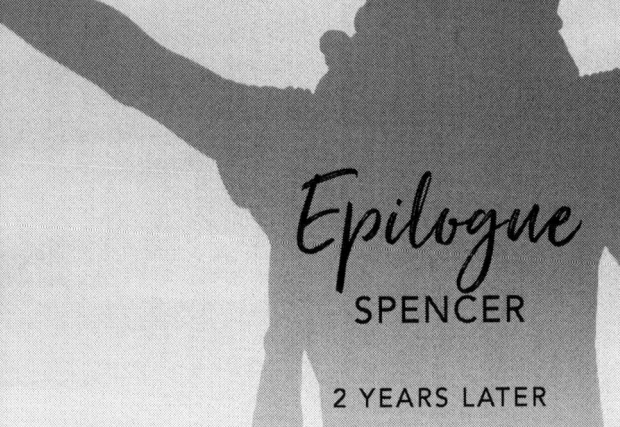

2 YEARS LATER

"Everything looks great," the ultrasound tech says as she's finishing up with the anatomy scan. "I'm going to go call your husband and kids in and we'll see whatcha got cookin' in here, okay?" she asks, patting my enormous stomach.

God, please let there be a girl. I nod my head as my throat tightens. I didn't think I'd be so nervous, but I'm shaking.

"Are they taking the babies out now, Dad?" Kyle asks as my guys flood into the tiny room.

"No, Savage, we're just going to see pictures of them in your mommy's tummy."

Yes, you read that right. Twins...again. What are the fucking odds?

"All right, y'all just kinda stand against that back wall there while I get this thing going again," the tech instructs. When she squirts the warmed petroleum jelly onto my belly, it makes a fart sound. Before he's even opened his mouth. I cringe, waiting for Savage to react.

"Did you hear that fart, Dad?" Kyle asks, giggling. Cooper sucks in his lips, trying not to laugh. The big kid turns his head to the side so our son won't see his smile as he shushes him.

"Get off of me." There is the sound of shuffling behind my head. "Mom, tell Lake to get his arm off mine."

My eyes close as I release a resigned sigh. *Why must they make everything so freaking difficult?* You'd think that by the age of fourteen this bullshit would have stopped, but sometimes I think it's only gotten worse. This is supposed to be a beautiful moment for us all—like the shit you see on the Hallmark channel. But as usual, my gang is only fit for Comedy Central.

"Boys!" Coop says in that sexy, authoritative tone he's developed over the years. I never thought it would turn me on so much to hear someone else correct my children, but let me tell you...when Cooper James does it, it's *hot*.

The room falls silent as the tech begins to move the wand around my stomach. The boys, including my husband, all stare in awe as they try to decipher body parts.

"Okay, this is twin A. See the spine here," she says touching the screen. "This is a hand here...and here we have a...a hamburger!" *A girl.* Oh, thank God. *Thank you, thank you, thank you!*

"When did you get a hamburger, Mommy? I'm hungry. I want one, too." Kyle squints his eyes, glaring at me with a huff, and I bust out laughing.

The boys and Cooper stew in their quiet confusion as the tech explains. "Hamburger is our code word for girl, because the girl parts look like a burger. If it's a boy, we call it a hot dog."

"Oh no," Kyle says with a worried look on his face. "You got our order wrong. We ordered hot dogs."

Oh my God, I feel like I'm going to burst from laughing so hard. Even the boys are balled over in hysterics.

When she is once again able to find her voice, the ultrasound tech responds. "Oh, honey, we can't change your order...You kinda just get what you get." Her face scrunches.

"And you don't throw a fit," Kyle finishes in a very blah tone.

"That's right, but, we have one more." She perks up moving the wand over to twin B who is being a little more modest than A. After shaking my belly and poking around a bit, she finally gets the baby to spread its legs. "I'm so sorry, buddy," she says, addressing Kyle. "It's another burger."

"Two baby girls, Cooper," I whisper through a torrent of happy tears. My husband, however, appears as if he's just seen a ghost. His mouth droops and he continues to stare at the screen, taking a moment to process the news.

"No!" Kyle shouts. "We're not having girls. Girls are gross."

Being the stellar mother that I am, I use the moment to rub salt in his wound. "Looks like you lost our bet, bucko... Someone's gonna be picking weeds when we get home," I taunt.

"Girls..." Coop finally finds his voice. He leans over, kissing my forehead and squeezing my hand. "God help us all." He shakes his head with a laugh. "What are we going to do with girls, Momma?"

I beam. "We're going to fill the house with pink!"

Kyle stuffs his pointer finger down his throat and gags. "I'm movin' out."

Acknowledgements

Writing this book was a team effort, and no one sacrificed more than my husband and children. Thank you, Adam, for being my biggest supporter. For the weekends you and the children spent visiting family and friends without me just so I could have a quiet place to write. For putting up with my absentmindedness and self-induced stress. For all the late nights you spent alone watching *CSI* while I was tied to the computer. I know how much of a sacrifice it was ;). Your support makes this dream of mine a reality.

To my brain, Nicole. I don't know how I'd do this without you. You love to downplay how vital you are to my writing process. I cherish all of our late-night brainstorming chats and depend on your advice. You are my sounding board, and I trust you implicitly. Thank you will never be enough.

Danielle, thank you for your eagerness and willingness to help. Your love for my characters and their story is everything. I'm so lucky to have found such a great beta and friend in you, and I hope you're here to stay!

To all of my beta readers: Nicole, Danielle, Edee, Kate, Nikki, and Selene. THANK YOU!

Juliana Cabrera, I don't know what I'd do without you. From your beautiful cover design and formatting to an invaluable friendship, thank you for always having my best interest at heart. I'm so blessed to have you on my team and in my life.

Edeerie...we did it! You, my love, are one hell of an editor and an even better friend. Thank you for all of your advice and for making my words beautiful. I can't even imagine trying to do this without you, and I don't ever want to.

To every single blogger, reader, and author who has supported me in any way. From sharing teasers and my cover to pimping my release all over social media, for reading, reviewing, and your heartfelt messages, thank you. I am so very grateful.

To the girls in my reader group, Heather's Hunnies. Thank you for all of your support and your friendships. To those of you who helped proofread the ARC, THANK YOU!

About the Author

Heather M. Orgeron is a Cajun girl with a big heart and a passion for romance. She married her high school sweetheart two months after graduation and her life has been a fairytale ever since. She's the queen of her castle, reigning over five sons and one bossy little princess who has made it her mission in life to steal her Momma's throne. When she's not writing, you will find her hidden beneath mounds of laundry and piles of dirty dishes or locked in her tower (aka the bathroom) soaking in the tub with a good book. She's always been an avid reader and has recently discovered a love for cultivating romantic stories of her own.

If you would like to connect with
Heather M. Orgeron, you can find her here:

Facebook: facebook.com/AuthorHeatherMOrgeron
Reader Group: facebook.com/groups/1738663433047683/
Twitter: twitter.com/hmorgeronauthor
Instagram: instagram.com/heather_m_orgeron_author

Printed in Great Britain
by Amazon